INAUGURATION DAY

Other works by Claude Salhani

Islam Without a Veil: Kazakhstan's Path of Moderation

While the Arab World Slept:
The Impact of the Bush Years on the Middle East

Black September to Desert Storm:
A Journalist in the Middle East

INAUGURATION DAY

A THRILLER

Claude Salhani

YUCCA

Yucca Publishing books may be purchased in bulk at special discounts for sales promotion, corporate gifts, fund-raising, or educational purposes. Special editions can also be created to specifications. For details, contact the Special Sales Department, Yucca Publishing, 307 West 36th Street, 11th Floor, New York, NY 10018 or yucca@skyhorsepublishing.com.

Yucca Publishing® is an imprint of Skyhorse Publishing, Inc.®, a Delaware corporation.

Visit our website at www.yuccapub.com.

10 9 8 7 6 5 4 3 2 1

Library of Congress Cataloging-in-Publication Data is available on file.

Cover design by Slobodan Cedic for Yucca Publishing
Cover photo credit: Courtesy of the National Archives

Print ISBN: 978-1-63158-063-5
Ebook ISBN: 978-1-63158-076-5

Printed in the United States of America

For my children, Justin and Isabelle

ACKNOWLEDGMENTS

A very hearty thank you goes to two people who each in their own way offered tremendous help: Stephanie Thompson and Micha Tanios.

1

BEIRUT, LEBANON

Paul Hines was very nervous. This was somewhat unusual for a man who was known for being calm and collected. Those who knew him well knew he was not a man who would panic easily, even under the most strenuous circumstances, even under fire, something Paul Hines had experienced more than few times in his long and distinguished career. Paul Hines was what some people called a spook. He was, simply, a spy for the Central Intelligence Agency. Yes, they still have those, except that few people knew what he really did for a living. To many people's knowledge, Hines was employed by the US embassy. He was a commercial attaché; one of many, although he was under no illusion the people who needed to know, knew what his real job at the embassy was all about.

Hines had been a spy most of his adult life. He was good at it and he liked what he did. He believed in what he did. But at the same time he was also a realist. Times had changed. The Company had changed. Things are not as clearly cut as they were in the past. His mind drifted back for a moment to the days of the Cold War when life seemed so much simpler. At least then

2 | INAUGURATION DAY

we knew who the enemy was, Hines reflected for a brief instant. Today the lines were often blurred. Sometimes the good guys were behaving like the bad guys. Hines knew his Company had done many things one could not be proud of, especially in the past decade, but it was a nasty world out there. And hey, the bad guys were doing far worse things. When dealing with bad guys, you need to be as ruthless as they were if you were to get results.

Now nearing retirement age, whenever he got himself into a tight spot he began to feel as though he had used up his quota of good luck. As the years went by, the more he found himself in tricky situations and the more he thought he might never make it back to the United States alive. Those who did not know him well were surprised to learn his age: sixty years and climbing. He still had a full head of hair; it was graying, but still there. He kept himself in top physical shape through a rigorous morning exercise regimen that many much younger men could not keep up with.

Hines was an optimist by nature. He was not one to look on the dark side of things, always taking an optimistic approach to a situation, regardless of how dark the cloud's lining might be. Paul Hines always managed to extract something positive from any task he handled and his positive attitude seemed to rub off on those he worked with. Those who knew him well also said that you needed to have that kind of attitude if you were doing the kind of job Paul was doing, and living in a place like where he was living. As the CIA Beirut station chief, working out of the US embassy in Lebanon, he knew there must have been a long list of those who wanted him dead. Indeed, his job was not something anyone could do. It required nerves of steel, especially in a place like Beirut, where there were no secrets—and Paul

Hines had them. Officially he was accredited as a commercial attaché, and other than the ambassador and his deputy chief of mission, no one else was supposed to know his real function. But everyone did. Though they pretended not to. Hines was often invited to dinner parties hosted by Beirut's elite, where some of the women tried to seduce him so that they could later brag to their girlfriends that they had slept with a real CIA spy. With one or two exceptions, Hines avoided them.

It was the same on the Lebanese side; only the head of the country's internal counterintelligence services and the head of the military's Deuxième Bureau were supposed to know of his real functions at the embassy, but Hines was certain that minutes after his arrival in Lebanon, all concerned intelligence agencies, from the Lebanese militias such as Hezbollah to the Syrians and Palestinians and Iranians, had a dossier on him. But that was part of the job and he accepted the risks.

Yet try as he did, there was absolutely nothing positive to be drawn from the frantic telephone call he had just received from his top informant in the country. Something today just didn't feel right. After years of staying one step ahead of those who wanted him dead, and often tried to kill him, he had developed a certain sixth sense. Common sense told him to stay away from this hastily-called-for meeting requested by the informant. It had all the markings of a trap. But Paul Hines also knew that the information his informant had obtained was most likely vital, or he would never have made the call. After having worked in the field as long as Hines had, sniffing out danger became second nature.

His intuition was right, because the intelligence his inform-ant had inadvertently stumbled upon was worth more than his weight in enriched uranium. Hines was soon going to learn that his agent had inadvertently stumbled on a plot to assassinate the president of the United States. It had happened in the most unexpected manner. One would assume that people in the business of assassinating the president of the United States would have taken a few more precautionary measures, such as making sure the room was clear before sitting down to discuss such issues. But that was a lucky break for "the good guys," as Hines would say.

Hines did not know of that plot yet, but he felt that whatever his informant would tell him in a short while had to be huge. He was, however, right to worry about today, because he also did not know that he would be dead in less than three hours. His death would put an end to a brilliant career with the Central Intelligence Agency, one spanning forty years and more than fifty countries. Hines had been responsible for bringing down at least six governments—three in Africa and three in the Middle East—but few people knew that and it was not something he wanted to brag about. It was just part of the secretive nature of his work. Some things were better left in the dark.

The short and frantic telephone call from his most valuable source in Beirut left him wondering why his contact broke all the security protocols by speaking on an open telephone line. Hines ran the conversation back through his mind over and over. It was short, and lasted just a few seconds, but long enough to tell there was fear in the informant's voice. Genuine fear. That much he could tell.

The fear he heard coming from his informant over the telephone line was not prompted or faked. That meant there were three possibilities: one, the contact was in imminent danger and had to get the information to him before the person or persons following him got to him first. The informant must have been followed, otherwise he could have made a run for the US embassy in the hills above Beirut and sought refuge there, seeing his cover was blown anyway. If he phoned rather than drove to the embassy, that meant he was unable to shake his tail, or they could be waiting for him.

Two: The contact was already in the custody of whoever had him and forced him to make the call in order to get to Hines. But if that was the case, why did the informant not use the agreed-upon code word indicating he had been compromised and was acting under duress? It was a simple code word that no one would catch other than those looking out for it. The contact didn't use it, so this reinforced the first theory.

Three: The contact had been turned by his intended target and was setting him up for a trap. That was unlikely, given his background. Either way, it did not look good.

Hines chose to focus on the first theory: that the agent was running for his life after stumbling onto something he was not meant to have heard or seen. Whatever it was, it did not look very encouraging. Paul Hines tried to reassure himself that he had been in tight spots before. But try as he may, Hines was unable to shake that nasty feeling; that gut feeling that something would go terribly wrong before the day was over.

2

His eyes closed, Sheik Hamzi al-Haq waved his hands in a gentle motion over his face as he finished reciting the evening prayers. The old sheik remained in a sitting position, resting his aching body on his folded legs and lowering his hands into his lap. Years spent in an Egyptian prison with regular beatings kept him in nearly constant pain. He opened his eyes and stared at his palms for several long minutes. Every now and then, he stroked the long, gray hairs of his beard, as if the motion offered him some inner strength. The decision the sheik had just reached had not been an easy one. The old Egyptian had been agonizing over it for days now, hoping that somewhere there would be an answer. But there wasn't. The new weapon was finally delivered and ready to use. Even the American raid would not stop them now.

Sheik al-Haq opened his eyes and felt around for his thick eyeglasses; he was practically blind without them. In the distance, a call to prayer went out from a muezzin and was echoed by several other mosques, each a second or two apart. The sheik listened to the familiar sounds; they somewhat soothed him. He picked up his glasses and put them on. The small, bare room slowly came into focus. The sheik found a microphone that was attached to a small battery-operated tape recorder and turned the switch to the "on" position.

"In the name of God the merciful and the almighty. In the course of his lifetime, man is forced to face a multitude of avenues and to choose the one that will take him to the gates of redemption and to the Kingdom of Allah. Other roads, those of temptation, will result in a direct path to eternal damnation and a life with the devil. It remains man's responsibility to identify the right road to follow and remain true to the teaching of our faith and our prophet, peace be upon him."

The sheik continued recording for another twenty minutes; his voice—already broken by repeated prison terms, beatings, and torture—sounded even weaker, thanks to the inexpensive recording equipment being used. Yet there was a certain serenity about his voice, something reassuring. Perhaps it was the calmness he projected, the deep thought, the self-assurance with which the sheik continued speaking for about twenty minutes, after which he turned off the tape recorder and removed the cassette. He raised himself and walked to the door, where one of his bodyguards was waiting outside.

"They are waiting for you downstairs," said the aide, taking the sheik's arm and gently guiding him down the long, narrow staircase.

"Let us go then," replied the sheik, handing the cassette to the aide. Like others before it, the cassette would be copied and tens of thousands would be distributed at mosques around the country, to disciples of the sheik, following the Friday prayers. Some would find their way to believers as far away as Afghanistan,

Pakistan, and even Indonesia. There were faithful people ready to follow the sheik all over the world.

On the lower level of the two-story building in a working-class neighborhood of Cairo, a group of five men had been waiting for the sheik. The men sat around a small coffee table on two red velvet sofas covered with cheap thick plastic to protect and prolong the life of the cheap imitation velvet. The summer heat made sitting on the plastic uncomfortable. The room was shuttered and there was no air conditioning. But it wasn't the heat that preoccupied these men.

One of them reached over on the coffee table and took a cigarette from one of the many packets lying on a large round dish that was meant to hold fruit. He took a lighter from his pocket and lit his cigarette. Two of the other men were also smoking and the blue smoke lingered in the room like a morning fog.

The five men rose in unison when the aging sheik entered the room and greeted him warmly. "*Assalamu alaikum,*" they intoned, wishing peace on their leader.

"*Wa alaikum assalaam wa rahmatullah,*" replied the sheik, motioning the men to sit down. The sheik chose the armchair between the two sofas and sat himself down. "The time has come to act and we must do so at once," said the sheik, looking at the five men in front of him. "For the sake of the Arab nation, we cannot allow the Americans to go unpunished. We cannot allow the traitors to sign the treaty. We must act quickly or we will be sidelined and our movement will become irrelevant."

"We are ready now, your holiness," said Abdelwahab, the man in the wrinkled gray suit. He opened his briefcase and took out a small black metal box. He placed the box with great care in the center of the table. The man opened the box to reveal a metal tube, slightly larger than a cigar. The tube was resting in a bed of foam and cotton. "Here it is, your holiness," said Abdelwahab. "We got this out of Sudan before the American attack."

The sheik stared at the small metal vial for almost an entire minute without speaking. Although the contents of the vial were not visible to the men in the room, it was as though there was some mysterious force emanating from the container. It was almost as though the vial contained some magic, or some supernatural force that could transform the lives of those in the room.

"How powerful are the contents of this container?" the sheik finally asked.

"Enough to eliminate five city blocks, your holiness. This is only the first batch. Unfortunately, we lost the Khartoum facility last week. That set us back a while. We were only able to produce the little we have here. However, we do expect Kabul to become operational within two or three months at most, if all goes well."

"What about the Americans?" asked the sheik.

"They suspect nothing," replied the man whom the sheik knew as Abdelwahab. "What we have done, your holiness," continued the man in the gray suit as he adjusted his thick glasses on his nose, "is still experimental, but it worked fine in our laboratory. To obtain the results we need, and be able to smuggle the weapons in adequate quantities, we had to find a more powerful ingredient." The man paused to see if the sheik was following his explanation.

"Go on," said the sheik.

"It is relatively simple, for the scientists, that is. And that is largely thanks to the training they received in American institutions of higher education." The man paused to let the irony sink in. "What we have done is combine two very lethal toxins, *Bacillus anthracis*, otherwise known as anthrax, and VX. The new combination is about a hundred times more powerful than either of the two other compounds." The Egyptian took another cigarette from the tray, lit it, and continued. "To give you an idea, one pound of anthrax alone has the power to kill everyone in an area as large as Manhattan, while a single drop of VX the size of a pinhead is also lethal. This new combination is even more powerful. When this new toxin is released into the air and absorbed through the lungs or skin, it inhibits the release of acetylcholine at neuromuscular junctions."

The others, including the sheik, gave him a puzzled look.

"In other words," said the man known as Abdelwahab, a scientist who had received his degree in Great Britain, "it leads to instant paralysis. The lethal dosage is only 0.02 milligrams per ten seconds, per ten cubic meters. That is very powerful. You see, ordinary botulinal toxins take about six to eight hours to take effect. This combination works within seconds, minutes at the most. The symptoms are combined. Instant dizziness, sore throat, dry mouth, excessive weakness of the muscles, paralysis, bleeding from the nose, mouth, ears, and eyes. There is only one downside to the new compound."

"Go on," said the sheik.

"In order to stabilize this new mixture, we had to add yet a third compound." The man looked at the sheik, as if waiting for his prompt.

"Continue," said the sheik.

"Unlike ordinary anthrax, if this compound comes into contact with water, the effect is greatly reduced and might even lose its lethal edge. But we don't expect to drop this in a body of water and thus we have to transport lesser quantities. Lesser quantities to transport means less chance of being stopped at a border."

"Fine," said the sheik. "We must strike right away."

"We are ready," said one of the other men. "Our Iranian friends will deliver this vial to our man in Washington when we get closer to the operation window."

"So be it," replied the sheik. "Let it happen, then. We must make sure the peace process does not go through! Have you identified the right person for the job?"

"Yes, your holiness, we have. His name is—"

"Don't tell me his name," interjected the sheik. "I don't need to know it. Don't tell anyone his name. They don't need to know it either. The fewer people who know, the fewer chances of information leaking out."

"Granted, but how do you want to refer to him?"

"Good question. Let us call him Omar. Yes, that sounds good. We shall call him Omar, after an Arab hero."

"Omar it is."

"Who else knows about him?" asked the sheik.

"No one but Kifah Kassar, the deputy commander in Lebanon, and of course the Doctor and his deputy, Zeid."

"That's fine," said the sheik. "They are all trustworthy people."

"Of course."

"Anyone else?"

"Two others who assisted in the training."

"See that they don't talk," said the sheik.

"Of course. You mean—"

"I mean nothing," the sheik cut him off. "I leave it up to you to make sure there are no loose ends. Tell me more about Omar.

His background, his experience, his skills. I take it he is clean. No dossier on him with any intelligence agency?"

"He is clean as a virgin on her wedding night. Depending on which story you choose to believe, our 'Omar' was born either in Iraq or in Lebanon. Some versions have him born in Afghanistan. I am not even sure that he knows for certain where he was born. I once heard him tell someone that he was born in Kuwait to Palestinian parents. He speaks all the local dialects and can easily pass for anything from Egyptian to Saudi, or Iraqi to Kurdish. He is excellent when it comes to picking up accents. He is like a parrot."

"That is interesting," interjected the sheik. "Do go on."

"As I was saying," said Abdelwahab, "he was probably born in Iraq to Palestinian parents. He lost both parents to a car bomb during the US invasion, when he was still in his early teens. He saw them die. He saw them burn and was unable to help them. Needless to say, that affected him greatly. One does not see such a scene without being marked for life. He blames the Americans for the death of his parents and is driven by his desire to take revenge. But what is interesting in his case is that he wants to do this in a calm and collected manner. People who are driven by a blind rage and want to see blood are dangerous to our organization and I, for one, tend to avoid them. Omar, on the other hand, is cool and calculated. He is a danger to his enemies and an asset to us."

"I agree," said the sheik. "That is an excellent assessment. Please continue."

"Thank you. He was adopted, so to speak, by one of the local militias in Baghdad, the Doctor's people. After the death of his parents he had nowhere else to go, no one to turn to. The Doctor's people took him in and took care of him. These were very difficult times in Baghdad with much fighting everywhere. The lads chipped in whatever they could spare to buy him some clothes and shoes. The poor boy had lost everything. He started accompanying some of the fighters wherever they went, including, at times, into combat. His first tasks were simple ones: to carry ammunition to a team firing mortars on US forces in the Baghdad area; to carry messages back and forth when the boys did not want to use cell phones or two-way radios.

"One day he volunteered to accompany a two-man team sent out to fire mortars on a group of US Army troops who tried to move into a neighborhood under our control. The two fighters were killed by gunfire from a US Army helicopter that was flying overhead, providing cover fire for the troops on the ground below. Instead of running away, as he should have, as would be expected—as most people would have done—or at least seek temporary shelter until the helicopter flew away, he stood his ground, showing no fear. He pushed the dead fighters out of the way, as they had slumped over the mortar tube. He adjusted the mortar for height and fired his first mortar ever, and scored a direct hit on the American helicopter, downing it and killing all its occupants."

"Quite a feat," said the sheik.

"Indeed. Mortars are not typically used as anti-aircraft weapons. But he made it work. He then readjusted and fired off about ten rounds, one after another, picked up his tube and ran to safety before the first round even hit the ground. The rest of the mortars rained down like fire from hell and there was no way to stop them. The troops never knew what hit them, and they had nowhere to retaliate."

"But then the Americans must have a file on him," said the sheik.

"Irrelevant for our needs. Although he continued hitting US troops with accuracy, getting better every time, he was arrested in a raid on one of the safe houses when the Americans were looking for Abu Mussab al-Zarqawi. We knew he would never talk, even under pressure. Even under torture. His hatred of the Americans was so strong that it would override every other sentiment in his body. Because of his young age, the Americans thought he was the coffee boy. They never tied him to the mortar killings. They have a file of a young man whose name has since been reported as dead. As far as the Americans are concerned, the young lad they knew under a different name has long been dead."

The sheik nodded in approval.

3

CAIRO, EGYPT

Chris Clayborne glanced casually around without really turning his head, allowing his eyes, protected by dark sunglasses, to glance from left to right and back. He did not want to make it look as though he was scanning the surroundings, checking to see if he was being followed, which he probably was, as most foreign journalists in Egypt were. Normally he could not care less, except this time he was specifically told by the man he had flown all the way from Washington, DC, to meet, to ensure he was not being followed.

Clayborne stopped outside a shoe store on busy Kasr el Nil Street, one of the major thoroughfares in the Egyptian capital. He took in the beehive activity of the Egyptian city, the largest in the Arab world, and the largest city in Africa, through the reflection of the store window. He was quite sure no one had followed him from the airport, but it was impossible to be sure. And he needed to be certain. He was quite certain that no single man or woman had followed him, but if there were numerous people on his tail, and they relayed themselves, it would be impossible to detect a tail. The reassuring factor was that when journalists were followed in Egypt, it was typically by the same tail, from arrival until departure. Clayborne knew that as a journalist, he was not high enough on the food chain of the intelligence services to merit more than one flunky to follow him and make note of whom he would meet, and then hand those notes in to a superior who would look at the list of names.

Names of government officials would be ignored. Members of the opposition or of the workers' unions and syndicates, or Egyptian journalists known for being opposed to the regime, whose names were on the list would be summoned to the intelligence headquarters and asked—politely at first—to recount their interview. It rarely went further than that, unless the foreign journalist later published a story that portrayed the country or its leaders in a negative manner. Then the interviews at intelligence headquarters could get somewhat more unpleasant.

Still, the Middle East had taught Clayborne that one could never be too cautious. He had been to Cairo dozens of times in the past, and as far as he could tell, whenever he was followed, it had always been a single tail. His old instincts had suddenly returned as he stepped out of his hotel. And he was more curious than ever to learn why his old friend and one of his most trusted contacts, Walid Barakat, had suddenly called him in Washington and asked him to come meet him in Cairo. Clayborne had met Barakat nearly two decades earlier, in Beirut, back when they were both based in the Lebanese capital. At that time Clayborne was a young journalist, just starting out in the business, and the Palestinian had proved to be a good source. Make that a damn good source, thought Clayborne, someone who got him more than one exclusive story and helped propel his career in the right direction.

Clayborne knew right away that if Barakat asked him to fly to Cairo, it would be well worth the trip. He was not the sort of person who would exaggerate a situation to give himself greater importance. The hardest part was convincing his editor to let him fly five thousand miles from Washington, DC, based on a cryptic telephone call. And in business class, no less.

But it was, after all, such instincts that helped him survive and excel as a journalist in the Middle East and to come up with the exclusive stories and the exclusive interviews. Now, at nearly forty, his senses for survival were stronger than ever.

Leaving the sanctuary of the Cairo Hilton, Clayborne ventured into the bustling city, pushing away a gaggle of street urchins eager to sell him faded postcards and a handful of fake souvenirs. The sun had begun to set, rendering the heat more bearable. A gentle breeze was beginning to blow in from the Nile, making this early September evening quite pleasant. Cairo metamorphosed at night. Once the crowds started to reemerge from their afternoon hibernation, the city would find its maddening pace once again.

Clayborne was glad to be back in the Middle East. The Cairo Peace Conference was finally going to take place in a few months. Even the recent spate of terrorist attacks against American embassies, followed by retaliatory raids by the US Air Force on suspected terrorist sites in Sudan and Afghanistan, was not going to deter the accords. Both the Palestinians and the Israelis were set on signing this historic peace treaty.

Yes, it felt good to be back. Washington, which he now called home, had become tedious. The abundance of political scandals had turned once serious journalists into nothing more than tabloid reporters. He hated that. This was a good time to go back on the road, to be in the field, covering a real story. It was also good to be away from Washington and the egocentric politicians and the media hordes that believed the world stopped rotating outside the Washington Beltway.

Soon after the war in Iraq, Clayborne was promoted to a desk job, given a big raise, and transferred to Washington. He never really adapted. He disliked Washington and home-office politics, and missed the Mideast and his friends. He had spent nearly two decades in the area, most of them chasing godforsaken conflicts that no one really seemed to care about, in places that most Americans couldn't pronounce properly, let alone place on a map.

The afternoon air carried abundant sounds and smells of Cairo, mingling them with the throngs of people who darted between dilapidated automobiles, donkey carts, and overcrowded buses that seemed as though they would collapse at any given moment. Gray clouds of exhaust fumes drifted slowly above the streets, adding to the decades of grime that turned once virgin-white buildings into darker shades, ranging from dark gray to ebony black. Drivers leaned furiously on their horns, adding to the cacophony of shouts emanating from street vendors trying to lure customers for a final sale of the day.

Clayborne took in the atmosphere. Cairo was truly a city that never slept; it was unique in the Arab World. There were always crowds on the streets, no matter the time of day or night. Yes, he reflected, it was good to be back.

Only this time, he could feel the difference in the air. It was in the people's eyes. Clayborne had learned to pick up these signs. It was almost a sixth sense. The eyes were different.

Clayborne knew the extremists could easily derail the talks. The recent bombings had accomplished nothing except create more hatred against the United States. American embassies from Rabat to Islamabad were on full alert and bomb threats had become a daily occurrence. And if one were to take the State Department's warnings seriously, no American in his right mind should be traveling in the Middle East at this time. But no one in his right mind would travel to war zones for a living.

Clayborne reflected on the telephone call. What information did the Palestinian have that required Clayborne to come all the way here? Two days earlier, Barakat, now one of the principal advisers to the Palestinian president, got Clayborne on his office phone and said, "It would be nice to see you."

That was his traditional code word. Barakat would never say something like "I have something important for you," or "Come right away." It was always something very low-key, such as, "It would be nice to see you." Only this time, he added: "I have an item you might find a little interest in." Then, after what seemed a little hesitation, "This has something to do with the bearded boys. I cannot say more on the telephone," added Barakat, referring to the Islamists. Chris Clayborne knew the Palestinian well. If he asked Clayborne to make the trip, he knew it was big. Years ago it was Barakat that had gotten him inside a terrorist training camp. That was a real scoop!

Clayborne used a circular pedestrian crossing to traverse Tahrir Square, a large piazza in the center of the city near the Egyptian Museum. It would have been sheer madness to venture across the large avenues amid scores of buses and hordes of taxis. There seemed to be absolutely no logic in the traffic pattern. Clayborne walked casually towards Kasr el Nil Street to Filfila, a small restaurant that served *foul* and falafel. He entered from the front of the restaurant, made his way to the back, and went out the back door. No one followed him. He continued for another block until he reached Groppi. It was a pleasant walk that took him about ten minutes. At the once fancy tearoom, Clayborne selected a table in the back of the café, close to the wall, but that faced the entrance. He ordered Turkish coffee.

The man Clayborne knew as Walid Barakat arrived ten minutes later. The Palestinian looked much older than his forty-seven years. His hair, or the little that was left of it, had turned white, and the once svelte guerrilla fighter had put on an additional thirty pounds around his waist. Walid greeted Clayborne with a kiss on both cheeks and a firm handshake. "My dear Chris, it is so good to see you again. How is Washington?"

"Quite boring, I am afraid, my dear Walid, quite boring," replied Clayborne. "Far too many money scandals involving members of Congress, right-wing lunatics pushing for war against any country that objects to US hegemony in the greater Middle East, and crazy Republicans bent on proving the president is not really an American. Meanwhile the Democrats are going all-out, behaving worse than the Republicans to prove that they are just as red, white, and blue as the other guys."

"Ahh, I suppose one cannot have it all," replied Barakat, with a loud laugh. "My dear Chris, you are beginning to sound like an angry Arab. There may yet be hope for your salvation."

"And how is Gaza?" asked Clayborne. "I see you are well." He gestured towards the Palestinian's waistline.

"Oh, Gaza is still the armpit of the world," said Barakat. "We have no sex scandals to speak of, since our friends with beards have decreed that women should be veiled, even on the beach. We have no money scandals, because basically we have no money," added the Palestinian, with a loud laugh.

"So why are you staying in Gaza?" asked Chris. "Why don't you move to the West Bank? Ramallah or Jericho? Or even Jerusalem?"

"The president wants me in Gaza," replied Barakat. "I have an excellent network of informers and agents working for me. And today, learning what the boys with beards are concocting is far more important to us than spying on the Jews. Listen, Chris, I don't have much time as I must get back to the president, so let me get quickly to the point." Clayborne nodded and took a sip of his sweet Turkish coffee.

"The president knows fully well that only peace will bring prosperity to the Middle East. His predecessor missed a golden opportunity to have a Palestinian state declared and recognized. Even if it would have been far from perfect, it would have given us a state to call our own. This president is sick, he is dying, he knows it, and he wants to be remembered as a peacemaker. He wants it to succeed. Call it his legacy to his people. He wants to lead them out of their political wilderness."

Walid lit a cigarette, took a long puff and looked around to make sure no one was close enough to hear him before he continued. "Chris, this is completely off the record. I never said any of what I am about to say. Feel free afterward to do what you want with it, but we suspect Doctor Hawali and our dear friend Sheik al-Haq to be in possession of biological agents and they may be planning an attack on the US."

"So the raid on Khartoum was justified?"

Walid smiled and nodded his head. "We believe so. We know that Hawali and those opposed to the peace process will want to strike and abort the conference. And our information indicates this will happen sooner rather than later. Certainly before the conference starts. They want to derail it."

"How solid is your information?"

"Solid."

"Can you share the source?"

"You know better than that. But you heard about the killing of the American agent in Beirut last week? We know it is related to that."

"So why are you telling me this?" asked Clayborne.

"We want to save the peace talks, yet we cannot go public. We want the world to know, public opinion to know, that we want peace. We have had enough war and enough fighting. I have with me photographs, photographs which I will give you, that prove the Sudan plant was hot."

"And as usual, these come from 'unnamed sources.' Right?"

"Right. You found these on your doorstep."

"I'll have to check with other sources."

"Officially, we cannot confirm or deny. But Chris, the entire peace treaty is in jeopardy. We are afraid these actions by the extremists will set us back thirty years, maybe forty years if not more, and will bring more bloodshed to the region."

"Why don't you go directly to the Americans with this information?" asked Chris. "You have high-up contacts at Langley."

"Yes, of course I do, but there is also a mole in Langley working for the bearded boys. I have double-checked. There is an insider at Langley passing everything we have to the Islamists."

"What can I do?" asked Clayborne.

"Expose the story, but don't expose me. If you do it, if you expose them, if you publish this information, you will upset their plans. They can no longer continue and risk being exposed. But please be careful, my friend, be very careful of who you trust. One more thing—while we don't know where or how, we do know the date on which they plan to strike. Next January 20."

"January 20? You sure you got that date right?"

"Why, what's so special about January 20?" asked the Palestinian.

4

SAN DIEGO, CALIFORNIA

Republican presidential candidate Richard Oren Wells was hot on the campaign trail. With only a couple of months until the election, all reports placed him ahead in the polls by a healthy 12 percent over his rival, the incumbent Democrat first-term president. And by George, Wells intended to keep it that way. His campaign policy, "Clean Up America First," had been paying off. Brilliant idea from his powerful campaign manager, Pete Roff. He was a very shrewd political manager who knew how to operate behind the scenes.

"Give the American people something they can get their teeth into," Roff advised early on in the campaign. "Forget Afghanistan and Pakistan and goddamn Palestan," he advised.

"You mean Palestine," a junior aide tried to correct him.

"No, son. I do not mean Palestine. I mean Palestan. And when I want your advice, you fresh out-of-college know-nothing piece of shit, I will ask for it. Now, as I was saying, most Americans couldn't care less about what the rest of the world does. And you know what? As long as the rest of the world does not get to vote in US elections, it matters as much as rat's shit what these people think. If I am to get the senator elected to the White House, as I intend to do, then I want to know what the people of Iowa, Nebraska, Alabama, and Tennessee care about, and I want them to know that Senator Wells cares about them, thank you very much."

With that in mind, the senator from South Dakota argued that the American people were tired of meddling in the affairs of far-off countries, when the much-closer-to-home Latin drug cartels were flooding the US with their lethal products, killing American kids. All the polls and prognostics seemed to indicate that Wells was going to be the next president of the United States.

High on his agenda was his promise to put a stop to the drug trade across the US southern border and take on the Mexican drug cartels, even if that meant sending boots on the ground in pursuit of the traffickers. His current campaign stop was in San Diego, California. His promise to fight the drug lords made him popular not only with conservatives, but also with many in the Hispanic community, who traditionally voted liberal, but were now fed up with what was happening in their old country, where the vast majority of Mexican Americans retained some form of family connection. Many were simply fed up with how much Mexico had fallen to the drug lords and where law and order had turned into anarchy. There was hardly a day when newspapers didn't carry some report of a gruesome killing, reports that bodies were found, hands bound, shot in the head, decapitated, or worse. Many Mexican Americans were frightened of going back home. And their votes in the United States counted.

Senator Wells stepped up to the podium in front of a huge crowd gathered in the San Diego Convention Center. There were hundreds of Hispanics in the audience, a point that Senator Wells did not miss. Or rather, that Pete Roff did not miss.

"My fellow Americans, my opponent has ignored what is happening right here on our very doorsteps, right here in this beautiful city of San Diego, and just a tram ride away from here where a real war is being fought. The war on drugs: a war that is killing dozens of innocent people every day in our neighboring country. A war that is infecting our very future, infecting our children with narcotic drugs. I PLAN TO PUT A STOP TO THAT!" The senator banged his fist down on the dais with every word of his last sentence for greater emphasis. There were wild cheers from the crowd.

"My fellow Americans, just a tram ride away . . ." He lowered his voice for effect and repeated his sentence enunciating every word. "Yes, just-a-tram-ride-away, just a tram ride away is a war threatening our very sons and daughters AND THE DECENT PEOPLE OF MEXICO. *Y TAMBIÉN A NUESTROS AMIGOS MEXICANOS.*" Huge cheers burst from the crowd, especially the Hispanics, now standing and clapping loudly.

"We started out waging a war on terrorism when my party, the Republican Party, fought terrorism when it threatened America in our cities. When terrorists attacked New York City and Washington, DC, we took the war to the terrorists. We sent our armed forces, our army, air force, navy, and marines to fight the terrorists. Today, not only New York and Washington are under attack, but so too are Phoenix, and Sacramento, and San Francisco, and Denver, and Chattanooga, and Boise, and hundreds of other cities across this great land of ours. And my opponent, ladies and gentlemen, my opponent sitting now in the White House is doing nothing to combat this real and present danger, this real threat to the security of the United States of America. And the threat is also endangering this great city of San Diego, JUST A TRAM RIDE AWAY. JUST A TRAM RIDE AWAY FROM ONE OF THE GREATEST CITIES IN AMERICA." Wild cheers from the audience.

"My friends, AMIGOS, COMPAÑEROS, what, you ask, has my opponent been doing these last four years to address this problem? Nothing. NADA. Do you want four more years of that?"

"No."

"Let me ask you then, can you afford four more years of that?"

"NO!"

"If you want to ignore the dangers that threaten you and your sons and daughters right here in America, then vote for my opponent and get another four years of the same, by which time the threat will no longer be just a tram ride away, it will be right here on your doorsteps, right here in San Diego. You want them to continue this policy of poisoning our children, then vote for my opponent." A few boos started to be heard in the audience, triggered by a handful of interns strategically placed around the hall.

"But if you want to change the way Washington deals with the drug trade, and if you want to see the drug criminals thrown in jail with harsh prison sentences, if you want to bring security back to your streets, then give me your vote, put me in the White House and I promise you this much . . ."

More cheers, and some people began shouting, "We want Wells, we want Wells!"

Senator Wells held his arm out, asking the crowd to let him continue. "I promise you this much . . . I promise you this much . . . I will take on those who threaten our security right here in San Diego. I will take this war away from our doorsteps and throw it in right at the doorsteps of the drug traffickers. The Mexican and Colombian drug lords are killing our children, infecting our youth. Their threat is as real today as Al-Qaeda was ten years ago. We did not hesitate then when we faced a real, clear, and present threat to the security of this great nation, and we will not hesitate now to apply needed force to defeat the terrorists, be they Islamo-fascists or narco-traffickers. WE WILL NOT SHY AWAY FROM OUR RESPONSIBILITIES.

"We must now apply similar force to deal with the real and present threat that we face every day from Latin American drug cartels. What I propose is a comprehensive plan to work with the government in Mexico, to send our special forces to train their troops, to send our troops to the border areas with authority to pursue the narco-terrorists inside Mexico so they can no longer continue to hide behind an international frontier, one they chose to cross at will. My plan calls for the eradication of the drug traffic, once and for all. I will ask the Department of Justice to create a special court where we will be able to expedite the trials of drug traffickers and see that they get the justice they deserve. I will ask the Department of Health and Human Resources to create a program drug users can turn to for help. I will make sure the narco-traffickers never get the chance to get on that tram ride to our borders. I will make sure they get a ride, but not in that tram to San Diego, my friends. I will make sure they get a ride up the river and a stay behind bars—for a very long time.

"My fellow Americans, give me your votes! We are blessed in this nation to have the right to vote freely; let's do our civic duty, get out and vote, and help me clean up America first. God bless you, God bless San Diego, and God bless the United States of America. God bless Los Estados Unidos. Good night and thank you."

5

TIJUANA, MEXICO

Among the millions of viewers watching Senator Richard Wells live on television addressing the crowds in San Diego was a small group of men just across the border in Tijuana, Mexico, not very far from where the senator was giving his speech. They were just a little more than a tram ride away, but close enough to worry about the man who could very well become the next president of the United States.

The six men were very powerful and feared in their respective communities, each representing one of the most influential families of Mexico's drug franchises. Between 2006 and 2012 they were responsible for the deaths of more than 47,500 people.

The men were meeting inside a heavily fortified compound with armed guards patrolling the impressive mansion grounds. There were sharpshooters on the rooftops and even a helicopter with armed men flying in a large figure-eight formation overhead. Although these men in the meeting room did not vote in the United States, they nevertheless remained extremely concerned by what they had just seen and heard. The business these

men represented had enormous investments riding on the out-
come of the next US presidential election. If the United States
was going to declare war on them, they could ill afford to lose
that war.

The six men were somewhat reassured when Antonio Juan
Ortega, whom they called Paco, entered the room. They were
nervously chatting about what the American president had just
said, and it worried them.

"This gringo is just loco enough to send his marines to
Tijuana. Then what do we do?" asked one of the six men.

"He cannot do that; it would be an invasion," said another.

"And when did that ever stop the Americans?" said another.
"You have not been watching CNN? You think they were invited
to visit Afghanistan and Iraq?"

"Now, gentlemen, if you will be so kind as to turn off your
cell phones and hand them over to your drivers or assistants
who will be entering any moment now," said Paco. The six men
complied.

"*Señores, señores,* please stay calm; we have nothing to fear,"
said Paco. "I told you a couple of weeks ago that I was working
on a plan and that I was going on a trip to Europe. The truth
is that I did not go to Europe, but that I went to the Middle
East. I went to Beirut, Lebanon. Wonderful place. There is even
a so-called Mexican restaurant there. But I did not ask you here
today to talk about international cuisine. I told you before I left
that you had nothing to worry about and I repeat it now: there is
nothing to worry about."

"Paco, this man is loco. He wants to send his soldiers here to
fight us. We cannot take on the whole damn US Army," said the
man sitting at the end of the table.

"Gentlemen, I am asking for your participation. Our friends in the Middle East are willing to take care of this little problem for us, but it will cost."

"How much?" asked the one wearing a bright Hawaiian shirt.

"Sixty million American dollars buys us a new president in Washington," said Paco. "Ten million dollars each."

"That's a lot of money," said the man smoking a cigar. Yes, agreed the others, ten million dollars was a lot of money.

"Yes," echoed Paco. "It is a lot of money, but think of it as an investment with a very high rate of return. Look at it this way. You can choose to invest ten million or choose not to invest. If you invest, you are guaranteed to make your money back ten-fold within a few short months. If you refuse, then you will not be allowed to partake in the advantages of a confused United States and move your merchandise without hassle—I repeat, without hassle—across the border. In fact, if you refuse to participate, then you will fail to take advantage of the situation. I give you three minutes to reach a decision." He turned and left the room.

Three minutes later, Paco returned. "What I need from you now is your generous financial contribution that will GUARANTEE—gentlemen, I underline the word 'guarantee'—that Mr. Wells never makes it to the White House. Before we start, I need from you two things. First, your participation of ten million dollars that will finance this operation. You can have the money wired into my account from the secure laptops in front of you. And second, I would like to remind you that this conversation does not leave this room. If you are having doubts about anything, walk out now. In either case, this conversation does not go further than here."

"But what guarantees do we have . . ." began the cigar smoker.

"None," Paco cut him off. "Just my word and the support of the best terrorist outfit in the Middle East working for us. Now, gentlemen, if you will be so kind as get on your laptops." The six men complied. They really had little choice. If one of them had wanted to walk, the others would have never let him walk out alive armed with that information. Paco had played this beautifully.

"I have to share with you that this wonderful plan I have set into motion, like many good ideas, this one came to me while on the toilet. I was looking through old issues of *Time* magazine and I came across these photos showing that one day, every four years, when all the members of the US government are gathered in one place . . ." He stopped to relight his cigar. "All except one."

"Why?" asked one of the men.

"Why what?" said Paco with a look of disbelief on his face.

"Why they make one guy stay away?"

"You are not serious?" retorted Paco.

"Oh, I get it. They don't want them all in the same place in case of an accident. Right?"

"Oh, you are such a fucking genius, you are," said Paco. "Of course, you fucking moron, in case of an attack, at least they still have someone who can become president and keep the affairs of state moving along. But whoever that one person is who gets to play interim president will be so swamped with all sorts of problems that we will be way down his list.

"Anyway," said Paco, "this is what I thought after a while. I had this crazy idea. Then later that night I watched this movie, and then I think, hey, why can't we do that? So I call my travel agent and ask him to arrange a flight to Beirut. I talk to our man there who handles our merchandise and we go out for dinner and this plan begins to take shape. We chat for a while and develop the plan some more. I tell him about the event, the movie, and the mortars, and he says he has the perfect man for the job. He wants one hundred million dollars. I tell him he is crazy. We talk more, I offer twenty-five, he says seventy-five. I say sixty, he says sixty-five. We drink some more. He brings in girls. Very classy ones. We spend an hour or two fucking these women. I say okay, but at sixty. Deal. We shake hands. They want the money half now, half on delivery."

"What the fuck are you talking about, Paco? What movie, what mortars? You sound almost as though you have been using some of your own product," said the man in the Hawaiian shirt. The others all laughed.

"Oh! The movie, man, you gotta see this movie. It's about the army in World War II and how they use mortars. So I get this idea, see?"

The others just shook their heads, not understanding what he meant by that.

"Anyway, additionally, you will be happy to know that besides that, our sales are going up in the Middle East. The market is expanding and our partners are projecting rising revenues. Especially now with this new democracy thing taking hold in a number of countries in the region, that means laxer laws, that means greater freedom for our people to go out and market our products. More open societies mean more jobs; more jobs, that translates as more spending money. However, I don't need to remind you that if that son of a bitch Wells makes it to the White House, we are screwed. Big time.

"We can take the matter into our own hands and make sure Mr. Dick Wells does not become president in the United States.

Or we can sit here and lament and allow ourselves to have our businesses shredded to pieces by this *norteamericano maricón*. Yes, sixty million dollars is a lot of money, but trust me, if Wells is elected, we might as well pack up and go home now. But what would happen if America became too preoccupied with its own internal problems to react to an offensive?"

"An offensive?" shouted out one of the six men. "You don't mean a military offensive against the *norteamericanos*? That would be suicide."

"That's out of the question altogether," said the man with the pipe. "There is no way in hell these goons you have on the roof are ever going to go fight the real US Army. You must be loco, Paco, excuse me."

Paco smiled and said, "I did not mean that we attack the US, amigo. Of course not. What I meant is that we follow up with the plan I agreed to and get that asshole Wells out of the way. The beauty of this is that it will appear to be a politically motivated assassination. If we get our Arab friends to do it, and we are kept out of it—no retribution. For this operation to be financially feasible for us, the timing of this operation is essential, which is why I will share with you this information. But I remind you, not a word must leave this room or we are dead men. Only seven people in all of the Americas now know of this plan. I am not about to tell anyone outside this room. That leaves six of you. Not a word, especially not among yourselves on the telephone. Not a word to your wives, your mistresses, your children: no one."

Paco looked straight into the eyes of the six men, one by one. His message was clear: You talk, you die. They all knew Paco well enough to realize he meant what he said. When it came to killing people, Paco always kept his word.

Paco felt he needed to explain in greater detail how this worked. "Now, supposing that America gets completely involved with a very serious domestic issue, such as the death of the former president and the current president-elect, the vice president, and the entire cabinet, save one. That would cripple the American machine and the system would probably grind to a halt for months until they hold new elections. The authorities would not know how to react to any major foreign or domestic event. The United States would go through months of political campaigning until a successor was elected."

"In that case, the chief justice, their minister of justice, or the secretary of state would assume power," offered the man closest to Paco.

"No, not so, Eduardo, in the unlikely event that the president and his vice president should both die at the same time, the American Constitution gives Congress the power to provide the succession. I have done my homework here, amigos.

"The 1947 Congress established that presidential powers would be assumed first by the speaker of the House of Representatives and secondly by the president pro tempore of the Senate. In the highly unlikely event of both their deaths as well, then presidential power goes to the heads of departments of the executive branch, beginning in the order in which the departments were created. In this case it would be the departments of State, Treasury, and Justice.

"But they would all be dead too, or at least very seriously wounded, placing a far less powerful figure, like the secretary of labor or education, in power. In any case, it would be someone without any experience in international affairs and who would be completely caught up in domestic matters for months to come, trying to sort out constitutional laws. The country would be going through a second election campaign so soon after this one. Their politicians would be exhausted and broke. We could easily buy some of them off, if need be. But I think there will not be any need for that. There would be a terrible void in the American government that would take months to fill.

"The American media and public opinion would be far too preoccupied by their domestic issues to worry about a little more drugs on their streets. Actually a lot more drugs. We would sell at rock-bottom prices, which will open up the markets for new clients, younger clients, then when the time is right we would jack up the prices, and this will create greater confusion in the US. The system would be stretched to the limit, which would be even better for us. We will be making billions of dollars. Their press would be occupied covering the home story. Just look at how involved they got over a simple sex scandal. Their press completely ignored all the world's issues to concentrate on this silly little intern and what the president may have said or done to her."

"Yes, I agree about the American media. But the chances of what you just described happening are extremely remote, my dear Paco. Surely you are just dreaming," said the man with the pipe. "Such a coup would be impossible to carry out. Impossible. And you want us to pay ten million US dollars each for that dream?"

"No, I am not just dreaming, my friend, not just dreaming. What I have just outlined is feasible. And not only is it feasible . . . we have put the plan into action, so if anyone wants to leave, do so now before I continue."

Two of the six men, the one with the pipe and the one called Eduardo, had second thoughts. Under normal circumstances they would have stood up and left, but given the level of secrecy demanded, they knew that they would not leave the compound alive.

"Excellent," said Paco with a gleam in his eyes. "Well, then, this is the rest of the plan . . ."

"Well," said the one of the others. "The total absence of a government in Washington would certainly give us three to four weeks, ample time to move in our merchandise in heavy quantity and disseminate it, hide the rest, and wait."

"But are you talking about taking out the entire American government? How would you manage such a feat?"

"As I said, not only is it possible; it will be done. And preparations are underway as we speak."

"This is an incredible plan, excellent, excellent," said the man sitting at the end of the table. "How are you going to get the entire American government together in one place to kill them all?"

"On Inauguration Day," said Paco. "On January 20. You should all have your merchandise ready to roll immediately to take advantage of the confusion. Come Inauguration Day, there will be total pandemonium in the United States. You will be able to move your merchandise without hassle and the sixty million dollars you so generously gave will fetch you dividends many times over. You will be given specific instructions regarding border crossings where your trucks will roll through unhindered, after we bribe or eliminate some guards. Gentlemen, to our success."

6

BEIRUT, LEBANON

Najah Mansour was on the run. He was sweating profusely as the Beirut sun beat down mercilessly on this hot, humid August morning. It was not even nine o'clock and the temperature was already above one hundred degrees Fahrenheit. The humidity hovering around the 100 percent mark made his cotton shirt stick to his body, but that was the least of his troubles right now. Najah Mansour knew he would be dead before the next sunset unless he managed to get out of the country within the next few hours. But that seemed an insurmountable task, with those who were after him already watching Beirut International Airport and the Beirut Port.

By now they certainly had people looking for him at the two main border crossing points between Lebanon and Syria, and assuming he somehow managed to get past them into Syria, they could get to him there, too. The only way out, he believed, the only way to save his life, was to get to the relative safety of a US embassy car and be driven inside the embassy, then get onto a helicopter that would take him either straight to Cyprus or to one of the US Sixth Fleet aircraft carriers, one of which is constantly on patrol in the eastern Mediterranean, along with the usual accompanying task force of battleships, cruisers, and detachment of US Marines. But chances were, those who wanted him dead also had people on the roads approaching the embassy. His only chance to stay alive was to use the information he had stumbled upon as collateral. What he had learned was more than explosive. He would give the Americans just enough information to whet their appetites and get him out of the country; then he would give them the rest. After all, his information was priceless. It concerned the life of the president of the United States of America.

Mansour darted into the underground parking lot of what was once the luxurious Piccadilly Cinema, just off Beirut's fashionable Hamra Street. The darkness of the vast underground complex was soothing, if for no other reason than it was about ten degrees cooler than the outside. He hid behind a parked car and waited, trying to catch his breath. No one followed him in. That was reassuring, somewhat. He pressed the button illuminating the digital readout on his wristwatch, covering the watch with his hand so as to minimize the light protruding from the watch. In as dark a place as this vast underground complex, the light from his watch might be seen from afar, giving his position away. It was only ten o'clock. It would be another two hours before the man from the American embassy, the man he knew as Paul Henry, would arrive. Two long and interminable hours to go, in which every minute would seem like an hour and every hour would feel as long as a day.

As Paul Hines, known to his contact as Paul Henry, approached the rendezvous point, he wondered what could have frightened his informant that was worth blowing both their covers. The information provided over the past several years, ever since Hines had recruited Najah Mansour, trained him, and acted as his controller, had been priceless. Indeed, Mansour had become an important asset for the American spy handler in Beirut.

The information Najah Mansour was able to pass on to the Americans had been very valuable and had saved at least a dozen American lives. And for that he was rewarded handsomely. But Najah Mansour did not go to work for the CIA for the money alone, although it was nice to be able to afford just about anything he wanted—within reason, of course. There was no sense in alerting the curiosity of the neighbors and starting rumors unnecessarily if he chose to live extravagantly. So Najah Mansour contended himself with a modest car and a modest apartment, not too far from the American embassy, a few miles north of Beirut, that Paul Hines passed at least once a day on his way to or from the embassy, depending on how he alternated his route for security reasons.

Najah Mansour had a deeper reason for wanting to help the Americans track down jihadists, and specifically those belonging to a group known as the Final Struggle Front (FSF) that also went by the name of the Popular Struggle Front. Whenever they wanted to avoid being directly blamed for something they would use the name Final Struggle Front. Najah's older brother, Mohammad, had been killed by the FSF because he had taken a job with the US Army as a translator in Iraq. Unable to find work in Lebanon, his brother had gone to work in Iraq before the outbreak of the war, when the Iraqi economy was in full bloom. But then 9/11 happened, and the United States launched its invasion of Iraq, and Mohammad found himself stranded in southern Iraq without work and without the possibility of leaving. While the arrival of American and coalition forces in Iraq was detrimental to the country in many ways, it turned out to be a godsend for the older Mansour. His English was fluent, and he had never been a great fan of the Iraqi dictator to start with. So he applied and was given the position. Soon after, the jihadists approached him and asked him to place a bomb inside the base where he worked. He refused. When they insisted, he turned them in. A few days later, a group of masked men armed with machine guns grabbed him as he was leaving the camp just outside Baghdad. And a few days after that, his mutilated body was found not far from where he had been picked up. His throat had been slit.

Mansour met Hines three years ago in a café in downtown Beirut, and, as is common in the Middle East, small talk soon turned to politics. Mansour wasted little time telling his newfound friend what he really thought of the fanatics in the FSF, a group that was founded in Iraq during the war and that had implanted itself quite successfully in Lebanon, Syria, and, to a lesser extent, in Jordan. Mansour told Hines he was going to avenge his brother's death by killing the man or men responsible for that crime.

By the fifth meeting, or maybe the sixth, when Mansour told Hines he had amassed enough money to travel to Iraq and begin his search for his brother's killer, Hines told him this was the wrong approach.

"If you go and try to kill them, you will most likely fail." Hines leaned closer to Mansour and lowered his voice even more. "Even if you manage to get into Iraq, how long do you think an outsider like yourself will last once you begin asking questions about the whereabouts of a master terrorist? They will probably kill you as they did your brother," said Hines.

"I have a far better idea. If you are interested, it will help eliminate the entire FSF. That would be your ultimate revenge," added Hines. "Get them all, not just one or two who can easily be replaced. Get them all."

With Hines's guidance, Najah Mansour learned to infiltrate the FSF's operation in Lebanon, where the group had an important operation and some of their top leaders lived, when they were not in Damascus or Baghdad. With a heavy US presence in Iraq for the moment, the FSF leadership preferred residing in the relative safety of the Palestinian refugee camps in Lebanon, where local authorities dared not enter.

The Final Struggle Front tried to pass itself off as a pan-Islamist movement and, as such, tended to operate with greater liberty from its base in Lebanon's West Bekaa Valley than it did in Iraq. The Americans suspected the FSF to be responsible for the deaths of at least thirty-five Americans in Iraq and countless numbers of Iraqis. It was also responsible for the death of at least three top Israeli diplomats, one killed in Cyprus, one in Athens, and the third in Istanbul. There had been a number of other attacks also believed to have been carried out by the FSF, though never confirmed.

Then there was the connection to the South American drug cartels. The Americans had long suspected that the FSF was nothing more than a bunch of mercenary drug smugglers hiding behind the mantle of jihadi and Islamist groups to find recruits and foot soldiers to help move narcotics throughout Europe and the Middle East. The bombings and political assassinations were carried out as sideline, or contractual work for intelligence services in the region that preferred not to get their hands dirtied. Interpol seemed to confirm that. It was a very lucrative sideline, as it brought millions of dollars every year into the front's coffers. The FSF functioned much along the same principles as the infamous Carlos the Jackal, who operated in the seventies: renting themselves out to the highest bidder. Despite this, the Final Struggle Front's business plan was on a far greater scale, with billions of dollars pouring in from the highly lucrative narcotics trade, giving the group added clout and tremendous outreach through contacts in the underworld.

Paul Hines was still wondering what could have been so paramount as to push his informant to go counter to established protocol and call him on his cell phone. Cellular connections were traceable and voice conversations could be easily tapped into and recorded. It was agreed that the informant would hang a red shirt on his clothesline over the balcony of his Beirut apartment. That meant he had information to pass on and requested a meeting.

The protocol was later that day, at twelve thirty; the two men would stop for coffee on the Corniche, the seafront promenade along the coast where Beirut residents from all walks of life mingled at all times of day and night. The presence of an American diplomat would not attract much attention, especially given that Paul Hines, with his olive skin and grayish-black hair, could easily pass for a European or even a Lebanese. He spoke fluent French and Arabic and had no trouble speaking with a Lebanese accent. This, and the fact that he had spent many years living and working in the Arab world, made him the candidate of choice when Langley needed to find a new station chief for the Beirut embassy. Paul Hines jumped at the chance to go back to Beirut, where he had spent eight wonderful years growing up when his father served two consecutive tours as a political officer at the Beirut embassy back in the sixties.

Beirut of the sixties and the Beirut of today were different worlds altogether, Hines reflected as he pulled into the underground parking garage of the Piccadilly Cinema. The once posh cinema was now abandoned, the lobby turned into a women's shoe store with the rest of the establishment left decaying. Hines allowed himself to dream for just a few seconds of the old days, when he and his chums from the American Community School would skip class and sneak into what were called stereo clubs, where it was so dark that the waiters carried flashlights to guide patrons to private booths.

Hines chased away the memories of yesteryear. He needed to concentrate entirely on the task ahead. He placed his right hand over his hip and felt the reassuring bulge of his gun, a Glock 34. He removed it from the black leather holster, flipped the safety lock to the off position, slid the barrel back in order to chamber a round, and then placed it carefully in his lap.

He waited, remaining still in his car, eyes scanning back and forth, looking for any telltale signs, anything out of the ordinary. He had arrived a whole hour ahead of his scheduled appointment, hoping to avoid any nasty surprises.

Najah Mansour heard the sound of the approaching vehicle and closed his eyes when the car's headlights came into view. He had gotten accustomed to the dark and wanted to retain that advantage. He opened his eyes once the car passed him and recognized the diplomatic plates with the US embassy numbers. Paul Henry was an hour early. That was good. He waited some more, then slowly found his way to the car driven by the American.

Hines almost shot Mansour when he tapped on the passenger's side window. "No! Don't shoot, it's me," shouted the

Lebanese informant. Hines unlocked the doors and Mansour jumped into the back seat and threw himself on the car's floor. "Let's get the fuck out of here, please," said Mansour. "They are onto me and will not hesitate to kill us both."

"Not before you tell me what the fuck is going on," said Hines, placing his Glock back in his lap.

"Go, please, go. Go. Go, go. Now. I'll tell you everything. But let's move fast."

"Okay. Who is trying to kill you, and why?" asked Hines.

Najah Mansour started to tell his handler how he had over-heard a conversation between one of the FSF's principal com-manders in Beirut, a man called Dr. Ibrahim Hawali, and an Egyptian he had never seen before, and they seem to be talk-ing about an imminent attack on the United States. "I heard them say it would happen as planned for January 20," said the informant.

"Shit!" said Hines. "Are you certain you heard the right date, January 20?"

"Why, what's the significance of that date?" asked Mansour.

"That's Inauguration Day. January 20," said the American. "Are you sure?"

"Of course," said Mansour. "I was not supposed to have stayed in the office that late, but I fell asleep on a couch, and when they found me they tried to have me detained. I knew I would be killed, so I made a run for it."

"Do you have anything more?" asked Hines.

"I'll give you everything once I am safely out of Lebanon," said Mansour.

"Goddamn you, man, I'll get you outta here ASAP. Tell me what else you know." Hines noticed the black SUV, a Range

Rover with tinted windows and several antennas on its roof, following him. He had taken three consecutive turns and the Range Rover did too. He had seen the vehicle before and realized who the men were inside the vehicle. "Lift the back seat up," Hines told Mansour. "You will find an M203. Take it out and take out the grenades that go with it. I think we have a tail."

Hines activated the hands-free gizmo connecting him to his iPhone and dialed a number in Langley, Virginia. By now they were driving as fast as they could in Beirut traffic, heading north along the coastal highway. The Range Rover was closing in fast. "Stay down and wait until I tell you, then fire that M203 into the black Range behind us."

The number in Virginia connected and Hines shouted into the small microphone: "This is Paul Hines, Station 129. Section Red. Situation critical. Identification number 228-98-7919-1407. Code word Buffalo Bill."

He could hear the man on the other end typing rapidly into his keyboard. After about three seconds, which seemed far longer, the voice on the other end said: "Sir, please stand by. I am connecting you."

"State your emergency," the new voice said.

"Did you locate me on your screen?" asked Paul Hines. He knew that by now Langley would have pinpointed his location on their electronic screens, thanks to the GPS he had in his cell phone and on his car.

"Affirmative."

"Take this down. Condition and urgency crimson. We have unconfirmed intel from known and trusted source that an attempt may be directed at POTUS on Inauguration Day. Source and myself are in imminent, repeat imminent danger, and need immediate assistance. Have a black Range Rover on my tail, about twenty yards back. Need assistance ASAP."

"Standby one," said the voice from Langley. Two more black SUVs had now joined the chase.

"Where is our closest carrier?" asked the duty officer in the Langley crisis room who had spoken to Hines. "How soon before we can get a Cobra over to him?"

"The Abraham Lincoln is off the coast of the port of Haifa, Israel, to the south, about seventy miles away," replied a junior officer. "The Cobras can reach the target in just about—" he punched some numbers into his computer and continued "—in just under thirty minutes."

"Scramble them NOW," said the senior officer. The junior officer relayed the orders via secure satellite transmission to the carrier, then told Hines he was patching him through to the fleet command in the control room. Within seconds, the commanding officer standing behind the radio operator plugged his headset into the control board.

"Buffalo Bill, this is the USS *Abraham Lincoln*. Hold your current course and we should be with you in less than thirty. Do you copy?"

"Copy. But would be much appreciated if you stepped on the gas. We might not have thirty."

"Roger that. We're sending you the best we've got."

With a maximum speed of 173 miles per hour and a range of 358 miles, the AH-1 Cobra attack helicopter carrying one M197 three-barrel 20 mm gun with a maximum capacity of 750 rounds of ammunition—basically, a Gatling gun—sixteen Hellfire anti-tank missiles, and 76 x 70 mm folding-fin aerial rockets, all designed to kill combat tanks, could very easily take out an armored SUV.

The two US Marine Cobra helicopter pilots were already running out of the briefing room before the first burst of the alarm alerting them to scramble stopped. A US Navy officer ran along with them as they darted across the deck of the USS *Abraham Lincoln*, heading for their Cobra attack gunships.

"This is a top-priority clearance mission," the Navy officer shouted to be heard over the din of the activity around them. You are cleared to engage and terminate with extreme prejudice. Do not waste time checking with Command and Control before engaging your target. Identify the target and eliminate it."

7

BEIRUT, LEBANON

Paul Hines was driving as fast as he could, given the heavy volume of traffic traveling on the busiest of Beirut's highways. He was trying to outrun the three Range Rovers behind him, who had started to fire at them with AK-47s. He wasn't worried about that. His car could withstand fire from an AK. But he knew that the men in the Range Rovers must have had other weapons. A grenade launcher or an RPG, most probably. He thought, with some cynicism, that they probably also had a couple of US-made LAWs (light anti-tank weapons). They were easier to carry than the Russian-made RPGs, and easier to conceal, as they were shorter. The disadvantage was that they could only be used once, and could not be reloaded as an RPG could.

Paul Hines opened the sunroof of his SUV and told Mansour to prepare himself with the M203, now loaded with a grenade.

"Now," shouted Hines.

Mansour stood up on the rear seat, stuck his head out of the opening, took aim, and fired. The grenade hit the first Range Rover dead center in the engine, sending the vehicle and its occupants flying in a great ball of fire. The other two cars plowed ahead, firing frantically. Najah Mansour ducked back inside the relative safety of the embassy vehicle, and the ping of bullets from the two Range Rovers could be heard hitting the car.

The Cobras came in low over the waves, flying barely a few meters over the calm waters of the Mediterranean Sea. The pilots were homing in on the GPS reading and were closing in fast. The lead pilot could now see the sudden burst of flames as one of the cars exploded. His first thought was that he was too late and that his package had been taken out of the fight. The pilot pushed his throttle forward, giving his engine an extra little push. He banked left and within seconds found himself within firing range. He fired his first rocket straight into the center of the Range Rover that was closest to his package. The car and its occupants practically disintegrated.

Hines and his informant began to feel better. Two of the three SUVs following them were out of commission. Their chances of survival suddenly improved.

The Cobras banked hard left, swung back, and made a second pass over the remaining SUV. A quick burst from the lead helicopter's machine guns and the threat was neutralized.

Their mission accomplished and already running low on fuel, the two Marine Cobras turned left and headed out to sea and their floating base aboard the USS *Abraham Lincoln*, but not before banking their machines left to right and then left again, in a symbolic salute to the men they had just saved.

Or so they assumed.

Just one mile down the highway waiting on an overpass, were two men, friends of those just killed in the three black Range Rovers. They allowed the US embassy car to approach, and as it neared, one of the men rose and fired a rocket-propelled grenade into the car. The car, now on fire, and its two occupants badly wounded, kept moving forward, passed under the overpass, and came into view on the other side of the bridge, where the second man fired his RPG into the car, this time killing Paul Hines and his informant instantly.

At about the same time that the Beirut CIA chief was killed on the coastal highway along with his chief informant, the sheik, in Cairo, was being briefed on the choice of the candidate who had been selected to be the president's assassin. He was one of the rising stars of the movement.

"You see," said the man in the gray suit, briefing the sheik, "Omar had always known hate. Since his birth, whether he was born to Palestinian parents and grew up in the Palestinian refugee camp of Tel al-Zaatar, as some think was the case, or if he was born in Kabul, it makes no difference. In fact it makes it all the better, as he can be claimed by many countries.

"In any case, between the moving about from one Arab country to the next, there was not much room for love in those camps. He grew up around too much hate. He thrived on hate and it made him function. Hate was his leitmotif, it kept him ticking; it was in many ways his internal clock. It was hate and anger trapped deep inside of him that made him who he is. He wanted—and still wants—to avenge the death of his mother and father."

"Interesting. Continue," said the sheik.

"I have heard several versions of who he is and what he is, all are true and all are perhaps exaggerated. In reality, sometimes I think even he doesn't know where he is really from. And for our purpose, this is to our advantage. It adds confusion and makes it harder to track him. In fact, he is a chameleon; the perfect man for the job. His story of his exodus from Palestine, in fact, could be that of any of the tens of thousands of refugees. One version—the one I heard—has it that after their exodus from the Promised Land, Omar's parents arrived at a United Nations relief camp in south Lebanon, where they spent their first years. These were the hardest years, as they faced cold and wet winters, uncertainty, and unemployment. The rain soaked right through their puny shacks, constructed haphazardly with whatever they could lay their hands on: bits of cardboard, tin, and slabs of plywood. Pushed by lack of work and Israel's proximity, they headed farther north to the relative safety of Beirut, where Omar's father made a living repairing cars in a small garage on the outskirts of Beirut.

"Like the majority of Palestinians who dwell in exile, Omar's parents blamed Israel, the West, and conservative Arab regimes for their ills, but more than all, they blamed America. Omar's parents raised him hating the Jews who stole their land, hating the Jews who stole their house, hating the Jews who forced them to live as political outcasts. His mother had lost her ability to love. Although she still cared for him and his father, her whole life became overshadowed by the Great Tragedy.

"The Naqba, or the Catastrophe—that's when they lost Palestine. Omar's mother spent most of her time lamenting the loss of her nation and her house. One of Omar's first recollections as a child was of his mother sitting outside their shack on an empty can of cooking oil and reminiscing with neighbors who shared the same predicament. Omar once said it was the equivalent of being in perpetual mourning, except the dearly departed was not really dead. Palestine was alive, at least in their hearts.

It was present. It was there! They could see it! They could smell it. Only now it was called Israel and was ruled by strangers who spoke an alien tongue and came from Russia, Poland, Germany, and other faraway places. Zionists, they were called. And America footed the bill.

"Omar's world was a desperate one. It was a world where tenderness and affection did not belong and where love had been unable to survive. Born into a violent society, in turbulent times, Omar belonged to a generation where understanding ceased. Dialogue had long been replaced by violence.

"For sixty years, the Levant was the theater of four major wars, numerous revolutions, and a cluster of coups and counter-coups. The Middle East witnessed a major war every decade. Over the last sixty years, every generation had been raised amid war, death, and hatred. Now, this so-called peace with the Zionist enemy forced on by the Americans made him yearn for action even more. For Omar, it is worse than all the wars put together.

"From birth, Omar never knew peace. His world was embedded in chaos and disorder. For Omar and those like him bound by the same predicaments, one thing mattered now. Only one thing: revenge! The little patience there was had long run out. For them, the younger generation, it was time for action. No more idle talks. Talk had gotten them nowhere. The examples to follow were those set by the youth in Egypt, Libya, and Tunisia. Take to the streets. Take action. That's what Omar and many like him believe. Many of today's youth feel that the olive branch had fallen like a withered autumn leaf and the time had now come to raise the gun.

"A few years after the death of his parents, Omar became convinced that talks alone were not going to liberate his occupied homeland or to push the Americans out of Iraq and Afghanistan and bring about true freedom for his people.

"Growing up with stories of Israeli atrocities on his people, and then amidst the mayhem of postwar Iraq, had made Omar a violent man. He knew that violence merely attracted more violence, but he grew to accept that fact. He lived with it every day. Every raid against the Americans was met by far greater retaliation. He knew that the Americans would reciprocate with air strikes for IEDs planted by Iraqis along the roads they used. US forces would launch massive raids in certain parts of Baghdad to find those responsible for the IEDs. They would bomb from the air, killing hundreds of civilians. With every raid of coalition troops, he knew more innocent people would die. Children playing in filthy alleys would be caught in a deluge of fire and steel. That is the way things are in the Middle East. They had always been that way, and unless his generation took matters into their own hands, he believed, this one and the next generation were doomed.

"Growing up amid the mayhem of the war in Iraq, the killing and the mass arrests, the torture stories of places such as Abu Ghraib, Omar believed his part of the world stood no chance to see peace anytime soon. This region, this part of the globe called the Middle East, seemed cursed for some reason to have all the wrong leaders. And this was nothing new; it was the same throughout the ages. Even before the Americans came, the Zionists came, and before them came the British, and before them were the Ottomans, and before them the Crusaders, and the Romans, and the Greeks, and the Babylonians. It was hard to keep track of the number of armies that had fought over this piece of land. Omar, like many of his people, believed armed struggle was the only feasible solution to achieve their goal. Their ultimate goal: the total liberation of their Sacred Land, Palestine! Ejecting the infidels from the land of the two rivers and from Afghanistan. Not by selling out to the Zionists, not by accepting deals for a small portion of the sacred territory. What was Jericho alone? It would be equivalent to the Vietcong accepting the liberation of a single hamlet in the Mekong Delta."

"Interesting fellow," commented the sheik.

"Yes, very."

"Continue."

"Well, unlike the infamous Carlos, Omar is not a master activist, or as the Westerners refer to us, 'terrorist.' He is just an ordinary refugee who worked his way slowly up the ranks, much as a business executive would climb the corporate ladder. Up until now, our Omar is unknown to the Mossad, the CIA, the French, British, and even unknown to the Jordanians, who have quite possibly the best intelligence service in the Middle East, as you well know. But he has great potential. Both his instructors and the few people who have worked with him attest to that effect."

The sheik allowed himself what could have passed for a smile. Yes, he knew quite well the Jordanians and their intelligence services, having been a "guest" of the king for seven years. "Yes, I know them well," he said.

"So he is a newcomer in the intelligence community. There was, and is, no active file on him. When the Americans arrested him in Baghdad, he gave them another name. And for the purpose of this mission, he will be using a whole set of new documents."

"What kind of education does he have?" asked the sheik.

"Omar's only education came from attending a few years at the local elementary school, along with rudimentary geography and history. But he is extremely street-smart. He taught himself English in just the four months he spent in an American jail in Iraq. He speaks it almost without an accent, and with a southern drawl when he wants to, which he picked up from a prison guard who was from Alabama.

"He loves to read. He has read just about every author you can name, and many that you and I could never name. He has read them. When he runs out of books to read he will grab anything he can get his hands on: newspapers, magazines, periodicals, et cetera. He will even read the labels on soda cans and boxes of pasta. He has an insatiable appetite for reading. And he retains it all. His mind is like a computer. During the course of his training, I was told, he read every book they had in the camp," said the man in the gray suit.

"And he knows what to expect in Europe and America?"

"Yes, we have been showing him films, so he should not be too disoriented."

"You have done an excellent job. Thank you."

8

The mood around the conference room at CIA Headquarters in Langley, Virginia, was somber. The Agency had just lost two valuable assets in the Middle East, just as they were about to uncover more information on a plot to kill the president of the United States. They didn't know who, they didn't know how, but at least they knew when. That was something concrete to go on—not much, but it gave them something. But who were they looking for? Where to start?

"What's that goddamn group called again? Who did Paul Hines say was planning this operation?" asked Phil T. Monaghan, Deputy Director of Operations of the CIA. Those who knew him well were allowed to call him P. T. "The Final Combat?"

"The Final Struggle Front, sir," replied Patrick Brent, his deputy, a former Middle East hand and a former US Marine with whom Monaghan had served in Beirut and in the Gulf War.

"So we can safely assume that it's them, this FSF, who plan to carry out the attack. That's what our man in Beirut said, isn't it? Play that tape back one more time."

Brent motioned to an assistant who ran the recording, the last message from Paul Hines. It was not clear, as his voice was covered by the sound of gunfire and explosions. But it certainly sounded as though Hines said "FSF."

"Play the recording back once more," said the director. They could hear much shooting. The specialists had identified the sounds as incoming AK-47s and outgoing M16s and M203s. They could hear the screaming and they could make out the high level of stress in Hines's voice.

"Listen up, people," shouted the deputy director. "We need you to be quiet for just a minute."

Paul Hines's voice came through the speakers again. He was shouting to be heard over the gunfire. ". . . I say again, the FSF, Foxtrot, Sie . . . Fuck it . . ." Then came the loud explosion.

"Run this by the techies, have it cleaned up and let's listen to it again," said Monaghan. "Right. Who is their front man? Their top dog in Beirut must know. Can we plan an extraction? We have SEALs in the area? Let's do it."

It was Brent who spoke now. "The FSF's top dog, sir, is Dr. Hawali, but he is extremely well guarded and it's doubtful that he would get involved in operations. The man we need to talk to is a guy called Kifah Kassar. All trainees go through him. All ops go through him. Anything that this group does goes through Kassar."

"Okay. Let's get this guy," said Monaghan. "Let's get this son of a bitch now. Let's nab the son of a bitch." Turning to Brent, he asked, "How long would the SEALs need to pull this off? It's August; the inauguration is in five months. We need to move fast."

"I figure a couple of weeks of training, recon, et cetera. Three to four weeks at the earliest, and that's pushing it. We'll need to reroute some satellites and get some overhead intel," said Brent.

"Well, needless to say, this gets top priority," said the Director. "We need to liaise with the Secret Service and the FBI. Set up a meeting with their directors, ASAP. I'm not about to allow the president of the United States to be killed on my watch."

"One more thing," said Deputy Director Monaghan. "We need to replace Hines in Beirut, like yesterday. Do you have anyone in mind? It needs to be someone working outside the embassy. We need to start playing dirty again. We can't post someone in Beirut and have them work out of the embassy; it's a dead giveaway. We need someone who can go in deep and set up a new network using whatever trusted sources we still have. Anyone fit the bill?"

"Could be, sir. I started looking into this as soon as we heard about Paul. I have a possible candidate, but I need to speak to you in private first," said Brent. "Let's grab lunch outside. Meet you out front at thirteen hundred hours. We'll take my car."

Along with the deputy director's security detail, comprised of three black SUVs, they pulled up in front of an Italian restaurant at Tyson's Corner, and the director and his deputy jumped out, followed by two bodyguards who kept discreetly behind them.

"What's on your mind, Pat?" asked Monaghan.

"Well, sir—" said Brent.

"You can cut the 'sir' crap when it's just you and me, Pat." The two men, both former US Marines, had a long history together. They had been under fire in more places at more times than they cared to recall. That close camaraderie bonded them and they had full trust in each other. That was why when Brent asked to speak to him outside the office, P. T. knew his longtime friend would not be wasting his time.

"Well, P. T., it's like this. I pulled all the files on all the likely candidates and I come up with one name every time."

"And?"

"And you're not going to like it . . ."

"No! Don't tell me it's who I think it is . . . not Laura Deadwood."

"Yes, P. T. It's Laura *Atwood*. I know you dislike her, but she is good. She proved herself."

"She also embarrassed the Agency."

"That was five years ago. And she was not wrong. She called it as it was. She proved herself in Iraq; she was right, goddamn it. She took the fall for her guy. You and I would have done nothing different," said Brent.

"You and I would not have had an affair with a terrorist."

"Come on, P. T., she didn't know he was a terrorist."

"She should have. Anyway, why do you think she is the only candidate?"

"Because, first, she speaks fluent Arabic; second, she is the only one crazy enough to take on an assignment in Beirut at this current time. Third, she has contacts in that city and can establish a network pretty fast. That's how she works. With Paul dead, so is his network. We are basically blind in Beirut right now. "

"Anyway, you didn't ask to talk to me outside the Agency to discuss Lara Croft. We could have had this conversation in the office, so what's on your mind?"

"Well, we need a cover for Laura, one that will allow her to roam the country freely without raising suspicion, particularly in a place like Lebanon, where they see a spy under every bed."

"And?"

"In a place like Beirut, there are only three professions that allow you to travel freely around the country. One, diplomat, and you ruled that one out. Two, spy, and that rules itself out; and the third is journalism. And President Ronald Reagan ruled that one out when he passed a law banning us from using journalism as a cover."

"Oh, shit. I thought you were going to say that. We can't; it would be breaking the law."

"But you said just half an hour ago that you wanted to start playing dirty."

"I didn't mean for us to go breaking our own rules. I meant we can break a few bones if we feel it is absolutely necessary."

"P. T., the lives of our government officials—of the president of the United States—are at stake, and we don't have the luxury of time on our side. Can we or can we not have your order to proceed? Proceed, but keep this only between us."

"OK, do it, make it happen, but no fuck ups this time."

"And P. T., one more thing."

"Yeah?"

"This is the real reason I brought you out of the office." Monaghan looked Brent in the eyes. "We have a mole in the Agency."

"How good are your sources?" asked Monaghan.

"Solid," replied the deputy director's deputy.

"Okay. Until this crisis is over I want you to personally take charge of that dossier. Does Atwood have a code name yet?"

"She does," replied Brent. "It's Qadi. That's Arabic for *judge*."

"Okay. From now on, we never mention her name. We refer to our agent in Beirut as Qadi. I will start compartmentalizing various bits to see who picks up what and how, and what they do with it. You know, the usual stuff."

9

BAGHDAD, IRAQ

Laura Atwood loved living in Baghdad, but she knew she could never call it home. Baghdad was one of those places where you could spend an eternity but never quite fit in, unless you were Iraqi, of course, and even then you had to belong to the right sect and reside in the appropriate neighborhood, or else risk getting abducted and having your throat slit. A complicated place it was, but an exciting place all the same, especially at this time. Atwood, now thirty-five, single, a couple of not very successful romantic affairs behind her, and with no immediate prospects of attaching herself to any particular man—not that she needed to—she devoted all her energies to her job, at which she was very good.

Her first real love affair had been with Jean-Louis, a Frenchman she met while working on her first major assignment for the CIA in Europe. Because of her fluent command of the French language—her mother was French—she had been sent to liaise with an official of the French counterespionage on the matter of a defecting Syrian who was French-educated. The CIA, who had worked with the French to help extradite the man from Syria, wanted someone who could understand all that was said firsthand and not rely on the translation.

Jean-Louis. Dear Jean-Louis. Only trouble was, it turned out he was married, and not very bright to think he could lie to an agent of the Central Intelligence Agency and get away with it. He had since divorced his wife and never remarried, or so he said. But when they exchanged a couple of emails in the last few years and he told her he was in Paris, something inside her told her to check the source of the email. A revealing bit of data found in the hidden header attached to every email sent allows one to pinpoint the sender's location within ten yards. And that's using websites and software available to all over the Internet. At the CIA they have slightly more precise means at their disposal. Still, you don't have to be a James fucking Bond superspy to figure this out. The email placed him at his wife's address on the wife's family farm in Normandy. She never called him back or replied to his emails after that.

The second love affair happened right here in Baghdad, with a handsome and debonair Lebanese businessman who, it turned out, was helping funnel large sums of money to Hezbollah in Lebanon. That was what not only broke her heart, but nearly ended her career, splashing mud on her face and on the Agency.

The affair was quickly hushed up and the press never got wind of the story; otherwise they would have had to pull her out of Iraq. The only reason she was still employed by the Agency was very likely because Pat Brent looked out for her. She and Brent had a short but passionate affair many years ago, before Brent married. The romantic attraction passed away with the years, but their friendship grew steadily and Brent watched her back as much as he could.

Atwood was of average build, with a very attractive face, straight black hair that ran down to her shoulders, and unusual green eyes that gave her a feline look. At times she would wear red lipstick that outlined her sensuous mouth, making her look like she might belong on the cover of a fashion magazine. She described herself as average, but was actually more on the petite side. Yet what she lacked in size, she amply made up for with self-esteem and self-confidence. She had a black belt in several martial arts philosophies, was an expert sharpshooter, and could kick the ass of any male twice her size.

Late one night, she took on five Iraqis who thought they would have an easy time raping a lone woman on a deserted Baghdad street. Two of the Iraqis ended up in the morgue with snapped necks; the other two in the hospital with broken collar bones, broken tibias, and shattered knees. The fifth one was probably still running. But she loved the work she was doing and she believed it was helping—albeit in a very small manner— the overall stability of the country. No one was going to impose democracy on Iraq overnight, over a year, or even over a decade. As a matter of fact, she was not sure anyone could ever impose democracy in that country, ever. Iraq, much like the other countries in transition in the region, had to grow up on its own. The people needed to find democracy on their own terms and decide when they would be ready of their own accord. The US could not bring democracy to Iraq, or any other place, for that matter, by dragging the people to the polling booth kicking and screaming. The Iraqis—as with any other people—needed to realize that in order to get ahead in the world they needed to mature as a nation first, something they were not doing at the present time. The country of Iraq, like many parts of the Middle East, was created by the Western powers. Its borders are haphazardly drawn across the sand, which is partially why there is so much strife in the region.

When the call came earlier that morning asking her to fly to Paris right away to meet with Patrick Brent, she knew it meant that change would occur in her life. She was ready for that change. All Brent could say on the phone was, "You have nothing to worry about, just meet me in Paris tomorrow at the usual place."

The last five years had been tough, both professionally and emotionally. There was the cock-up with one of her sources, someone who turned out to be a double agent, who had accused a valued US source working for the other side.

Laura sat back in her large, comfortable bamboo chair in a small inner courtyard of a house in Baghdad's "safe" neighborhood. It was unbearably hot and the air conditioning had stopped working. She liked sitting outside late at night when sounds carried far and the city was somewhat more at peace, except for the forces working in the shadows. She listened to the sounds of the night. A child was crying in the distance, and a woman's laughter filtered up from a house or two down the street where a party was in progress. That was one of the things Laura liked most about the Middle East. People still managed to party even in times of war.

Somewhere not too far away, a car could be heard struggling up a steep hill. In the distance, Arabic music was playing from an old, scratched record, a reminder that this was still very much the Middle East.

Baghdad seemed so peaceful now. She thought of her pending trip to Paris and how she would enjoy it, what restaurants she would eat in, and she would maybe even call Jean-Louis. She smiled at the thought.

10

BEIRUT, LEBANON

It had been a few years since Laura Atwood was last in Paris and she was happy to be back, even if it was most likely not going to be for more than a few days. Laura went through customs and immigration and took a cab to the Hotel Baltimore on Avenue Kléber in the sixteenth *arrondissement*, the "usual place" referred to by Pat Brent. She checked in and called Langley, who informed her that Brent was due to arrive within the hour. She changed into a dress and decided to wait for Pat at a small outdoor café, the weather being so charming at this time of year. Brent arrived in time for lunch.

After Brent briefed her on her new assignment, Laura Atwood, now working under the alias of Laura Craft, arrived in Beirut and established herself at the Commodore Hotel, just off Hamra Street. The Agency had arranged for her things in Baghdad to be shipped back to a storage facility in Virginia, and she was given cash to buy everything she might need as far as personal effects went, from clothes to perfume.

For her cover, she was set up in a cozy apartment on Rue Vaneau in Paris's seventh *arrondissement*, not far from Les

Invalides. She opened a bank account with Banque Nationale de Paris, in which she deposited about thirty-five hundred dollars in euros. She also opened a savings account, in which she deposited about ten thousand dollars in euros. She was issued a press card by a fictitious magazine that existed only in the minds of its CIA web developers. The site came complete with masthead, with real email addresses that all went to the same small group of recipients: four CIA analysts specially recruited for this assignment by Patrick Brent. They were set up in a separate office in Tyson's Corner, Virginia, rented for the occasion by a front company. Had anyone bothered to check out the credentials of Miss Laura Craft, they would have been amply satisfied of her authenticity as a working journalist.

Upon arriving in Beirut, Laura called on an old contact, Charbel Assaf, a man she met years ago towards the tail end of the Lebanese Civil War who once ran the Lebanese Forces' intelligence unit and whom she had trained back in Langley. She told him she needed some hired help, musclemen who could think on their feet. Men she could trust. Assaf provided her with three names of men who would give their lives for him. They were like brothers—more than brothers. She hired them on the spot. One of them, an Armenian by the name of Kevork Nazarian, showed he had promising skills with his battered gray taxi.

After checking back into her room at the Commodore Hotel, Laura Atwood connected her laptop to the high-speed Internet offered by the establishment. She connected to an Internet site and signed in using her username and password.

She was instantly transferred to a high-security intranet server somewhere in Virginia, not very far from Dulles International Airport. She entered a second password and was granted access to an extra secure server and one more password would allow her to get into her mailbox. She clicked "Send" on her laptop. Seven seconds later, the message went to an electronic mailbox. Had anyone traced her call, as happened with most calls by the foreign press, they would have learned that she called a commercial computer network system based somewhere in Ohio that provided easy access to its members worldwide. Also, had anyone bothered to check further, they could have learned that Laura had sent her message to the editor of an American women's magazine.

What no one would have ever been able to trace, however, was that the electronic mailbox Laura Atwood had messaged could be accessed from any telephone, anywhere in the world, without the caller ever revealing his geographic location. In fact, the "American editor" happened to be a group of CIA desk officers in Tyson's Corner, just outside Washington, DC. Their job was to publish the fictitious publication, keeping it current in case someone checked up on it. They reported directly to Brent and no one outside the group except for the deputy director knew anything about this operation.

The reply was sent to Laura's electronic mailbox in the same way. An hour later, when Laura Atwood called the US number again, she was prompted with a message flashing on her screen: YOU HAVE ELECTRONIC MAIL WAITING. She retrieved the message, which simply said: "TO: /Bei Ex Foreign Desk/DC. Acknowledge your earlier message. Hope you are having a great time. Stay safe. Regards Dougherty/DC."

Laura Atwood hit the ground running. On her first night in Beirut she was invited to a party thrown by a journalist she met in the lobby of her hotel. It was here that she first noticed Chris Clayborne. She instantly felt attracted to him. Laura got herself a gin and tonic and sat back, taking in the crowd. She recognized an American television reporter, James Wallace, from one of the American networks. He looked about as arrogant in real life as he appeared to be on television. Half drunk, the man was relating to a captive audience his past exploits.

"Those assholes in New York don't know shit," said the correspondent in a loud voice, holding his drink between two fingers and waving his arm around so much that half the contents spilled out onto his trousers. "It does not matter," he said. "It does not matter. Because in the end we will all be dead when the Israelis start to bomb the place again, as they did in '82."

He took another sip from his drink before continuing, this time spilling more contents down his shirt. "It does not matter. Does it matter?" he asked a young female assistant producer who seemed to be worshiping his every word. "It does not matter." He turned to the young woman, "Ask Shirley, here."

"Sheila," corrected the young woman.

"Shirley, Sheila, what the fuck. Sorry sweetheart, of course I know you are Sheila. Not Shirley.

"Anyway, Shirley, Sheila, anyway, I told those shitheads in New York that we were exclusive with the footage from the south and they refused to run it. Too fucking gory, they said. Too much blood and guts. Man, this is a fucking war; people get killed. What do they expect? It's a fucking war we're covering here, not some goddamned political convention. There ain't no balloons and ribbons here."

"You ain't seen war yet, mate," offered an Australian writer, looking down into his beer. "Those misbegotten bastards in Dixie are gonna waltz right up to downtown Beirut in their bleedin' Merkava tanks one of these days, mate. Right up to bleedin' Hamra Street. Just as they did back in 1982. And mark my words, mate, then you'll see what bleedin' war is all about."

"Dixie?" asked a young reporter. He had just arrived a few days earlier and was unfamiliar with the jargon used by the press corps in Beirut. "What does the southern United States have to do with the Middle East?" asked the young reporter to one of the older veterans sitting next to him at the bar.

"Dixie is how we refer to Israel," said the more experienced journalist.

"Why?"

"Israel is a taboo subject in most of the Arab world. And sometimes just mentioning the word 'Israel' can get you in trouble, so we call it Dixie. You know, south of the border . . . Dixie?"

"I still don't get it," said the young reporter.

"Oh, you will soon enough. The next time a pre-pubescent nine-year-old kid sticks his AK-47 into your back and tells you he is going to kill you because you are a Zionist spy, you'll get it." The older reporter picked up his drink and walked away.

Meanwhile, across the bar, the others were still at it. "Shit, just listen to the fuckin' Aussie. He's gonna give us that Vietnam shit again. Hey, all right, I wasn't in 'Nam, buddy," retorted the American network correspondent. "I was too young then. But I sure as hell know a goddamn war when I see one."

"Yeah, right, mate. Right on," replied the Aussie.

"Don't let them impress you." Laura turned around to identify the source of the voice addressing her.

"Hi, I'm Chris Clayborne. You're new here, right?" The man held out his hand. He had a strong and firm handshake. He was in his late thirties and good-looking, thought Laura. Well-tanned from working outside in the sun. This one, she guessed, did not spend his days in the safety of the Commodore bar.

"Yes, I am new here, my name is Laura Craft. I arrived yesterday."

"The greatest danger that can happen to this bunch," said Clayborne, pointing across the room, "is that they might fall off their bar stools after too many drinks. Especially Jounieh Jim there," he pointed to the TV correspondent.

"Jounieh Jim?" questioned Laura.

"Yes. We call him that after the port of Jounieh, about ten miles to the north of here. During the Israeli invasion in 1982, Jim used to spend every weekend there because it was safer than Beirut, but continued to report as though he was on the front lines. He'd interview his cameraman over the phone and then report to New York, as though he was there. Paid his sound-man extra bucks to mix in sounds of explosions and bullets. He would even duck to avoid bullets flying over his head. I'm a journalist with IPS, International Press Syndicate. Whom do you work for?"

"I'm freelance, mostly for women's magazines."

"So where is home for you?"

"Right now, the Commodore Hotel; otherwise, Paris. And you?"

"I grew up in the US, in the DC area, in Virginia, and went to school there. A boring little place called Burke, where the most exciting thing that ever happens is when the local volunteer fire department drives around the neighborhood every Christmas with Santa standing on the back of the truck."

"Are you serious?"

"Very."

"Clayborne?" asked Laura Atwood. "Is that Scottish, Irish, English?"

"As a matter of fact, I have Hungarian origins," replied Clayborne. "My great-great-grandfather came from Budapest to Quebec. My great-grandfather couldn't stand the cold and moved further south to the US. I was born just outside New York City. Then my parents decided to move to the DC area. The family name was changed from some unpronounceable name for the US immigration officer at Ellis Island when my great-grandfather moved here."

Across the room, the obnoxious television reporter was now shouting at the drunken Australian about how a war should be covered.

"So what brings you to the Paris of the Middle East?" asked Clayborne.

"The usual: I want to do a story on the aftermath of the killing of the US diplomat."

"Kind of unusual for a women's mag, wouldn't you say?"

"Well, yes, we're actually doing a piece on the diplomat's widow."

"You know, it was no big secret here, but the diplomat, as you keep calling him, was really the CIA's man in Beirut. He was the local spook."

"Are you certain?" asked Laura.

"Unless you know many dips who carry M203s—that's an M16 that fires grenades as well as bullets—in their back seats and have the capability of calling in Cobra attack helicopters for help in the middle of the day on the main coastal highway. Not even the ambassador has that kind of clout."

Chris Clayborne took a long sip of his Jack Daniels, savoring the burning sensation as it went down his throat. It was his first drink of the day and it felt good. When Chris Clayborne first arrived in the Middle East as a young journalist, more than two decades ago, he had found the story exciting and instantly fell in love with the place. His mentor and boss, Charlton MacClarty, had given him the opportunity to prove himself and sent him to cover the war during his first month on the job. Fresh out of college, Chris Clayborne proved he could produce great stories and compete with newsmen who had been in the field many years more than he had. He had a knack for getting to the right place at the right time.

But the violence soon got to him. The more bloodshed he saw, the greater his love for peace grew and the more he despised war. Yet he could not get himself to leave the place. There was a certain attraction that kept him hooked to Beirut and the Middle East. It was a love-hate relationship. At times, Chris Clayborne felt as though he was living his life to the fullest, yet at other times, he was really tired and fed up. There was a certain *joie de vivre* in the Middle East that was lacking in the US. Even during the worst days of the war, life in Beirut was still pleasant and exciting. People took the time to enjoy life. Every minute of the day was lived to the utmost, as though it might have been the last minute of life—and sometimes it was. There's a limit to the amount of bloodshed you can bear. There were days that he missed being able to walk quietly down a crowded street. To go to a movie, to the beach. To see normal people. To get away from the guns and the war. Well, at least Beirut was quiet now. The guns had finally fallen silent. He liked his present arrangement where he spent half his time in the Middle East and half in Washington. This way he was getting the best of both worlds.

11

BEIRUT, LEBANON

Two months after Laura Atwood arrived in Beirut, Kevork Nazarian was at the wheel of his battered Mercedes taxi. Although the old gray and beaten car had seen far better days, it tended to blend in with the rest of Beirut's aging taxi fleet, yet Nazarian's taxi was no ordinary taxi. Rather, it was the driver that was out of the ordinary because he possessed amazing driving skills that were hard to match. Nazarian was able to manipulate his car with incredible agility. He had learned his skills while working as the personal driver and bodyguard to one of the Christian Lebanese Forces leaders, until his boss got blown up one day while riding in the car of a fellow militia leader. Kevork's armor plating saved him from injury as he was driving close behind the other car. Although the vehicle's bodywork left much to be desired, it was what was under the hood that really mattered: a V8 engine kept in perfect working condition and capable of outrunning most, if not all, cars on the road.

The driver of the nondescript taxicab waited anxiously outside a quiet residential Beirut apartment building, three buildings away from where his "package" worked. The driver of the battered gray Mercedes chain-smoked American cigarettes as he waited. He had been waiting for well over an hour. The woman he was waiting for usually left the building, where she worked as a cook for a wealthy Lebanese couple, shortly after eight every night except Sundays.

This particular night, however, the couple had dinner guests, and asked the woman to remain a while longer. The driver, of course, did not know that, but he had no option but to wait. Finally, the woman came out and the driver turned on his engine as she emerged from the building. The driver threw the car into first gear and slowly approached the woman from behind. Hearing the sound of the car's engine in the otherwise deserted street, the woman turned around. She usually had to walk a few blocks to the corner of the street before she found a taxi. She thought luck was with her tonight and hailed the taxi to stop. Instead, the driver stepped on the gas, running straight into the unsuspecting woman, knocking her to the ground.

The driver had practiced this maneuver dozens of times. The trick was to knock the victim down without killing her. It was a tricky maneuver in which one had to take much into consideration, starting with the gender, age, and physical condition of the intended victim. The climate needed to be considered, as people wore thicker clothes in winter. It was also important to pay attention to the surroundings so the victim did not fall into incoming traffic. And, just as important, the driver had to make sure there would not be police officers or security guards around to try to stop him fleeing the scene.

The driver called the police on one of three cell phones purchased a few days earlier and reported the hit-and-run incident. He described the car as a blue Toyota Corolla. Yes, he was sure that's what it was. He hung up before the police had a chance to ask his name. He repeated the exercise with the second phone, only this time he spoke using heavily accented Iraqi Arabic. A man walking his dog witnessed the scene and called for help but his statement that it was a Mercedes car that knocked down the woman would be countered by two other witnesses saying it was a Toyota. In any case, no effort was going to be given by the Lebanese police—already stretched—to find the hit-and-run driver in a case involving a Palestinian refugee from the camps.

The driver then used the third phone to call his employer, a very pretty Canadian woman he knew as Madame Laura. The driver removed the SIM cards from two of the cell phones, broke them into little pieces, and threw them and the phones into a large garbage bin, then drove home for the night. Less than an hour after the battered taxi knocked down the woman in a Beirut street, a phone call from a number in Beirut was intercepted in Langley, Virginia, thanks to the wonders of satellite technology and the National Security Agency's highly sophisticated technology. NSA specialists had been monitoring all phone calls to parts of a remote camp in Lebanon where they knew Kifah Kassar had been staying and training his new recruits. Arabic speakers on duty picked up the message they had been waiting for without difficulty.

"Kifah, this is Mahmoud in Beirut. I know I shouldn't call you on this line, but there's been an accident. Your wife was hit by a car less than an hour ago and was taken to the American University Hospital. I thought you might want to know, comrade."

"How . . . how badly is she hurt?" asked Kifah Kassar, dazed by the news.

"We don't know, comrade, she's in the operating room right now. Still unconscious."

"I'll come—no, wait. I'll, umm . . . damn. I'll be there as soon as I can," said Kifah Kassar, slamming down the phone.

12

This is the one," said one of the Arabic speakers monitoring the voice communications near Fort Meade, Maryland. The information was instantly relayed to the CIA in Langley, where it was passed on to the Command and Control center in charge of this mission aboard the USS *Abraham Lincoln* in the eastern Mediterranean. Less than one minute had elapsed between the time the message was intercepted and the time it reached the Mediterranean. From there, the information was relayed to a team of US Navy SEALs who had been dropped by parachute from a height of ten thousand feet over a deserted road linking a remote FSF training camp in Lebanon's Bekaa Valley to the main Beirut highway. They used black directional parachutes, their faces painted black to blend in with their black uniforms, making them practically invisible just a few feet away.

The short burst came over the high-powered radio the team carried, "Phoenix One, this is Phoenix Base. Do you copy?"

"Phoenix Base. This is Phoenix One, go ahead."

"Phoenix One, please be advised the bird has left the nest. The show is on the road. Over."

"Phoenix One, copy and out."

"Stay awake, boys, time to rock and roll," said the SEALs team leader, like three other members of his team, a fluent Arabic speaker. He clicked the safety off his machine gun and waited. Each knew exactly what they had to do. The men had trained extensively every day for the past three months on how to carry out this mission. Hopefully there would be no deviation from the original plan, and all would unfold as it had during the training exercises. But he knew things could always go wrong.

Fifteen minutes later, a car was heard racing towards the Navy SEALs roadblock. Kifah Kassar could make out flashing lights ahead and picked up the outline of the roadblock with his headlights. Damn roadblocks, thought Kifah Kassar. There were probably another half dozen more between here and Beirut. That was going to slow him down considerably. He cursed the Lebanese Army for being overzealous, as these checkpoints were quite ineffective.

Kifah Kassar stopped at the checkpoint manned by the SEAL team, who had now all donned Lebanese Army uniforms.

"*Jabha*," shouted Kifah Kassar, slowing down.

"Stop, brother, stop," ordered one of the men Kifah Kassar thought to be Lebanese.

What are these clowns up to now, wondered Kifah Kassar as one of them approached him, shining his light into his face. "Turn that fucking light off before I shove it up your ass."

"Sorry, friend," said the man in the Lebanese uniform, "but we have reports that the Jews might have landed a team farther up the road."

"The fucking Jews are always landing farther up the fucking road. Now get out of my way. I am Major Kassar from the PSF. Now move."

"Yes, I know who you are," replied the native Arab speaker with a grin, as he fired two darts straight into Kifah Kassar's throat. "You are a motherfucking son of a bitch terrorist piece of trash," added the SEAL, in English. The Palestinian never heard that last part. He was out cold even before he had time to realize what was happening.

The gun used by the Navy SEAL fired special darts that would knock out a person instantly without killing the person. Hours later, Kassar would wake up with a very bad headache.

Before his head hit the dashboard, another member of the commando team jumped in the seat next to him and started pulling him out of the car. Among the items dropped by parachute with the Navy SEAL team equipment was a rather macabre item: the body of an Iraqi man, roughly the same age and build as that of Kifah Kassar.

The dead Iraqi brought by the Navy SEALs was dressed in the clothes taken from the Palestinian, along with his watch, and placed at the wheel of Kifah Kassar's car, which was then doused with gasoline and driven over the side of the road onto the rocks. The crash was not enough to ignite the car, but a small self-destructive timing device would take care of that in exactly five minutes, rendering identification practically impossible. As with Kassar's wife, Lebanese authorities were unlikely to spend much effort investigating the crash. The lateness of the hour and the empty bottle of booze in the front seat would make it an open-and-shut case.

"Phoenix base, this is Phoenix One: Birds are ready to fly home with the worm," said the group leader into his radio.

"Eagle down in four minutes. Stand by," came the reply from one of the two helicopters hovering high overhead.

13

NEAR PRAGUE, CZECH REPUBLIC

Kifah Kassar slowly awoke what he assumed to be several hours later. In fact, he had been heavily sedated and sleeping for about two days. His beard was shaved to let him think he was out for hours instead of days. He felt as though his mouth was on fire. After he was knocked out and taken aboard the helicopter, he was transported to a US carrier off the Lebanese coast, then, under medical supervision, put on a flight to Athens, and ultimately transferred to a secret CIA facility in the Czech countryside. Arrangements had been made to turn the facility into something resembling a Lebanese security prison. All personnel that came into contact with the prisoner—and those were few—were of Lebanese origin and spoke Arabic flawlessly with a Lebanese accent.

The Palestinian opened his eyes slowly, quietly taking in the scene around him. He was lying on a thin foam mattress that was placed on the floor of a tiny cell. It was filthy and bloodstained, and reeked of urine and vomit. A low-wattage bare bulb, suspended from a short wire protruding from the ceiling, illuminated the room. A dirty, dented bucket in the corner of the cell served as a toilet. The Palestinian instructor pushed himself up on his elbows. His throat felt sore. He rubbed his throat and his head, which felt like he had a hangover, the way he usually felt after getting drunk on cheap arak. He tried recalling what had happened, but his mind was not responding too well. He tried to stand up, but fell back onto the filthy, smelly mattress.

He remembered the roadblock. It must have been those Lebanese soldiers who kidnapped him. But why? He could hear screams coming from a distant cell, maybe another floor, and moaning from adjoining cells. Kifah Kassar didn't know it, but those were all recordings made by a professional Hollywood studio. Kifah Kassar shuddered. He rose slowly and started banging on the iron door. It seemed to no avail at first, but minutes later he heard footsteps outside. Several people were walking towards his cell. The heavy metal door was flung open, revealing three armed guards.

"What is the meaning of this," screamed Kifah Kassar. "Do you people know who you are messing with?"

"Keep your fucking mouth shut," ordered the oldest of the three guards. "Move your fat ass and come with us."

The men were wearing uniforms worn by the Interior Ministry police force, the ISF, or Internal Security Force. Why had the Lebanese arrested him? To be sure, the Front had been at odds with the Lebanese in the past, but relations at the present time were good. It simply did not make sense. This was a stupid mistake that would quickly be taken care of. He would be released in no time and with all apologies due.

Kifah Kassar was marched down the long, narrow corridor to a room where an officer was waiting for him. Kifah Kassar couldn't identify the man's rank, as he wore no insignia on his

clean, starched uniform. This was not unusual with some interro-
gators. The man did not bother to look up at him and continued
to study a file on his desk. Except for a single black telephone, the
desk was bare. A large color portrait of the Lebanese president
adorned the wall behind the desk. A map of Lebanon was crudely
taped to the far wall. There were no windows and no natural light
filtered through. The officer motioned him to sit in a chair placed
about five feet from the desk.

"What is this all about—"

"Quiet!" shouted the officer. "Quiet. You will speak only
when spoken to." The officer paused for a second. "Understood?"

It was more an order than a question. The officer returned
to his file. He did not expect an answer from the Palestinian.
After a few minutes, the officer lifted the telephone. Kifah Kassar
guessed that the phone was relayed to a switchboard, as the officer
did not dial.

"The colonel's office," he barked into the receiver. Then, in a
far nicer tone, he said, "He's here, sir," and hung up. No doubt
Lebanese, thought Kifah Kassar, Lebanese, but why, why?

The officer removed a pack of cigarettes from his tunic
pocket and handed one to Kifah Kassar, which the Palestinian
happily accepted. The officer pressed a buzzer and a soldier
brought in a large glass of water, which Kifah Kassar drank to
the last drop.

No more words were exchanged until the door swung open
as a short man wearing a colonel's uniform strode in. The colonel
was an evil-looking man, with thick, yellow-tinted eyeglasses partially hiding toady eyes. In a flash, the other officer rose, darted
around the desk, and grabbed the cigarette out of Kifah Kassar's
mouth, throwing it to the ground.

"The colonel does not like people to smoke in front of him," he said. He handed the file to the colonel, who sat himself at the desk. Nothing was said for several long, agonizing minutes as the colonel studied the file. Finally, the colonel spoke, addressing Kifah Kassar in a soft but threatening voice.

"You are being held by the Lebanese security forces in a prison in Beirut, near the racetrack. We regret the inconvenience but knew that if we did not bring you here you would not have come on your own," said the colonel. "I am a very busy man. I have several important questions to ask you and I don't have time to play games. If you answer me quickly, and correctly, you will be released. However, if you choose to fuck with me, this will be our last interview. And I will hand you back to this lot," he motioned towards the guards who had brought him to the interrogation room. "And if that were to happen, you will regret the day that the whore you call mother gave birth to you. I am a civilized man and don't like to hurt people, but my friends do. So help me help you. I will say only this to you: think very carefully what you say before you say it, because I know when you lie and if you lie, I will be very angry."

The colonel leaned back, allowing his words to sink in before continuing. The colonel had done this before and was good at it. He could see his words had the desired effect on Kifah Kassar. "I want to know who ordered the killing of the American agent and of the Lebanese man with him, and why. We know your group was involved, so please don't insult my intelligence by denying it. We don't particularly care about an American spy dying but we had spent a lot of time training our man to infiltrate the US spy network, only for you to kill him. I am not happy. So quickly, who and why?"

"We did—"

"Remember," said the man in the Lebanese colonel's uniform, "no lies."

"We did not know he was an American, and we did not know the other was Lebanese and working for you," said the Palestinian. "In all honesty."

The officer ignored Kifah Kassar's last remark. "We have reason to believe that our agent was killed because of something you did not want him to know. What could be so important that it merits killing someone for?"

"I would like to find out how my wife is doing first. She had a bad accident last night . . . yesterday," he said, looking at his watch and suddenly remembering the reason for his sudden departure from the safety of the training camp in south Lebanon. God Almighty, how could he have forgotten about her? He also had no idea what time it was. His watch said 6:10, but with no windows to look out, he could not tell if it was morning or night.

"Tell us what we want to know and you can go home to her this afternoon," said the colonel. "Otherwise, we have somewhat perfected the trick the Americans used at Abu Ghraib and in Guantanamo. You know, the waterboarding. Well, we found that if you add certain unpleasant elements to the water it tends to make people talk faster. And my friend, you know that no one resists. All end up talking. You understand? It does not matter how strong you are or how loyal you are. In the end, everyone talks. It's just a matter of how much pain you can take before you break. You know the French in Algeria had developed this device they called the bicycle. It was, as the name indicates, part of a bicycle that powered a small generator onto which the prisoners were attached through car jumper cables and with their feet in a basin of water. Extremely uncomfortable and painful. Many could not support the pain, and died. You know what the Front de Libération National asked of their cadres? To try and hold out from twenty-four to forty-eight hours. Just twenty-four hours, to give the cell members enough time to escape and change their locations. And you know why the FLN asked their militants to hold only that long? Because they were realists. They knew that in the end, everyone talks. For them it was just a matter of saving other members of the revolution. In your case, my dear Kifah Kassar, you have no one to protect but yourself. So save yourself the trouble."

14

BEIRUT, LEBANON

Chris Clayborne did not want to admit it, but he was rapidly falling in love with Laura. He had not been in love for many years—since his marriage broke up five years earlier, and his wife of fifteen years left him for some seedy pseudo-sailor living in Portsmouth, Virginia. Laura was young, beautiful, intelligent, witty, and seemed exceptionally different from most other women hacks he had known. Laura seemed to understand the Middle East situation far better than some so-called old hands.

Clayborne could see the candlelight reflected in Laura's bright green eyes as she sipped her wine. Laura allowed a tiny drop of Bordeaux to drip down the side of her mouth, like a red teardrop. She let Clayborne wipe it away with a gentle stroke of the back of his hand. Laura's eyes also revealed a deep, hidden pain, a burden from her past that seemed to have affected her, to sadden her; yet she never wanted to talk about it. Maybe it was a love affair gone sour? Laura avoided talking about herself and although he felt she liked him too, she somehow always managed to keep him at bay, to keep her distance. She didn't want to get involved. Well, maybe that was a good thing. Beirut was not the kind of place one should start something like that, Chris told himself. But why not? Nothing made him want to love more than all this hatred around him.

Clayborne's thoughts were interrupted by the waiter offering to take their order. Yes, they were ready, said Laura, sensing Clayborne's sadness. They were also famished. Chris ordered for the two of them: fettuccine alfredo for a starter and then fish, the *rouget*, a specialty of the house. Both the pasta and the fish were always perfectly served at La Plage, a cozy restaurant sitting so close to the water's edge that sometimes the waves would actually touch your feet. They also ordered a bottle of Château Musar, a delicious white Lebanese wine.

Clayborne took Laura's hand across the table, gently squeezing it. At times Laura reminded him of a frightened and confused little girl, while at other times she seemed hard and dedicated to her work. "So, what's this terribly important story that forces you to leave so suddenly?" asked Clayborne.

"Can't say. You know," she smiled at him, shrugging her shoulders, and placed her other hand on top of his, "exclusive stuff and all that. We can't have the wires go after it, now can we? It would hardly be an exclusive, would it?"

"Laura, you know I don't care about that. I care about you."

"No, Chris, stop. Please, I can't get involved at this time. I really can't. I can't explain, but the timing is just not right. I like you very much, I really do. But things are kind of crazy at the moment."

"Then why are you fighting it?"

"I have to concentrate on my career. I've always wanted to be a writer, and now I have the opportunity to do that. Tell you what: when I get back from Europe, let's go spend a weekend in Cyprus. Okay?"

"Fine, it's a plan." Chris lowered his voice and leaned closer to Laura. "Don't turn around now, but see that man at the third table by the stairs with the woman in a lilac dress? He is one of Dr. Hawali's closest advisers. He never lets anyone take his picture and no one knows what he looks like. In fact, not many people even know of his existence."

"So how come you know him?"

"I saw him briefly in Baghdad, years ago, at a conference. He had his bodyguards grab my camera and confiscate my film. But I never forget a face. No one even knows his real name. Outside of the Doctor's circle, people refer to him as 'the Thinker.'"

"Charming man. Just what does he think about?"

"Mostly second options."

"Second options?"

"Yes. He is the counterblow to the Front's policies and strategies. He will think up ways to make use of a situation and milk it to greater potential."

Laura looked perplexed. "What exactly do you mean?" she asked.

"It's really very simple. For example, the Doctor will go to the Iranians and ask for money to finance his operation. Well, the Thinker is the man who dreams up reasons why the Iranians should pay the money. He will tell the Doctor that they can take care of a bothersome dissident for them. Naturally, the price doubles and all sides walk away content."

"Except for the dead dissidents," interjected Laura.

"Details," said Chris. "Zeid, the Doctor's number two man, once confided that the Thinker believes there are two sides to every opportunity. Both sides can be made to work in his favor." Chris took a sip of his wine before continuing. "For example, by instigating an attack on a kibbutz in Israel, the Thinker knew that the Israeli Army would retaliate. That's exactly what he wanted. The peace talks were going too smoothly, and he needed to put the other Arab leaders on notice that the Palestinian conflict is far from over. It gave him leverage at the last Arab summit. It really matters little to him that innocent people will die. What counts is that Israeli planes bombing civilian targets in Beirut always make front-page news."

"And even you don't have a picture of him?"

"No one does. He is rarely seen in public. The only reason he is here tonight is probably because he wants to impress the woman he is with and take her to bed. She is very likely to be the wife of some Arab diplomat who has been recalled back to his country for consultation."

After dinner, Laura went back to Chris Clayborne's apartment. Chris had moved out of the Commodore Hotel and into a furnished apartment facing the Mediterranean. Washington insisted he cut back on expenses. The flat was situated on the waterfront about a mile from the restaurant. They sat close to each other on a comfortable sofa on Clayborne's balcony, overlooking the sea. Plagued by electricity shortages, the city was in total darkness. The only sound came from waves crashing on the shore across the street, or an occasional car driving by.

Clayborne went inside and returned with two very large tumblers of cognac and a cigarette filled with first-grade Lebanese hashish. Chris and Laura sat in silence listening to the waves, drinking cognac and getting stoned. Occasionally, a short burst of machine gun fire could be heard in the distance, interrupting the silence of the night, a reminder that this was still Beirut, after all, and that the war was never too far away. Clayborne placed his arm around Laura and she snuggled closer to him.

"Make love to me," she whispered in his ear. Laura felt she needed Chris's comfort. He brought her a certain amount of safety that temporarily made her forget why she was here and what would happen to her if she ever got caught. Langley had instructed her to use him, and right now this was what she needed him for.

Clayborne started to get up. "No, here. Make love to me here," said Laura. She slowly unbuttoned her blouse and removed her bra, revealing perfect, firm breasts. Clayborne reached over and unzipped her skirt, which she let drop gently to the floor. Very slowly, she removed her white silk panties without taking her eyes off Chris. She let Chris run his warm hands over her body. It felt good. She started undressing him, caressing the thick hair on his chest. She reached for the tumbler and took a sip of cognac, placed her lips on Chris's, and offered him some from her warm mouth. They kissed passionately, touching each other, feeling one another, caressing, and holding tightly, giving one another much needed comfort. Laura felt Chris's warmth as he entered her. They savored each other for the longest time, now totally drenched in perspiration. The cognac and hashish made their heads swim to the cadence of the waves crashing on the nearby rocks.

They continued to hold on to each other long after their love-making was over. There was something very special about making love in a war zone that brought out the most tender of feelings in a person. Maybe it was to make up for the hatred around them that people loved so passionately in war.

They remained clasped together for a long time, both lost in their thoughts. It was a near-perfect moment, and both Chris and Laura wanted to prolong their pleasure as much as possible, to make the moment last, to escape the violent reality that surrounded them.

A distant explosion brought them back to earth. "I could stay like this forever," whispered Laura.

"Yes, so could I."

"I bet you bring all your women up here and make love to them like this."

"A gentleman never tells," replied Clayborne, laughing. "The truth, Laura, is you're the first one I've made love to out here." Clayborne rose to fetch more cognac, hashish, and a blanket. With dawn nearing, it was starting to get chilly. He also brought out a transistor radio.

"When are you coming back?"

Laura had that melancholy look again, abruptly reminded of the real reason for her presence in Beirut. "Don't really know," she said kissing Clayborne on the nose. "Probably not too long. A week at the most."

"I shall wait for thee, my love."

"What time is it, anyway?" asked Laura.

"Almost time for the news," replied Clayborne, turning on the radio, which was pre-tuned to the BBC, in time to hear the announcer say, "And that's it from Sports Roundup. Next on the BBC World Service is a bulletin of world news."

"Damn, it's late. I must get home," exclaimed Laura.

"Too late now," laughed Clayborne. "It's almost four. No one walks around Beirut at this time of night. Looks like you'll have to spend what's left of the night here." He hugged her tightly.

"Love me again," said Laura, curling her legs around his waist.

"Wait, let's listen to the news first," replied Clayborne. "It's only seven minutes long." But neither of them could wait that long.

15

BEIRUT, LEBANON

In the end, Kifah Kassar ended up spilling more than the Americans expected, or even hoped for, but once he started to talk there was no stopping him. He was so sleep deprived and so mentally and physically exhausted and had so many drugs pumped into him that he just wanted to sleep and rest for at least an hour. Hell, he would have even been happy to sleep for fifteen minutes. He was so exhausted from the waterboarding that he became delirious and started to talk about the "special young man who would avenge the Arab and Muslim world." He described "Omar" so well that the former Lebanese Forces commando hired by Laura Atwood and driving a battered gray Mercedes taxi had no trouble identifying him when he emerged from the address also graciously provided by the Palestinian resistance leader.

When Omar left his apartment building near the Arab University, he failed to notice the gray Mercedes taxi waiting by the corner of the street. Traffic was always heavy around the university and lingering taxicabs were a common sight. Even the small dent on the taxi's front right side did not seem out of place with the rest of Beirut's battered fleet of *services*, or collective taxis. Carrying a shoulder bag, the young Iraqi-Palestinian walked a few paces to the corner and hailed a cab. The driver of the gray Mercedes waved to Omar, signaling he would pick him up, but was beaten to the fare by another taxi that suddenly swerved in front of the gray Mercedes. The driver of the gray Mercedes honked his horn, cursing at the other taxi for stealing his fare, but there was little he could do. The driver cursed his bad luck and followed Omar at a safe distance, keeping the automatic gun he kept hidden under his seat within easy reach.

The Armenian called Laura on her cell phone. She answered on the second ring. "Miss Laura, *marhaba*," said the driver.

"*Marhaba*," replied Laura.

"Miss Laura," said the Armenian, "we found your package. Tony and Elie are already on their way; I just called them. What you want I do?"

"Just stay with him. And keep me informed. Where do I hook up with you?"

"I don't know where they are going but one possible destination is the Front's headquarters on Mazraa. Just guessing."

"Okay, I will head your way and see where we can connect."

"*Trés bien*," said the Armenian, switching to French.

It was a good guess. Omar headed to the Front's headquarters off Avenue Mazraa. The driver of the gray Mercedes parked two blocks away, not wanting to be noticed by the guards. He was furious, knowing he had blown his one chance to pick up the terrorist Washington was so eager to get its hands on. Miss Laura had promised him a huge bonus if he managed to pick him up. A Navy SEAL commando unit waiting off the coast would sweep in and help ferry out the terrorist, once the driver or Laura gave them the signal by calling a number on their cell phones. Now the plan was derailed. Out of frustration, the driver bit off the filter of his American cigarette and spat it out the window.

Dr. Ibrahim Hawali greeted Omar warmly and explained what was expected of him now that his training was completed. Omar would have a chance to prove himself and once again repay the Americans for the injustice committed against his people. The Doctor left Omar with Zeid, who filled him in on last-minute details and handed him his new identity: a Jordanian passport in the name of Issam Abdelrazzak Haidar, given to the Palestinians through the good graces of the Syrian intelligence service bureau in Beirut in exchange for ten thousand dollars—peanuts when compared to the sixty million dollars the Mexican drug cartel would pay him. And even if they reneged on the full amount, the Doctor had already pocketed thirty million dollars. Omar was then left with Zeid, the Doctor's trusted deputy. He made Omar/Issam go over the procedures of the plans forward and backward. Zeid then gave Issam ten thousand dollars in cash and two credit cards in the same name, along with a Jordanian and an international driver's license. Zeid stressed the importance of the mission and repeated how paramount it was that Issam be certain that he was not being followed.

"More money will be sent to you in due time. It is suspicious if you travel with more than ten thousand dollars. It arouses suspicion and sends up red flags. So spend a couple of hundred in the duty-free stores. This way you will be able to truthfully say that you have less than ten thousand dollars.

"In fact," said Zeid, "you could say that your mission is in two parts. The first is to make sure you are not followed or caught, and the second part of your job is to complete the task with your mortars. Without succeeding at the first job, you will not succeed at the second task. You understand the importance of this mission: under no circumstances whatsoever are you to be caught alive. Don't think that the Americans will not get you to talk, because they will. They may not use some of the methods we do, they may not break your finger bones or pull your toenails out, but believe me, what they will do to you can be just as convincing. So let me be 100 percent truthful with you: do not let them catch you, and if they do, don't let them catch you alive."

Laura and Kevork Nazarian watched from a distance as Omar emerged two hours later escorted by a man with a slightly disfigured face. Laura recognized the man with the scars from photographs she had seen of him. He was the public face of the FSF, a man called Basil Sharraf. Also known as Zeid.

The two men shook hands, embraced, and kissed. Then Omar got into a white Peugeot with three other people. The three men, as well as the driver, were armed. The driver of the gray Mercedes slammed his fist into the steering wheel. Picking up Omar was now impossible. He remained three or four cars behind, and followed. They could be going anywhere, and the man was afraid to lose them. If they headed into the camps, it would be suicide to follow. There was only so much he could risk. There were areas in the camps that were even off-limits to the average Palestinian. At the end of Avenue Mazraa, the car turned left and followed the coastal road south, then turned left again. They passed in front of the Kuwaiti embassy and then veered right toward Beirut International Airport. The driver of the gray Mercedes prayed that they would not go into Chatilla, one of the largest refugee camps. No, thank God, the car kept going straight, to Beirut

Airport. The driver of the gray Mercedes was thankful for that. The airport was neutral ground and there was always a crowd there. It was easy to follow someone without being noticed.

Outside the airport, Omar left his escort and walked unaccompanied inside the terminal building. The driver of the Mercedes dropped Laura off in front of the departures area, parked his car, and followed inside. The two were joined by two more of Laura's recruits, also former Lebanese Forces fighters, Nabil Khoury and Tony Helou. Omar checked in at a Middle East Airlines counter. The crowds at the airport were greater than usual and this helped Laura and the driver blend in. It allowed them to then remain a few discreet steps behind their package without being noticed. Omar did not seem concerned by his surroundings; he walked straight ahead without looking behind to see if he was being followed. He headed for the Middle East Airlines desk, where passengers traveling to Brussels were checking in. Laura told the Armenian driver to remain in the queue behind Omar. She was going to get a seat on the same flight. When Omar presented himself at the counter, Laura was by a stroke of luck at the adjoining counter. She tried looking to see what name and what nationality the man she was following was traveling under, but was unable.

The flight to Brussels was fully booked. Laura tried to get a seat in first or business class, to no avail. There was not a single empty seat on the plane. She tried to bribe the desk agent, but that didn't work. Next she tried offering money to several passengers to give her their seats, but this didn't work either. She asked the Armenian to see who he could bribe, convince, cajole, or even threaten, if need be. Meanwhile, she called Langley on her cell phone.

The Armenian came up to Laura with a big grin on his face. "Madame Laura, I have one my cousins, his name is Harout, he going on same flight to Brussels. He okay for giving you his seat for one thousand dollars."

"Tell him it's a deal."

Kevork motioned to someone standing in the queue, who came over and was introduced to Laura. "Madame Laura, this my cousin, Mr. Harout. Mr. Harout, this my lady boss, Mrs. Madame Laura." The two then went into what seemed to be an interminable discussion in Armenian, and the cousin finally said to Laura, "Okay, we go tell agent you take my seat."

16

BEIRUT, LEBANON

Dr. Hawali found the Thinker in a jovial mood, which was unusual.

"My dear Doctor," said the Thinker, looking up from his desk, "we shall have our weapon on time. The backup facility in Kabul is proceeding at full strength. Our dear sheik in Cairo has agreed to continue funding the project completely. Even the attempt on his life last week did not deter him. He is convinced it was the Israelis who tried to kill him. So now he is more than ever committed to seeing the project through. If all goes well, we can have enough material within a few months."

"That is good news, but let's make sure it is no longer than two months. We are on a tight schedule."

BRUSSELS, BELGIUM

It was Omar's first time in Europe, and it felt strange. It was all the more strange because this time he had to impersonate someone else. He not only had to use someone else's name, but he had to begin thinking like someone else, too. He scanned his environs, moving his gaze from left to right and back. The area seemed clean, but there were numerous places where someone could hide, should they need to. Omar took in the scenery around him. Everything seemed in perfect working order. Everything was clean and tidy, everything seemed to be in its place, almost like those small dollhouses he often saw some of the younger girls in the camps play with. People were well dressed and they all seemed to have somewhere to go. No one lingered at street corners, like in the camps, or in most Arab cities. Even the cars looked new and polished; it was hard to find one that was dented or dirty. Drivers stopped at red lights, although there were no policemen at intersections to enforce the law. And car drivers didn't honk their horns, unless it was a real emergency.

For a while, it seemed to Omar, now travelling as Issam, as if this was a perfect world: clean, tidy, orderly, and elegant. But then a voice inside of him told him no. No! It was most certainly not! It was because of them, the Imperialists, the Europeans, the friends and allies of the dreaded Zionists that he, Omar, was a refugee, a man without a nation. He was obliged to travel on false documents, using a forged Jordanian passport, or, in this case, a stolen passport. Otherwise these *nice* people wouldn't even let him into their silly little country. Palestine and Iraq were synonymous with terrorism! And still, the Belgian embassy in Beirut had refused him a visa. The Arabs were not liked very much either. He finally obtained a Dutch visa. Since the establishment of the European Union and the signing of the Phares Schengen Zone, internal borders between the signatories were abolished. A visa from any one Schengen nation allowed the holder to travel to the other countries freely.

Suddenly Omar felt even more hatred for these so-called civilized people. Why should they enjoy their lousy little unimportant lives when his people had no country to live in and were forced to survive in refugee camps in filth and squalor? But now he had an important job to do and decided to concentrate on the task ahead. There would always be more time to hate later.

Once the seat belt sign was switched off, Omar started walking casually up and down the aisles of the plane as if he was stretching his legs, as many passengers tend to do on a long flight. But Omar had another reason to do this. He was studying the passengers, scrutinizing every face and mentally placing them in one of two categories. He was looking for those who could be a possible tail and those who could not. The ones who were obviously too old or too young to be spies he placed in the second category and discarded. In that second batch went also those who were obviously traveling with their families. Pregnant women (there were three). That left him with a good twenty-four people, among them Laura Atwood, whom at first he almost placed in the second category. But he caught a quick glimpse of her eyes and that made him change his mind. There was something about those eyes, thought Omar. They seem to be hiding something.

Omar first noticed the woman from the airplane before he noticed the man outside the airport. He initially put it off as paranoia. It was his first time outside the Middle East. No one knew him. No one outside a group of trusted people knew he was going to Brussels.

The man was definitely not on his flight from Beirut. Then he spotted the same man outside the Hotel Métropole in the center of Brussels. The man was sitting in a café adjoining the hotel. He was sitting outside, even though it was too cold and he should have been sitting indoors, as all the other patrons were. When Omar left the hotel, the man quickly paid for his coffee and followed. A car driven by a woman raced up to the curb and the man jumped inside. Omar felt, more than saw, the man behind him. But instinct and training told him the man was there. There was no rush, he said to himself. He had plenty of time before meeting his contact. It was Sunday and there were few cars on the streets of the Belgian capital.

How could they be on to him so soon? Omar pondered. Could it be the Israelis, or the Americans had somehow managed to infiltrate the Front? That was always possible. The Doctor was always worried that the Front could be infiltrated by double agents. Anyway, Omar was not worried. Let them follow me; for the moment I don't need to lose them, he thought. There is plenty of time for that later.

He walked from the hotel to the large open-air vegetable market near the Gâre du Midi train station. Omar was amazed by what he saw. The place resembled a Middle Eastern market, with hundreds of vendors, mostly Arabs, selling their produce in this weekly makeshift market. Thousands of housewives, Europeans, Arabs, Turks, and Africans mingled, jostled, and bargained for fresh produce. This was better than he had expected. He started to laugh. Whoever was following him would have a great time trying to identify his contact, as the sheer number of Arabs present in the market gave the young Palestinian a great idea. It was better than to try and lose his tail. He would confuse him. If he lost the man now, they might put another on him, and it would take Omar longer to identify a new tail. Omar stopped at almost every stall, looking at the fruits, vegetables, and flowers, inquiring about the price, chatting in Arabic with the vendors.

What a great place to meet another Arab. There were even some pro-Nasserites selling political newspapers and arguing with passersby. Omar bought a few bananas from one vendor, an apple from another, some sunflower seeds from a third, and Arabic sweets from yet another. He shook hands with every vendor and tried to make it seem like everyone he spoke to was his intended contact. An hour later, at exactly eleven thirty, Omar made his way to a stand selling french fries on the southern end of the marketplace. It was easily recognizable by the large sign advertising FRITES ET MOULES ALI BABA. An Arab-looking man and two women, probably the man's wife and daughter, were busy cooking and serving French fries in large paper cones which were then topped with mayonnaise and other bizarre looking sauces. Omar waited until he had the attention of the man and asked for "one fries and one falafel."

The man behind the counter hardly reacted. "We have no falafel. Only *frites* and mussels."

"But they have no mussels in the Arab world," replied Omar in Arabic.

"Then have some *frites*," the man said.

"OK, give me the largest Ali Baba fries you have. Without mayonnaise." The man handed Omar a paper cone filled with French fries. Had anyone bothered to hold the cone, they would have noticed that it was slightly heavier than other cones of the same size. Omar paid and left. He continued to walk, eating some of the fries. A few minutes later he placed the rest in one of the plastic bags with the fruits he had bought earlier and slowly made his way back to the Hotel Métropole. Omar went to his room and locked the door. He placed a newspaper on the desk by the bed and emptied the remaining French fries onto it. At the bottom of the pile, sealed in a small plastic bag, were the pieces of a 7.5 mm pistol wrapped in an oilcloth and a Moroccan passport stolen a day earlier from a hotel, where the passport's owner would not miss it or report its loss for another week. This would give Omar ample time to get to London and then discard the stolen passport.

Omar donned a pair of surgical gloves he had bought earlier at a pharmacy, and in less than two minutes had cleaned and assembled the pistol. The last item in the plastic bag was his itinerary for his flight to London and the name and address of his contact in the British capital. He memorized them, placed the papers in an ashtray and set them on fire, then crushed the ashes and flushed them down the toilet. But first he needed to lose whoever was following him. He packed his overnight suitcase and disposed of the fruits and seeds bought earlier along with the newspaper and gloves. He put on a pair of black leather gloves and balanced the gun in his hand. It was a small caliber, but Omar trusted it would do the job. He was confident that despite the fact that he was being followed, he could still pull it off. In fact, the Brussels and London stops were intended specifically to weed out potential tails. Yes, he could do the job well.

He had studied the map of Brussels for more than a week now and knew the streets he needed to know by heart. It was simple. He'd even foreseen the possibility of being followed and it would take him little time to lose his tail. He went downstairs, paid his bill in cash, and left.

His pulse was beating faster now. His mission was in sight. Omar drove his rented car from the Hotel Métropole to the vast underground parking garage that ran the whole length of Rue de la Loi. He parked near the Avenue des Arts entrance and walked up the staircase leading to the street next to the Banque Bruxelles Lambert. Instead of going straight out onto the avenue, Omar waited quietly at the top of the staircase. This was the heart of the business district and was totally deserted on Sunday. Omar didn't have to wait long before his tail ran up the stairs trying to catch up with him. The hit came so suddenly that the man never had enough time to react. As he rounded the corner onto the landing, Omar jammed his outstretched hand into the man's throat, slamming the man's windpipe between his thumb and forefinger. The powerful blow stunned the man, allowing Omar enough time to immediately follow with a powerful karate kick into the man's groin and a side kick into his chest. The triple blows sent the man crashing down the concrete staircase. The hit to the throat had cut the airflow, momentarily paralyzing the man. Omar followed the American agent down the stairs and before the agent could regain his balance, Omar snapped his neck in one quick motion. The only person in Europe able to identify the Palestinian was now dead. But then he recalled the driver. The woman who picked up the agent he had just killed. She had seen his face.

He concluded that the fact he was being followed, and not killed or arrested, indicated that the Americans were not sure it was him they were after. Or that they did not have the support of their local allies, otherwise they would have had the Belgian authorities pick him up. But on what charges? Traveling with fake documents? He would spend a few nights in detention and then be expelled. They really had nothing on him, and the fact that he was still free proved it.

They couldn't tie him to the death of the agent in the underground parking garage on the Rue de la Loi because no one saw him do it. He left no clues, no fingerprints, he wore gloves the whole time, and hadn't fired his weapon.

Omar needed time to think through his next step. Maybe the *frites* vendor had given him away. He didn't think so, but it was a distinct possibility. He was the only one to know of Omar's arrival in Belgium and that he would be visiting his stand in the marketplace at the Gâre du Midi. Still, Omar's instincts told him otherwise. Getting back to his car was too dangerous, as the body might have been found by now. He decided that he would change his travel plans. The airline schedule given to him by the *frites* vendor would have to be changed, just in case. Omar decided he would take the Chunnel train to London instead of flying. Considering the time needed to go to and from airports in Brussels and London, the boarding and deplaning, the security checks at airports, and the fact that one needed to be at the airport several hours prior to departure, the trip from Brussels to London aboard the Eurostar was about the same in cost and time required. Omar took a taxi to the train station, where he boarded the next train for London. But before boarding, he went into the men's room and disposed of the pistol he had been given by the *frites* vendor. He broke it down and dropped the pieces in the toilet flush tank. It would probably be several years before anyone would find it. And if and when they did discover the gun, there was nothing in the world that tied him to it.

By the time the Belgian police were alerted that there was a dead man in the staircase of the Rue de la Loi parking, Omar was already in France heading for the Chunnel, the high-speed train linking England to the Continent. The police had a hard time identifying the body because the victim carried no identification on him: no ID, no passport, no credit cards, no driver's license, not even the obligatory residence card issued to every foreigner in the country that Belgian law dictated everyone had to carry at all times. By the time it was discovered that the man with the broken neck was an American and the embassy responded (it was Sunday, after all), Omar was safely lost in the perpetual crowds of British railway stations.

The Palestinian terrorist was exhausted both mentally and physically by the time he reached London. The look in the American's eyes as he snapped his neck had remained with him throughout the train ride to London. For some strange reason, he could not rid himself of that image. The dying man's stare haunted him and kept him awake. Every time he dozed off, the frantic eyes popped back into his mind. He would relive that scene over and over and over, all in slow motion. Omar would see the face of the American agent he had killed appear in his dreams, but the face would be underwater and it would drag the young Palestinian with him. Omar felt he was suffocating, he felt that he could not breathe. And then he would wake up. When he arrived in London, he got in a taxi and asked to be taken to a pub.

Laura Atwood was furious. After she dropped off the Brussels agent in the underground parking garage, she drove back out, in case Omar had a car waiting for him outside. It was an old trick to park in an underground location, as he did, then run out and hop into a waiting car or a bus. The fact that Omar had killed the Brussels agent seemed to confirm that he must be on the move. Otherwise, why risk this?

Now they lost the trail and would have to start all over again. They had come so close to nabbing him. He was probably back in the quagmire of the terrorist camps in Lebanon, and it would take forever to flush him out again. She knew Omar was far too smart to return to the apartment from where he had been followed in Beirut.

From her room at the Amigo Hotel near the Grande Place, she placed a call to Pat Brent in Virginia.

"Think there is a slight chance he might still be in Belgium?" asked Brent.

"Sure, and if I hold my hand over the North Sea, it will part like Moses separated the Red Sea. This man is no fool. He's long gone by now," replied Laura. "Let's not waste any more time here. I'm going back to Beirut."

The return flight to Beirut seemed to last forever and Laura felt terribly depressed. The people in Brussels had screwed up the best opportunity to get their hands on the terrorist. She had a bad feeling about this. This man Omar was a cut above the average killer. He was smart and didn't waste time. He covered every angle. He did his homework and carried out his mission well. There were no clues, no traces to pick up, no fingerprints. Even the hotel room in Brussels offered no clues. There wasn't even any garbage to shift through. The Palestinian had removed anything that might help identify him. Sure, the Belgian police had promised results, but she wasn't holding her breath. They had nothing to go on. The hotel register and airport entry card were dead ends. There was no trace of him ever leaving the country, which meant he probably drove or took the train. If her instincts were correct, he had probably driven to France, Luxembourg, or the Netherlands. Cars were seldom stopped at the borders that were gradually disappearing with the Eastern expansion of the European Union becoming more of a reality every passing day.

Then there was this affair with Chris Clayborne. That bothered her too. Chris was getting too serious. She could not afford to get involved; not now. On the other hand, it provided her with a better cover. A male companion in the Arab world was always a good thing to have, but she was starting to feel guilty for using Chris as she did. Or was she really using him? At times she actually enjoyed being with Chris. She enjoyed making love to him. He was nice and kind to her. She needed the warmth he provided, and his contacts were valuable. Beirut was not an easy place to live, especially when you were a female American spy working for the CIA. If the Palestinians or the Lebanese or Hezbollah ever found out, her life would not be worth a devalued Lebanese lira.

17

LONDON, ENGLAND

Omar woke up startled. His first reaction was to reach for his gun, usually placed under his pillow, only his gun wasn't there. He was somewhat disoriented, and for about a second or two, unsure of where he was. Was he in Beirut, Baghdad, Brussels, or London? The complete darkness of the room added to his disorientation. He thought for a fraction of a second that he might be dead. Maybe that's what hell was: darkness. Total darkness. But Omar quickly recovered. It suddenly came back to him. Of course, he was in London.

Omar was drenched in perspiration, his hair clinging to the back of his neck. The nightmares simply would not go away. He had been having these same horrible dreams over and over, every night, since the Brussels affair. It had been several days now, but still they kept recurring, night after night. In his dreams, Omar kept seeing the face of the American agent he had killed. The face of a man who knew he was about to be killed looked at him. Looked straight into his eyes and asked, "Why? Why, my son, did you choose to kill me?"

In his nightmares, Omar saw the soldiers he had killed in the helicopter with his first mortar, back in Iraq. He saw the bodies flying out of the giant mechanical bird as they fell to the ground. Some were on fire. Only, in his dream, they didn't hit the ground—they would fly away. In his nightmares he could see the eyes of the agent he had killed in the parking garage, though in reality he hadn't even had time to see the man's eyes. It all happened so quickly. And every time he looked into those eyes, they suddenly turned into his father's eyes. Though by now, Omar was not sure what the eyes of his father looked like. He decided he wouldn't look at the dead man's eyes, but it was impossible. Why was this happening to him? He had killed before, in Iraq, and it never bothered him. He never even stopped to think about the killing he was doing before. There was a war, and he had to kill the invader. But now it felt so strange. Until a few days ago, until he came to Europe, these facts had never bothered him. Why were they getting to him now?

Then he dreamt that he was trying to escape and was being chased by a helicopter. The soldiers who were on fire were cursing him; some were shooting their M16 rifles at him. Bullets kept hitting his back, though they were ineffective. Omar laughed; he laughed hysterically. Then he woke.

Omar looked at his watch. It was still early morning in London, only six. The young Palestinian rose, took a shower, and ordered a cup of coffee from room service. The strong coffee made him feel better. Omar was bored with sitting still. After Brussels, he was eager to get to the US and on with his assignment. But he had to wait until he got the green light from the Doctor. Meanwhile, that meant staying in his hotel room and waiting for the phone call. Zeid and the Doctor were trying to figure out how word of his presence in Brussels was known so quickly. Was there an informer within the group? That's what they wanted to find out before proceeding with the plan.

A very young and very good-looking Kurdish maid came by his room every morning around ten to clean and make the bed. She could not have been older than seventeen, but was already married and had two children. She complained to Omar that her husband beat her. He was often drunk on cheap arak and would take his frustrations out on the poor woman.

The second week Omar was in the hotel, the maid entered the bathroom while he was enjoying a bubble bath. Embarrassed, the young woman was about to leave when Omar called her back. "Wash my back," he told her.

Instead, the pretty young woman removed her clothes, revealing a body as white as milk, and joined Omar in the bathtub. Her long black hair came down to her well-rounded buttocks.

Other than a couple of prostitutes, Omar had never had sex before. He was good-looking, with short, curly, jet-black hair, and kept his body in shape by exercising at least two hours a day. He felt the maid's soft skin touch his. He lay back in the soapy water and looked at the young maid. She straddled him, dipping her hand under the warm bubbles. She found Omar erect and gently guided him inside her, then started a slow up-and-down motion, creating gentle waves in the bathtub. Omar, as though possessed by a demon, started moving furiously. She shook her long, smooth, dark hair over Omar's head, partially covering his face. She placed her lips on his and whispered, "No, no. Slowly, slowly, relax, make the pleasure last."

Omar could not control himself and burst inside her moments later. They remained in the tub for more than an hour,

Omar caressing the maid's amazingly white, smooth body. Her large breasts felt good to touch. Omar then carried her into the bedroom where he made love to her once more.

Had it not been for the young Kurdish maid, Omar would have gone crazy locked up in that hotel room day after day after day. At least she provided good entertainment. Omar often wondered what it would have been like to have a steady girlfriend, to have someone to share thoughts and ideas with. To have children with. The maid was a good lay, but they hardly spoke to each other. When she had turned fifteen, the poor child had been married off to a fifty-seven-year-old man. Her husband was a vegetable vendor, carrying large crates of fruit and vegetables on his back from dawn to sunset. By the time the old man got home at night, he was far too tired to care for his young wife, whose sexual appetite never seemed to wane.

TEHRAN, IRAN

Shortly before dawn the following morning, the Doctor headed to Damascus by car, where he boarded an Iran Air jet bound for Tehran. After debating the plan all night long with the Thinker, an even greater plan had begun to slowly take shape. The sheik's initial blueprint was good; in fact, it was more than good—it was excellent. But the old man had failed to fully grasp the dynamic potential of his proposal. It had far greater consequences. Given the new biological weapons promised by the sheik, this would be the greatest strike by any group against the Americans and their Israeli allies in history. There was no doubt the world would wake up and listen to them after this strike.

In the Iranian capital, the Doctor needed to solicit the help of yet another party. By the time the plane landed in Tehran, the Doctor was satisfied with his revision of the plan. The Thinker was right: not only would the revised plan instantly derail the peace talks forever, but it would also cement the Front's role as leader of the resistance to the peace process. It would show the Americans that there could be no halfway solutions. Palestine was not negotiable.

An hour later, the Doctor was ushered into the office of Ayatollah Firamarz Kazemi. Officially, Kazemi was the head of the Islamic Reform Movement, a staunchly conservative fundamentalist movement grouping thousands of followers and encompassing several members of parliament, including two prominent cabinet ministers. Much to the dismay of the president, Kazemi's position commanded much power, both inside the country and abroad. Using a legion of sympathizers recruited by loyal agents through an intricate web of mosques and Islamic teaching centers scattered around Europe and the United States, the Ayatollah had constructed a vast network of supporters in his personal crusade against the United States and Israel, his sworn enemies. Kazemi's position was further strengthened through close ties he had cultivated over the years with various extremist Palestinian groups like the Doctor's PSF.

Kazemi was a tall, thin man in his late fifties. Like most members of the Iranian clergy, he wore a black beard, robes, and a turban. Six years spent in Evin Prison during the Shah's rule had fomented his hatred of America, which Kazemi blamed for supporting the Shah. After the Islamic Revolution, Kazemi was placed in charge of uncovering past relations between the CIA and Iran's SAVAK intelligence agency. The more he discovered, the greater his hatred for America grew. The Central Intelligence Agency believed he was responsible for numerous attacks against American and western European interests in the Middle East and Europe. The CIA also believed that Kazemi maintained close ties with al-Haq's group in Egypt. And they were not mistaken.

After the usual greetings, the Doctor came right to the point. "Excellency, how would you like the chance to strike at the very heart of our enemy, while the United States is rendered completely impotent?" asked the Doctor.

"What exactly is on your mind?" the imam asked, and avoided adding, "other than your insatiable need for more money."

"As you know, the Americans are in an election year. Both the president who is running for reelection as well as the number one contender representing the Republican party, Senator Richard Wells, are trying very hard to appease the Jewish lobby by flirting in a very dangerous manner with the Zionist state. The president is pushing the American Congress hard to pass a bill that will provide the Zionists with nearly $2.4 billion in financial aid, above what they already receive. The package will also lift the arms embargo, giving the Zionists practically an unlimited supply of American armament, including F16 airplanes, Patriot missiles, and advanced radar equipment."

"Yes, I am well aware of all that," said the imam, lighting a cigarette.

"All of our requests for greater justice, for consideration for the Arab Palestinians have gone unheeded. We are being ignored by both the present administration and Wells's people," continued the Doctor. "The Zionists are stalling while building more settlements in the West Bank and expelling more of our people. Since the collapse of the Soviet Union, the Americans have nothing to worry about, and are conducting themselves with even greater arrogance. It is time to show them and the world that millions of Arabs and Muslims cannot be ignored forever, just for the sake of a few votes." The Doctor paused to test the Ayatollah's reaction. It was what he had hoped for.

"Yes, my friend, you are right," said the Ayatollah, speaking slowly and in a low voice, forcing the Doctor to lean forward. "We cannot accept to have Zionists rule the world, to have them lead America by the nose. You know, my brother, that the Iranian people will stand by your side, by the side of justice. Tell me exactly what is on your mind."

"We will shortly have the chance to hurt the Imperialists and bring home a message to the Americans and the Zionists. We will strike hard. Very hard. Your Excellency, we have a plan that will make the very earth tremble in America. It will make every American wake up and react to the injustice that is taking place in occupied Palestine. It will be carried out with the greatest media coverage ever assembled. We will have the largest audience there to watch us, live on television. It will be the biggest coup in modern history. Your Excellency, as I said, we have to proceed very cautiously on this one. If ever one single word got out, the Imperialists will spare no effort to track every last one of us down and kill us all. Therefore, for your own safety, Excellency, and for the safety of the operation, and with all due respect, I will only tell you the minimum you need to know. I myself will only be told the minimum I need to know," lied the Doctor. The truth was that he did not fully trust the Iranians. But their help for the success of the operation was essential.

"Excellency, we are in a position to eliminate the next president of the United States with live world television coverage. We will strike one hard blow. We need your blessing as well as your political and financial backing."

"That is quite a feat you propose, my dear Doctor."

"Yes, Imam. We have the means to do it. We have a good plan. But we will need your help. The help of some of your diplomatic personnel."

The imam remained silent for a long time. The only sound came from a clock on the wall. The Doctor stared at the wall clock for nearly fifteen minutes, watching the hands move slowly before the imam answered.

"Very well Doctor, I accept. You shall have my backing. Let me know what you will need."

18

LONDON, ENGLAND

It had been two and a half uneventful weeks, during which time Omar practically never left the hotel room. His orders from the Doctor had been to lie low to avoid the risk of being seen. The time for action would come soon enough. This next mission was far too important to jeopardize now.

Finally, the day did come. Zeid appeared unannounced at the hotel one morning, surprising Omar with the Kurdish maid. He sent the maid away and told Omar he was to fly to the US in three days' time. In the meantime, they had a lot to go over: details to study and plans to finalize. The complete details of the plan were known only to the Doctor, the Thinker, and Sheik al-Haq. The final piece to the intricate puzzle of the attack was not even revealed to Omar. It was a shame that Omar would have to die in the attack, but there was really no alternative.

Omar's journey would now take him to the United States. He was to pose as a Jordanian electrical engineer and was given a passport bearing his photograph and the name of Marwan Raheem. It was a real passport that was stolen two days earlier from a Jordanian businessman staying in a Beirut hotel. It would be another week before the theft was reported, and by then, Omar would have thrown the passport away. It would have served its purpose.

But before proceeding to the United States, Omar had to meet a man called Sean O'Connor, an ex-IRA man who would help him on the final leg of his journey. O'Connor was a renegade who now sold his service to the Russian mafia, Sheik al-Haq, and any others willing to pay the asking price. Though a renegade, O'Connor maintained a code of honor and once he accepted a deal, he remained loyal and would never sell out his employer. It was how he managed to stay alive.

The rain and chilly London weather surprised Omar. In October, Beirut was still nice and warm. The ring of the telephone brought Omar out of his sleep. It took him a few seconds to situate himself. He picked up the phone on the second ring, glancing at his wristwatch. It was almost ten o'clock in the morning. He looked around the strange hotel room. He had left the television set on, but had killed the sound, and the flickering image threw frantic shadows around the room.

"My name is Sean O'Connor," said a man with such a heavy Irish accent that the Palestinian had trouble comprehending at first. "I understand you have a gift for me from the good Doctor."

"Yes, yes, I do," answered Omar, propping himself up on his elbow.

"That's grand," said O'Connor. "Have a taxi take you to a pub called the King's Arms, on Clapham Common, just south of the river. Ask for me at the bar. I'll be there at half nine tonight." The man hung up.

The pub was noisy, crowded, and filled with cigarette and cigar smoke. Omar made his way to the bar. Dozens of young people seemed to be enjoying themselves, men and women drinking different colored beers, ales, lagers, and other alcoholic beverages.

"Get you something, mate?" asked the barman.

"Where is Sean O'Connor?" A gentle hand tapped Omar on the shoulder. The Palestinian turned around to see the face of a handsome, clean-shaven man in his thirties smile at him. The man had long black hair that ran down to his shoulders. The man extended his hand.

"Omar, is it? I'm O'Connor, Sean O'Connor. My friends call me Connor. Come, let's sit upstairs."

Sean O'Connor grabbed two pints of Guinness from the bar and handed one to Omar before heading for the upper floor of the pub.

Omar followed Sean up a flight of stairs where they selected a table in the corner, in front of a large, round window overlooking the entrance of the pub. The back exit was only a few feet away. Years of living one step ahead of the law had taught the Irishman to always take extra precautions.

O'Connor had received his training with the Irish Republican Army. Much like the Palestinian, O'Connor too was opposed to a partial settlement in his native land. Northern Ireland was not to be shared with the Protestants. He fell afoul of the IRA after eliminating a British Member of Parliament without the IRA's approval. Since then, he had been on the run and used his old contacts to propel his new business. Sheik al-Haq found him most useful. Arabs in England stood out and were easily noticed by British Intelligence.

"You are being followed," said O'Connor.

Omar felt unprotected in this large city that he did not know. Unlike Brussels, London was overcrowded, making it much more difficult to notice a tail. He looked quizzically at his new acquaintance.

"I followed you from your hotel, to be sure, and you have a tail, laddie. Not bloody Brits though. We know the bastards, MI6 and the SAS—the bloody British elite force, you know, the Special Air Service—when we see 'em. Kind of smell 'em, you know. You get used to it after all these years. You know what I mean, laddie? Think it could be the Yanks perhaps?"

"Yanks?" repeated Omar. He had never heard that term before.

"Yeah, the Yanks, you know, the Americans. The fuckin' CIA . . ."

Omar shrugged. He hadn't noticed he was being followed. "Are you sure?"

"Bloody 'ell, man, yes I am sure. There are two of them, there are. There in that dark blue Ford Scorpio," said the Irishman, pointing out the large window. "One's a lass, a good-looking girl, too. We've never seen 'em before."

Omar glanced out the tinted pub window, and saw a man get out of the Scorpio and head towards the pub.

"There's no need to worry," said Sean O'Connor, reading Omar's mind. "The bastard won't be allowed upstairs." O'Connor made a slight nod toward the stairs, where two large men were sitting blocking the passage. "They're friends of mine," said O'Connor. "Drink your Guinness and we'll lose them in a short while."

"I have heard much about you," said Omar to the Irishman. "I heard through mutual friends that it was you who took care of the British soldiers in Gibraltar." Omar looked straight into the Irishman's eyes.

Sean O'Connor just smiled. "You have good friends," he said.

"The kidnapping of a cousin of the Queen last year, that was you too, I understand. It paid off. The English released four of your men in Belfast."

"Yeah, well, the bloody English have to be reminded every so often that the events can affect other parts of the bleedin' Kingdom of Great Britain and bloody Northern Ireland too, you know. It's not just Northern Ireland. We can hurt them here as well, and we have." The Irishman took another sip of his beer. "What about you, laddie? You seem to have impressed quite a few people, I understand."

It was Omar's turn to smile.

"But on to business. You will enter the United States using this passport," said the Irishman. He handed Omar an Irish passport. "It's real, not fake. It has been lent to us by its owner. The similarities are striking. Learn the details and memorize them. When you land at Kennedy, make sure you arrive any day of the week except Thursday and Friday. Then, at immigration, go only to booth number sixteen. Remember, only number sixteen. One six, got that?"

Omar nodded.

"We have a few friends in the American Immigration Service. Especially in the Boston area, but in New York too, where you are to enter."

"This is sure?" asked the Palestinian.

"You need not worry. Yes, we are sure. Our sources are excellent."

"Why New York?" asked the Palestinian.

"More people, larger airport, immigration officers have less time. They are overworked and our friends operate easier."

"You have done your research, I see," said Omar.

"We have many friends who are sympathetic to our cause," said O'Connor.

One of the burly Irishmen guarding the stairs came over and whispered something in Sean O'Connor's ear.

"The man, the Yank, he is asking about you at the bar," said O'Connor.

"They must die, then," said Omar. "If they have seen my face, they must die."

"Fine," said O'Connor, downing the last of his Guinness in one swig. "Let's go, then. I'll brief you more later."

O'Connor led Omar outside the pub just as the American agent headed back to his car. Omar stopped briefly outside the pub and looked at the Scorpio. A woman was sitting in the driver's seat. He glimpsed her face as the man opened the car door to get back inside the vehicle and the interior light came on for a few seconds. But it was long enough for Omar to get a good look at the woman and he instantly recognized her as one of the passengers on his flight from Beirut. She was the one with the eyes. Yes, he recalled clearly how he almost classified her as a non-threat. Then he saw her eyes.

Then, just as quickly, the interior of the car went dark again. Omar could not help but smile at her. A car came from the opposite direction and its headlights briefly illuminated the woman's face, giving Omar a clear view of the woman's face. Her eyes, that ice-cold look, those piercing eyes momentarily froze Omar in his tracks. There was definitely hate in those eyes. Although he only caught a quick glimpse of her, he could clearly see this was a woman on a mission; a woman with a purpose. It sent a cold shiver down his spine.

The rain had stopped, but it was still chilly and Omar pulled up the collar of his leather jacket. Omar and O'Connor walked south, towards Clapham Common, before turning right. The Ford Scorpio followed at a safe distance. Omar and the Irishman turned towards the fire station just off the Common. It was a one-way street and the man in the Scorpio was forced to leave the car and follow them on foot. They continued for a few hundred yards, walking slowly, taking their time, and then veered right into a small, dark, side street leading to Grafton Square: a nice residential block with a group of houses facing a small, fenced park. The man from the Scorpio followed the pair into the alley, when suddenly two pairs of hands grabbed him off the street into the lower entrance leading to the basement of a townhouse. Before the agent could react, a knife had already been inserted through his ribs, piercing his heart. He died without making a sound.

Meanwhile, the woman driving the Scorpio had gone around Clapham Common and pulled up outside the alley, waiting for the other agent who now had disappeared from view. At first, Laura Atwood took little notice of the drunk approaching her. She looked in her rearview mirror and saw the Palestinian and the Irishman coming out of the alley, towards her. The drunk had an unlit cigarette in his mouth and was looking through his pockets for matches. As the man neared the Scorpio, he pulled out a .45 with a silencer attached, aimed at Laura and shot repeatedly through the windshield. Laura stepped on the accelerator while ducking her head under the dashboard. She hit a parked Mini, ripping off its rear fender, but managed to free her car and race away. The gunman continued to empty his gun into the Scorpio. The windshield was shattered and the left rear tire punctured, but Laura continued to drive away at full speed. By now, Omar and the Irishman were just a few feet away. She saw they were armed too and had started firing at her. The car jumped the curb as Laura tore across the well-manicured grass on Clapham Common, zig-zagging as she drove. One bullet hit her side mirror, shattering it. Laura pressed down on the accelerator, pushing the Scorpio as hard as she could. The car skidded on the wet grass and Laura lost control, hitting a tree in the middle of the Common. Still partially dazed, Laura looked at her rearview mirror and saw the Palestinian and the Irishman approaching the car. Miraculously, a crowd of people, including a policeman on patrol, ran towards her. The Palestinian and his friend turned away and disappeared into the London night. Laura Atwood cut the engine, buried her face in the steering wheel and started to cry.

Laura Craft's cover was blown. She wasn't certain that the ter-rorist had actually seen her face clearly, or could even identify her, but going back to Beirut would amount to suicide. His friends had seen her. She was not sure how long they had been follow-ing her and when they had picked her up. They might have even photographed her. She knew Langley would order her immediate return to Washington. It was too dangerous now to venture back to Beirut. Besides, there was still the "taxi driver" in Beirut. He could identify the terrorist, and no one had seen his face.

Before leaving London, Laura called Chris Clayborne in Beirut. She told him she was being transferred to the States and that the transfer was immediate. Chris insisted she wait for him; he would fly to London in the morning. They could at least spend a few days together in London.

19

WASHINGTON, DC

The borrowed passport and forged US visa given to him by Sean O'Connor got Omar through British security, and he was now about to test US airport security. But first he needed to rid himself of all other documents. As the aircraft entered North American airspace, Omar locked himself in one of the plane's toilets and shredded all other documents before flushing them down the toilet. The next step of the operation was going to be critical. For about thirty minutes, Omar would be totally defenseless and at the complete mercy of United States Immigration officers. There was no other way. It had to be done if he was to enter the United States. But the Irishman in London was confident and seemed to know what he was talking about. Omar was confident that his plan would work. Besides, Omar had taken risks before. He knew he could fool the Americans. He had fooled them, and others, before. It seemed to be getting easier, fooling people, thought Omar. Deep inside him, he enjoyed raising the stakes every time. It had almost become a game between him and those chasing him. He had always managed to remain a step ahead of them. He was smarter than they were and he would continue to fool them. But it pushed him to go further and further every time.

There was always the risk that the Americans could turn him back, but Sean O'Connor's information was solid. His Irish friend had told him that their man in immigration at Kennedy Airport would look out for him if there was a problem. Still, he had to be careful. But then again, Omar had always been careful. He laughed at the thought. How can one do the job he was doing and talk about being careful? That was how he survived. He had been careful to the extent that this could be at all possible. There were no photographs of him. They didn't even know his real name. The only enemy agents to have seen his face had died in London. Or so he thought.

Omar queued up for passport control, along with hundreds of other arriving passengers, all foreigners. There was a separate line for US citizens and green card holders. Both lines were moving fairly quickly and within minutes Omar found himself in front of a US immigration officer who stamped his passport and waved him on.

Omar was relieved to walk out of the terminal building into the fresh air. He wiped his sweaty palms on his trousers and took a deep breath of afternoon air as he walked out into the open. Kennedy Airport was a mess and reminded Omar of an Arab *souk*. People were running around in every direction, pushing and shouting. Taxi drivers were screaming back at police officers who were screaming at them. Large buses were blocking roads already blocked by an armada of yellow taxis and other cars. Passengers pushed and shoved each other as they darted to catch their flights. A group of Hasidic Jews hurried by with a gaggle of children in tow. A squadron of

Japanese tourists followed a man holding up a small red-and-white flag.

Omar left the international terminal and took a shuttle bus to the TWA domestic building. He scanned the electronic board where arriving and departing flights were listed and randomly chose a flight leaving for Minneapolis, Minnesota, in one hour and twenty-five minutes. But he had one more thing to take care of first.

Omar easily located the Irish Tavern on the arrival level. The bar was crowded, but he found an empty stool on the far end of the room. The barman greeted him and asked what he would like to drink.

"A Guinness, please," said the Palestinian. "By the way, I am a good friend and acquaintance of Sean O'Connor from Belfast. I understand you have something for me."

The barman walked away without replying and returned a moment later with half a pint of Guinness and a menu. Omar opened the menu and found a small sealed envelope inside. He slipped the envelope into his inside jacket pocket, finished his beer, paid, and left the bar. He found the men's room and locked himself in an empty booth. He took out the envelope given to him by the barman and took out a Massachusetts driver's license bearing his picture. The name under the photograph said Stavros Papadopoulos and gave a fictitious address in Boston. There was also a credit card with the same name. He signed the card, copying the signature on the driver's license, pocketed both items, and left.

Omar returned to the TWA departure hall, where he purchased a ticket and paid for it in cash using the name of Stavros Papadopoulos. With his good Mediterranean looks, Omar could easily pass as a Greek or an Italian. Anyone trying to trace Devin Callahan would stop at a dead end outside Kennedy International Airport. The Brooklyn address did not exist, just like the Boston one. No one would ever realize that Stavros Papadopoulos, alias Devin Callahan, alias Marwan Raheem, was in fact Omar al-Kheir, one of the most deadly terrorists in the world. He was lost inside this huge country called America. Looking for him now would be like looking for a needle in the proverbial haystack. There was simply no way he could be traced, or found. It was a perfect plan. Omar smiled at the thought. Oh, how easy it was to fool these people. They believed too easily. Much too easily. By now Omar had fully regained his confidence. Victory would come soon enough.

By now Omar was quite certain that no one was following him. After entering the United States in New York, doubling back between terminals—giving the appearance that he was lost, had anyone taken notice—he flew to Minneapolis. He followed the same ritual there too, going back and forth between two airport terminals. After landing in Minneapolis, Omar changed planes once again, heading to Washington, and as he did on the previous flights and at the air terminals, he scrutinized the faces of every passenger on the plane. There were none who had flown with him from New York, he was quite sure of that. This time, he was certain that no one had followed him. The trail was clear and all links with his past were severed.

The US capital's brightly lit landmarks looked resplendent from the air as Omar's plane came in for landing at Washington's Ronald Reagan National Airport. Omar recognized the Pentagon, the seat of America's imperialist strength from where the American military commanded its troops around the world. The Capitol, with its large dome dominating one side of Pennsylvania Avenue, and the Washington Monument, that looked like an Egyptian obelisk, were visible from miles away. And there was the Potomac River, snaking its way between the capital and Virginia to the south. It was just like the films he had seen.

Omar suddenly felt the same excitement he had experienced when he entered Israel clandestinely several years ago. It was the same tingling sensation he felt before every mission, when all the pieces started slowly falling into place. It was a mixture of adrenaline and fear, of hatred rising to the surface yet again. It was the only time when anything started making sense to him. His palms felt sweaty, as they always did before every mission. That feeling would only go away once he was safely back on home ground, on familiar territory. Now, he was on enemy ground once more, and everyone around him was to be considered hostile and potentially dangerous. The Americans, who for so long had aided his enemies, were now going to pay. Revenge was almost at hand. But he had to be careful. Yes, the Americans were naive, but strong. Their intelligence service, the CIA—or was it the FBI—could still stop him, prevent him from accomplishing his mission. The Americans always claimed the CIA never operated on American soil, but Omar could not believe that. He had to remain alert. Whoever it was could still get to him. It was time for renewed caution. His survival instincts were not going to let him down.

The sheer number of Arab and Asian taxi drivers outside Washington's Ronald Reagan National Airport surprised the Palestinian. It was not something he had expected in America's capital city. A Pakistani taxi driver dropped him off at the J. W. Marriott on 14th Street, just a few blocks from the White

House, where he was able to get a room registering under his new identity.

Omar spent the first several days getting acquainted with the city. For his plan to work, he needed to know the layout of the town. The American capital was a pleasant city, and Omar found it easy to get around in. Much easier than London. The streets had numbers and letters of the alphabet. The numbers ran north–south and the letters east–west. The confusing part was the avenues bearing the names of various states that ran diagonally, but for the most part, he found it was not a difficulty city to operate in.

On his third day in Washington, Omar signed up for one of the tourist tours of the capital. He found it was a simple way to get around and study parts of the city he needed to discover and commit to memory. It was a perfect cover. No one really ever gives tourists a second look. Omar paid particular attention to the Capitol building, studying its layout and the surrounding buildings. He bought a tourist map and spent hours scrutinizing every street, every small detail. He found an army surplus store near his hotel, where he bought a magnetic compass. Next he found a large stationery store and bought a red felt pen and the kind of compass used by architects and draftsmen. He spent several days at the Library of Congress going over back issues of the *New York Times*, the *Washington Post*, and *Time* and *Newsweek* magazines. His only interest was in the January 21 editions of the papers, starting in 1900 and jumping four years to 1904, 1908, and so on, until he reached the most current editions. The publications were all on microfilm and easily accessible. The more he scanned through the microfilm, the greater his excitement grew. This was getting better all the time. Every photograph he looked at confirmed his idea. He returned the microfilms and walked out. He hailed a taxi and asked the driver to take him back to his hotel. On the way, Omar spotted a French restaurant and asked the driver to stop. He bought a copy of the *Washington Post* and found an empty table on the restaurant's outdoor terrace, where he sat and ordered lunch. He leaned back in his chair and looked at the date on his newspaper. It said November 1. He still had a little more than two months to prepare himself. So far, things were going just as planned.

Omar allowed himself to indulge in a good meal, ordering some of the most expensive items on the menu. After all, this was the sheik's money; he could easily afford it. After lunch, Omar hailed a taxi and asked the driver to take him to Union Station. He found a public phone and placed a call to a number in Athens. "I have arrived safely and all is well. Please give my best regards to my Doctor," he said before hanging up.

Later that afternoon, back in his hotel room, Omar placed the map of Washington on the floor, took out the drafting compass, placed the point on the steps of the Capitol building and measured fifteen hundred meters to scale. The map was in miles, and it took him a few minutes to recalculate the difference into kilometers. He inserted the red felt pen in the other end of the compass and drew a circle around the Capitol. There seemed to be plenty of real estate in the designated area to suit his purpose. The next part of the job was going to be the most demanding, from a logistical sense. If he failed to find the right location, his entire plan could fail. But Omar was confident he was going to succeed, as he always had in the past. He wiped his hands on his trousers once more.

PARIS, FRANCE

The Iran Air jet landed at Paris' Charles de Gaulle Airport only seven minutes behind schedule. Once its passengers and crew had disembarked and its regular cargo was taken off board, the plane was moved to a remote part of the Parisian airport where it was to remain for the rest of the night before its return flight to Tehran the following morning. As usual, a lone Iranian security guard remained onboard.

An hour later, the guard walked off the plane and scanned the surrounding area before returning to the cockpit, where he took a flashlight, pointed it towards a group of parked vehicles near the terminal building, and flashed three short bursts. Moments later, a tan colored catering truck pulled up to the plane and three men in white overalls emerged. The guard led them to the rear of the aircraft, and with his help they removed a metal case containing a single metal tube measuring roughly three feet long and weighing exactly 45.2 pounds. Along with the tube were two smaller wooden cases, each containing five smaller items. Those items weighed roughly four pounds each. Eight of the items in the two cases were painted olive drab and carried yellow labels, while those in the other case were clearly marked in light green and had red labels, the standard NATO coloring for the contents of the case. The three cases were placed inside the catering truck and driven out of the airport to the Iranian embassy, where they were placed inside a secure vault.

The following morning, Ali Moshtemi, an Iranian diplomat accredited to the United Nations in New York, arrived for consultations with the Iranian ambassador to Paris. It was a normal routine that Moshtemi carried out every other month. Since diplomatic relations with the United States had been severed, Iranian diplomats in New York frequently traveled to France, where the Islamic Republic still maintained a large diplomatic mission, one of its largest in Europe. Moshtemi welcomed the break. In New York, he was banned from traveling more than twenty-five miles from Columbus Circle.

Unlike the ambassador to Paris, a career diplomat, Moshtemi was a faithful supporter of Ayatollah Kazemi. By mid-afternoon, Moshtemi had completed his talks with the ambassador and other Iranian diplomats. Before leaving the embassy, he stopped by the office of a political attaché and picked up a suitcase containing a tube weighing 45.2 pounds.

An embassy car drove Moshtemi back to the airport, where he boarded an Air France flight to New York's Kennedy International Airport. As a high-ranking diplomat accredited to the United Nations, Moshtemi did not have to submit his luggage for inspection to US customs and was able to proceed directly to his apartment on the Upper East Side. He locked the suitcase in a specially built closet and kept the only key with him at all times. In any case, there was always an armed Iranian guard inside his apartment. No one alien to his department was ever allowed inside, and certainly no Americans. Even the cleaning crews were loyal Iranians.

Over the next two months, Moshtemi flew to Paris three more times, each time returning with several of the smaller colored items brought to Paris aboard the Iran Air plane. As usual, he walked straight through US Customs, protected by his diplomatic passport.

WASHINGTON, DC

It took Omar, now using the name of Stavros Papadopoulos, about ten days to find the right location. He ruled out going through real estate agents because they would be too easy to trace. There would be records: forms to fill out, papers to sign. He considered using the classified ads from one of the local newspapers, but rejected them for the same reason. Too many phone calls, also traceable. This made his task all the more difficult, but a lot safer. He spent several hours a day walking around the Capitol building, looking for the right place, for buildings with "For Rent" signs posted outside. He started his search a mere two blocks away from his target and gradually enlarged his perimeter by another street every day. His search was complicated by the sheer number of government buildings that could not be considered for his task. There were also numerous office buildings in the area that housed government offices. He wanted to avoid them too.

After a week of searching, Omar had identified three buildings that met his requirements. When he reached the intersection of Third Street SW and E Street, he knew he had found what he was looking for. It was the perfect location and there was a sign hanging on the building indicating there was space for rent. The apartment he visited was a spacious rooftop unit, situated exactly 1,326 meters from the steps of the US Capitol building. Omar calculated it gave him a margin of seventy-four meters. For his plan to work, the apartment had to be no more than fourteen hundred meters away from the Capitol steps. This would do perfectly.

The building was brand new and had eight floors. It was the top floor, the eighth floor apartment, which attracted Omar. The apartment itself was slightly smaller than others in the building, but it had a very large terrace to compensate for lesser living space. The terrace extended about ten yards from the large glass living room windows and ran the entire front of the building, making it about twenty yards wide. The closest building was more than twenty-five yards away, giving him ample privacy. The eighth floor rooftop apartment did not have a view of the Capitol, which was an added advantage. There were a number of taller buildings obscuring his view of the Capitol. If he could not see them, they would certainly not see him. That was good, very good.

Another added bonus was the proximity of the Metro; Federal Center SW was only 150 meters from the apartment. Omar had not given his escape plan much thought until now, but seeing the Metro gave him an idea. He got a map of the Metro system and studied it, scrutinizing all the destinations and connecting stations. Once he was satisfied he had exhausted all possibilities, he boarded the orange line, which he rode to New Carrollton, in Maryland. It was only nine stations away. From New Carrollton he could ride the train to Baltimore-Washington International Airport. It was an easy escape from Washington and it was a route he could use without having to drive. There had to be alternatives. After the mission, there would be chaos. He would need to be flexible. He had to have several options available.

The Metro stop also had a fairly large commuter parking lot and he could leave a car there, if needed. In fact, yes, he believed he would leave a car there, just in case. It was always good to have a backup plan. Plan for the unexpected, always plan for the unforeseen, Kifah Kassar used to say. The next day, Omar took a taxi to the airport and rented a car. He drove to the apartment building near the Capitol and from there to New Carrollton and on to Baltimore-Washington International Airport. The first time around, he missed the exit. He returned to New Carrollton and drove back to BWI a second time. It took him forty-five minutes. He drove back to the Metro stop and tried it a third time. This time it took him only thirty-five minutes. Just to be sure, he repeated the drive three more times. Now he was certain he knew the right route to take and which exit to use. There would be no room for mistakes later. There could be unexpected delays due to inclement weather, emergency road work, or just a simple traffic accident. Next, he would need to check airline schedules and make flight reservations.

The apartment contained two bedrooms, a generous kitchen that came equipped with everything one could need—a living room, a small dining room, and the substantial veranda. The veranda, or terrace, was very important. Omar would have preferred a furnished flat, but this would do nicely. Let the sheik spend a bit more money furnishing the place. He signed a one-year lease and paid a two-month deposit and three months' rent in advance, and in cash. He told the landlord that he had just arrived in the United States and had not been able to open a bank account yet. Banks in Greece are slow, he said. Not as efficient as those here in America. Between his business and personal matters, there was so much paperwork to fill out. Would the landlord prefer a check on a Greek bank? "No, thank you," replied the landlord, "cash would do very well, thank you." Cash was fine, especially since the landlord was returning to his condo in Barbados for the winter. As his occupation, Omar told the landlord he was opening a Washington branch of a Greek maritime company.

Omar bought a bed and mattress, sheets, blankets, a few kitchen items, and a large screen color television set. All was paid for in cash. Cable was already installed in the building, for which he was thankful. The fewer people that came into the apartment, the better. The hardest part was done. Now, he could sit back for a few weeks and allow the time to pass. But first he had to let Beirut know that all was proceeding according to plan. Once again, he returned to Union Station to call the same Athens number. The phone was answered on the third ring. Omar said he had a message for his Doctor. The Doctor was to be told he was feeling better and would not need medication. The man who answered the telephone in Athens noted the message and told Omar he had two numbers for him.

The two sets of numbers, each containing ten digits, might have easily passed for innocent telephone numbers with the area code. In fact, they were a simple code devised by Omar. The simpler, the better. If anyone had been listening, which Omar believed was a good possibility, they would certainly be looking for a complicated and hard-to-break code. To get the information he needed, Omar dropped the first and last three numbers of the first set. This gave him the street address. The second set of numbers provided Omar with a post office box number he needed to know, once he had dropped the extra digits. Omar hung up and walked back to the apartment on E Street.

Zeid was pleased with the call from Athens and immediately informed the Doctor. Early the next morning the Doctor headed back to Damascus, where he met Brigadier General Kamal Kader.

"I came to tell you that you should schedule the maneuvers for January 18 through January 28," said the Doctor. "Be prepared to strike at dawn on the twenty-first. You will get confirmation from the international media. Stay tuned to CNN or

Al Jazeera that evening, General. You will know when to strike. This strike will very likely solve your internal problems. After a coup like that, your party and the popularity of your party and of your president will skyrocket. It could quite possibly bring an end to your civil war. When we next meet, it will be after our victory. May Allah be with us."

WASHINGTON, DC

The polls showed Senator Richard Wells ahead of the incumbent president by a generous 37 percent. Senator Wells was campaigning in New York City and the camera showed him addressing a large crowd of Jewish Defense League members.

"My administration will stand firmly by our allies in Israel," shouted the Senator to the applause of the crowd. "We will not let our allies down. This administration will not abandon our friends in this time of great need. My friends, I seek your support in these crucial elections, in these crucial times, and I promise you that I will stand firmly by Israel. I will not force it to sign any hastily negotiated peace settlement that would only endanger its future and give strength to its enemies."

Standing along with his team of advisers, Pete Roff smiled. He had no doubt that his "client" would win the White House come November.

Omar, too, smiled as he watched the live broadcast on his large television screen. "Just wait a while," thought the Palestinian. "Just you wait. Things will begin to change soon enough."

20

LANGLEY, VIRGINIA

The director of the CIA convened an emergency meeting to be held at six o'clock in the morning at Langley. Attending the meeting were his top crisis people; those included his deputies, his top security advisors, and two senior analysts. As the matter at hand concerned the security of the president of the United States, and the fact that a foreign terrorist was believed to be involved, the director also asked the head of the US Secret Service and the director of the FBI to attend. With the head of the Secret Service was also the agent directly in charge of the presidential detail—the man who ultimately was responsible for the protection of the president.

With the date of the presidential inauguration rapidly approaching, the pressure was sure to rise. And of course, the men around the conference table all knew that the added pressure would be on the FBI, seeing as they were responsible for security inside the United States. At the same time, the pressure would mount on the CIA to get more intelligence on what was being concocted overseas. And as neither group progressed, at the end of the day, the pressure would be all that much more on the Secret Service to make sure the president remained alive and the events proceeded as planned.

The tipoff sent by the CIA operative in Beirut moments before he and his informant were murdered a few months ago had not yielded much to go with. They knew that the attack would take place on Inauguration Day. But how, where, when, and the most important question—who—remained to be answered.

William Potter, Assistant Deputy Director of the Federal Bureau of Investigation, in charge of Counterespionage, looked worried. He, as most of the other men around the table, had not slept more than a few hours a day for several weeks now. He was paler than usual on this cold January morning, Monaghan, the CIA director, noticed as he kicked off the meeting.

"Gentlemen, thank you for coming here at this early hour. I know you are all early risers, which makes it somewhat easier. There have been new and disturbing developments that came to our attention overnight. What I am about to tell you comes from a number of sources, including NSA intercepts and intel we have been able to compile through HUMINT and ELINT. The matter is much more complex than we initially thought. According to this information, our analysts believe the assassination of the American president could be the prelude to a wider plan by certain groups who intend to profit from the mayhem that would ensue."

"What could be bigger than the assassination of the US president?" let out the head of the Secret Service.

"Indeed," said Monaghan, "indeed. But here it is. It's quite possible that the Syrians might be up to something big. It appears that the regime in Damascus is concocting a dual-facet plan that would boost their popularity, extend the life of the current regime, which appears to be dwindling as we speak, while at the same time get their revenge on us for supporting the opposition in their civil war. They hope that with the assassination of the US president there will follow a short time frame when the US will be busy with domestic issues, thus ignoring the world stage. Syria, as you all know, has been in the midst of a devastating civil war that has taxed the military very heavily. However, Assad has not yet committed the top elite military units into the fight. Not just yet, anyway. He has been holding them in reserve for something just as big as this. He has two major units, each brigade size: the Special Forces and the special unit of the very elite Republican Guard have been held back just outside Damascus. Just a few hundred are deployed around the presidential palace.

"We have been getting reports over the last few days that Assad has ordered those troops into high readiness, one would presume to head into Damascus or some other hotspot of trouble. Maybe Aleppo again. However, the advance units have already started to move and everything suggests that the troops are heading away from the capital and towards the Golan Heights.

"We believe the Syrians will attempt to go for the Heights," said the director. "Mind you, this is more than just a crazy hunch at this point. NSA has picked up a lot of chatter from those elite units.

"Our intelligence from Syria indicates that the opposition was not involved in the multiple bombing attacks in Damascus yesterday," he continued. "We believe that it was in fact the Mukhabarat, their domestic intel group.

"Additionally, and we don't quite yet know for sure, but there seems to be a lot of chatter among the South American drug cartels. We picked up a report of one of Mexico's drug lords going to Beirut at about the same time that Hines was killed. And then we noticed a lot of money was being shuffled around between the Caribbean and the Middle East. We know that there has been for a while close cooperation between some Islamists and the Latin American drug lords, but what is going on here seems to be taking things to a new level."

"Do we need to get the DEA in here?" The question came from the FBI.

"It's entirely up to you," said the director of the CIA. "I have already had a conversation with them and they have been very cooperative. They have passed on some valuable data that will help the security of our agents operating undercover."

"If there is any truth to the rumors going around that they have financed this operation then I personally will go after them and get each one of those bastards," said Potter.

21

WASHINGTON, DC

Shortly after eight the following morning, Chris Clayborne parked his car at the International Press Service garage near the intersection of K and Sixteenth Street NW, and walked to the front of the building to wait for his old friend, Dieter Schiller, to pick him up. To kill time, Clayborne started doing the crossword puzzle. Reluctantly, he had returned to Washington to resume his duty as Managing Editor of IPS. The Mideast story was getting nowhere fast and the money people were losing patience in funding a non-story.

Clayborne hadn't seen Schiller in more than two years and was happy his old friend was going to be spending a few weeks in Washington. Schiller arrived moments later in the back of a shining black stretch limousine. Clayborne jumped inside and together they drove to the US Capitol building. Schiller always enjoyed traveling in style, which was easy to do when someone else paid for it. Schiller had always been a leftist at heart, but firmly believed the capitalist press whom he worked for could easily afford to spend the money. His work was excellent, a cut above the others, and his "owners," as he called them, never questioned a single expense account item.

Clayborne first met Schiller in Chechnya, back when they were both covering one of their first wars. It now seemed like a lifetime ago. Schiller was then on assignment for the German magazine *Der Spiegel*. The two men got caught in crossfire between Russian Army tanks and Chechen militiamen firing rocket-propelled grenades. They remained pinned down in a dirt-filled ditch for several hours as bullets and artillery whizzed right above their heads. They were both terrified, but somehow managed to find just enough courage to raise their cameras over their heads and snap a few frames.

Since then, a deep friendship had developed between the two journalists and whenever their paths crossed, they made it a point to cover a story together. Near the end of the Lebanese Civil War, Dieter Schiller was wounded in the chest by a sniper's bullet and Clayborne risked his own life to carry him out of the fire zone. Clayborne stopped a group of leftist militiamen and forced them to drive his wounded colleague to a nearby hospital, saving his friend's life. Later that afternoon, Chris returned to the spot where Dieter had been shot in order to retrieve his camera.

"Chrissy," said Dieter in his thick German accent, slapping him on the back, "it's so good to see you again, my friend. My Gott, you look like a real working journalist again. No fucking suit and tie today. You can't stay in that fucking office all the time, my friend. You must get out and see the real world again, ya. Or else you become a silly boss-editor like the one you used to bitch about all the time."

"Dieter, this city will kill me faster than Beirut ever did. Good to see you again. Yeah, it's great to get out. I see you still like to rough it, eh? Nice car. You could have at least chosen one with a Jacuzzi."

"Sure. If I don't come to America, you don't get your ass out of the office. Ya? You stay there all the day. You become grumpy old man. Boss-editor!"

"Truth be said, old friend, that I would have left the office even if your majesty would have stayed away. You know we have to tell the young ones how to focus their cameras these days."

"Ya, you see, you already are the boss-editor you used to complain about. That's dangerous, my friend."

With the presidential inauguration only ten days away, Clayborne and Schiller were planning to check on the progress of the construction being carried out on the press stands, the large platforms from where press photographers and television crews would cover the important event. Chris wanted to make sure that IPS photographers got the best angle.

Chris Clayborne had replaced his longtime mentor, Charlton MacClarty, as managing editor after the latter retired. It was MacClarty who recommended Chris be given the position, and it was also MacClarty who convinced Clayborne to take the job. At first Clayborne was reluctant to come out of the field. He loved his work and enjoyed covering the Middle East, even if at times he desperately wanted to get away from the everyday violence.

"You can't play cowboy forever," MacClarty told Chris over lunch one day. "Besides, IPS needs a good man here. Most of these assholes don't know shit from Shinola. You would be good for the company; take the job, kiddo." And Chris did. MacClarty retired to a small house in Annapolis overlooking Chesapeake Bay, and Clayborne took over as managing editor.

Now Chris rarely left the office. This last trip to the Mideast had been an exception. IPS had smelled a scoop, and Clayborne was the only one who could have delivered it.

Anyway, this was a good chance to get out and stretch his legs and enjoy a big fat lunch at company expense with his old friend from the Middle East. Hey, that's how most of DC lived. Take away those corporate expense accounts and half the restaurants in the city would go out of business. Most of Washington's lawyers, politicians, and lobbyists would be eating sandwiches out of brown paper bags if they had to pay for those expensive lunches and dinners out of their own pockets.

Clayborne was scouting the various fixed positions his photographers would be assigned on Inauguration Day. Using his iPhone camera with a new zoom app he had recently downloaded, he started to take pictures from the positions so that he could later discuss with the picture editors where to position their best shooters. He started shooting pictures of people who were passing at various distances from the press platform, while taking mental notes of the various angles. His 8x zoom lens worked beautifully and gave him clear images of faces more than fifty yards away. He was focusing on the Capitol stairs when a man with a Middle Eastern complexion walked into his field of vision, right into his frame. He snapped a few frames but only one was in focus.

"Hey, Dieter, look at that man in the brown leather jacket," said Clayborne, without removing his eye from the camera. "He looks familiar."

Chris followed the man with his lens as he went up the stairs of the Capitol. The man stopped and turned towards Chris, giving him an excellent front view of his face. Instinctively, Chris snapped some more frames. He wondered where he could have seen this man before.

"Just another Middle Eastern face," replied Dieter Schiller, also looking through his lens. "You are just nostalgic for that crazy part of the world."

"Like you are not. Tell me you are having a ball in Hamburg," replied Clayborne, keeping his eyes glued to his camera.

"Hamburg is a very civilized city."

"Sure it's civilized, but tell me you are having fun."

"I live very well, thank you."

"You are ignoring my question. Are you having fun? Are you getting laid, are you still getting stoned, are you getting published on the front pages of the *International Herald Tribune*?"

"I see you still have your priorities right. Fun, sex, hash, and then getting published, ya?"

"Not necessarily in that order. Sex could go first. Anyway, look at that guy, Dieter. Where have we seen him before? Come on man, use that Prussian head of yours."

"I don't have your memory of faces, my friend. All those beers and all the hashish you poured into me made me lose some of my memory."

"It's called old age. The beers and hashish never bothered you before. It's old age that makes you senile."

"I did not say I was senile, ya? I said I did not have your memory of faces."

"Big help that is right now. I still can't remember the man, but I know I have seen him before."

"Maybe he is an Arab diplomat, or journalist?"

"No, I don't think so. Look at his eyes, he seems to be making mental notes of things. There is something strange about him."

"And what are we doing? Not studying the layout?"

"No, look, he's different. Look at those eyes, Dieter. Look at those eyes."

"Uh oh. I sense your journalistic nose is acting up again. You smell the big scoop, ya? Remember what happens last time you dragged me into one of your intuitions. I get shot, ya."

"No scoop this time, but I just hate it when I can't remember a face. It rarely happens to me. I believe I have even photographed this guy before. But where, damn it, where?"

"Anyway, he's going away. See? He did not plant any suspicious packages, your Middle Eastern enigma. No bombs, no boom-boom today, ya? You get no scoop, I'm afraid. We let you out of the office one bloody day and you start seeing conspiracies. My, my. Washington has really gotten to you. We should get that three-piece suit and tie back on you and send you back to the office. Maybe you are better at being boss-editor."

"I never wore a three-piece suit. Now you are exaggerating."

"Not so. My sources tell me they saw you in a three-piece suit. Anyway, you can wear a tuxedo if you like. Let's go get some lunch; I'm starving."

"It's only eleven in the morning, Dieter. Are you still on German time?"

"So what difference does it make, ya, German time, American time, or Beirut time, we can get some beers first. Make it a long lunch, like in the old days. I was recommended a very good French restaurant. Very expensive. We also have champagne, and caviar, ya?"

After lunch, Chris Clayborne returned to the IPS office. He plugged his iPhone into his computer and downloaded the images taken in the morning. Minutes later he was examining the photos on a large screen. When he came to the picture of the Middle Eastern man on the steps of the Capitol building, he enlarged it as much as he could. He had only had time to shoot a single frame before the man walked out of his field of vision. He made several prints of the photograph, using a high-quality printer. He looked at the face that seemed to be staring back at him. He just couldn't get the man out of his mind. Where had he seen him before? Soon other business occupied him, and he momentarily forgot about the man from the Middle East until the technician brought the glossy color print to his office.

Chris left the office earlier than usual. The long lunch, the numerous beers, and the champagne he had enjoyed with Dieter Schiller had wiped him out. He was not used to drinking so much since he left the Middle East. He fell asleep a little before ten. But it was an uneasy sleep. He awoke two hours later, tossing and turning in bed, unable to fall back asleep. He got out of bed, poured himself a large glass of cold water, dropped two Alka-Seltzers in the glass, and turned on the television set to the News Network Channel. There was more disturbing news from the Middle East as radical Palestinians were now openly warning America's president-elect not to side with Israel. Iran also seemed to support the radicals, once again calling for jihad. Another car bomb went off in Cairo near the home of Sheik al-Haq, but he escaped unhurt. In an unrelated story, Syria had scheduled large-scale maneuvers on the Golan Heights for the following week. And the Washington peace talks were stalling once more.

The Middle East again, thought Clayborne with nostalgia. He wished he were back in Beirut. He thought briefly of Laura, of the good times he had with her, before the face from the morning suddenly came back to haunt him. Where had he seen it before? Chris walked into the small room he used as a study.

He turned on his desktop computer, waited for it boot up, and dialed into the IPS photo bank computer database. He placed the glossy photograph next to the computer. Chris Clayborne punched in his password and within seconds was connected to IPS's vast photo library, allowing him to view millions of photographs at the stroke of a single key. But that was precisely the problem. There were millions of images in the database, far too many photographs to select from.

Not knowing exactly where to start, he punched in CLAYBORNE/BEIRUT/BEIRUT/?/? and pressed enter. The computer prompted him with the line SEARCHING, PLEASE WAIT . . . while a tiny globe rotated. A few seconds later the screen showed him the following:

AUTHOR: CLAYBORNE, CHRIS
SUBJECT: DATELINE: DATE: CAPTION:
NUMBER OF PICTURES: 32,756
PRESS F1 TO VIEW PHOTOGRAPHS OR MAKE A NEW SELECTION.

Great. There were nearly thirty-three thousand photographs taken by Clayborne relating to Beirut alone. Clayborne calculated that it would take him at least 2700 hours to view all those pictures, assuming he spend only five seconds on each. He needed to narrow his search down. He typed CLAYBORNE/ PALESTINIAN/BEIRUT/?/? and hit the enter button.

BEIRUT, LEBANON BEIRUT, LEBANON NOT SPECIFIED NOT SPECIFIED
AUTHOR: SUBJECT: DATELINE: DATE: CAPTION:
NUMBER OF PIX:
PRESS F1 TO VIEW PHOTOGRAPHS OR MAKE A NEW SELECTION.

He was still way off. He poured himself a Jack Daniels on the rocks and returned to his computer. CLAYBORNE/ PALESTINIANS-FIGHTERS /BEIRUT/?/? and enter.

CLAYBORNE, CHRIS PALESTINIAN BEIRUT, LEBANON NOT SPECIFIED

NOT SPECIFIED 3,245

AUTHOR: SUBJECT: DATELINE: DATE: CAPTION: NUMBER OF PIX:

PRESS F1 TO VIEW PHOTOGRAPHS OR MAKE A NEW SELECTION.

Well, at least the number was coming down. Where could he have seen that man? He was certain he had photographed him. Like many photojournalists, Chris never forgot a picture he took. Or did he actually take the picture, if indeed there was one?

CLAYBORNE/BEIRUT/PALESTINIANS-FIGHTERS/ CONFERENCE/?/?, enter. The computer informed him he had 436 pictures. He hit F1 and started looking at mug shots of Palestinians he had photographed over the years, comparing them to the one sitting on his desk. An hour later, he had only viewed half of them. Most were of prominent leaders; some showed fighters in Beirut or the south. Damn, there had to be another way. Think, man, think. Clayborne rubbed his eyes and fixed himself another drink. He could not place a name on the man and could not remember where he had photographed him. Yet he knew he had taken his picture once before. He kept looking at the print next to his computer. By five in the morning, Chris gave up and went back to bed.

The following morning, Chris could hardly function. He was tired from having stayed up a good part of the night, but this

Middle Eastern man bothered him. He propped the color photograph taken a day earlier in front of him, leaning it on a frame holding a picture of Laura standing next to a group of Palestinian commandos. Julia, his secretary, stuck her head into his office to remind him he was running late for the morning editorial meeting.

CLAYBORNE, CHRIS PALESTINIANS-FIGHTERS BEIRUT, LEBANON NOT SPECIFIED

NOT SPECIFIED 1,245

"I'll be right there," he replied. But the photograph acted like a magnet. He was unable to leave it, unable to get away. Five minutes later, Julia returned. "They are starting without you," she said. "And Franklin is furious. Says we are days from inauguration and desperately wants your input." She moved into Chris's office, closed the door behind her, and said in whispered tone, "I think he really needs you. He gets lost and begins to panic when he has to cover such a big story. You'd better go save his ass."

"Thanks, Julia, I'll handle him." Gerald Franklin was the executive editor and senior vice president of IPS. He had come to IPS from a small Midwestern paper and brought his small-town mentality with him. The morning editorial meeting was sacrosanct to Franklin, and any department head who failed to attend had better have a good excuse. He was technically Clayborne's boss, but as he knew nothing about the news end of the operation, he left Chris alone, most of the time.

"Julia," Chris called out. "Send Peter upstairs." Peter Griffiths was Clayborne's deputy.

"You know Franklin won't like that," she called back.

"That's all right; I'll handle him."

Chris Clayborne grabbed the image off his desk and walked over to the photo archives department, situated at the opposite end of the floor. He found Angelica Gonzalez at her desk, as usual, sorting through piles of black-and-white images. Angelica was in charge of the archives and she knew almost every image in her library.

"*Buenos dias*, Angelica. How are you today?"

"*Hola*, Señor Chrees. How nice to see ju." Angelica was in her late sixties and had been working in the IPS library since she graduated from college more than forty years ago. She had never married and the photo library was her life; she treated it like the child she never had, refusing to retire. A fact for which Chris was forever grateful, as no one knew the files like she did.

"Angelica, do you recognize this man?" asked Clayborne, showing her the color photograph of the Middle Eastern man standing on the steps of the US Capitol. Angelica changed her eyeglasses and scrutinized the photo for several seconds before replying. "No, señor. I am sorry, but this image does not recollect a bell for me. Ees it important?" Clayborne smiled. Angelica had her own way of mixing idiomatic expressions. "*Sì*, Angelica, *es mucho importante*. I want you to drop whatever you're doing and see if you can match this with something from the files. I need it yesterday. *Muchas gracias*."

When Chris got back to his office, Franklin was there waiting for him. "Just where the hell have you been, my dear man?" Franklin had the nasty habit of addressing everyone as "my dear man."

"Something urgent came up and I have to get to the bottom of it," replied Clayborne. "Could be a big story."

"Would you care to share with us?"

"It's too early to reach any conclusions, but I have a hunch this could be big. Very big."

"Well, it better be big, because so is the president's inauguration. And that's only nine days away, my dear man."

"This could very well have to do with the inauguration, believe me."

"I'll see you at this afternoon's planning session," added Franklin as he stormed out. "Be there."

After lunch, Clayborne returned to the archives to help Angelica search the thousands of images and completely forgot his afternoon meeting with Franklin. By the time he left the office and made it home, it was well past ten. He looked in his refrigerator for something to eat, pulled out a slice of cold pizza, and opened a bottle of red wine before returning to his computer. He spent the next few hours searching through the database, without finding what he was looking for. At four thirty in the morning he gave up and went to sleep, totally exhausted.

An hour later, he awoke with a jolt from a deep sleep. It suddenly struck him. He himself had never seen the man before. He had not actually taken the picture, not the original picture anyway. He had only copied a photograph given to him by the Palestinians, by Zeid to be precise. It was a handout. He remembered that day now, soon after he returned to Beirut. With renewed vigor, he jumped out of bed, returned to the computer, and as soon as he was connected, typed in:

HANDOUT/BEIRUT/PALESTINIAN-FIGHTERS/?/?; seconds later the computer gave him the following prompt:

AUTHOR: SUBJECT: DATELINE: DATE: CAPTION: NUMBER OF PIX:

PRESS F1 TO VIEW PHOTOGRAPHS OR MAKE A NEW SELECTION.

HANDOUT PALESTINIANS-FIGHTERS BEIRUT, LEBANON NOT SPECIFIED NOT SPECIFIED 135

Chris hit F1 and a mosaic of small images instantly filled his screen. He placed the cursor on the first and hit enter. The mosaic disappeared and a large 10 x 4 black-and-white image appeared in its place. Chris's heart was beating faster now. The first picture displayed was not the one he wanted. He hit F2 and the screen was instantly replaced by the next picture. Not it either. He looked at the next, and the next. It was the sixty-fourth picture. That was the one. The photograph showed three young Palestinian fighters holding their AK-47s and smiling for the camera. Chris zoomed in on the man on the right and enlarged the photograph. The man appeared a little younger than he did today, but then again, the photograph had been taken more than a year ago. There could be no doubt, it was definitely the same man. The same eyes. Chris zoomed in on the eyes. He compared them to the color photograph on his desk. It was the same man. He pulled up the caption. It read:

"Beirut, Lebanon, December 25, 2012 - A photograph distributed by the PSF (Popular Struggle Front) today shows three unidentified Palestinian youths as they prepare for a suicide attack against Israel. Shortly after this photograph was taken, the group attacked a school in a kibbutz in northern Israel, killing several Israelis and wounding scores of others, including a number of children. The Palestinian commandos who carried out the attack were reported to have been killed by the Israeli army. CC/IPS HANDOUT"

"It's showtime," said Chris to the computer screen. "I got ya." Chris moved the cursor to the following picture. It was identical, except that this one had been cropped to exclude the fighter on the far right, the one Chris had photographed on the Hill. He read the caption. It was almost identical, except for the last line that indicated that only two of the commandos had been killed. "The third is believed to have survived and is reported to have escaped," the caption read.

That was it. This man was definitely the same one. What the hell was he doing in the US, right there on Capitol Hill? Chris made a print of the photograph, scribbled the picture number on a note pad for future reference, and signed off.

Chris Clayborne downed the rest of his wine. It now all came back to him. He remembered the frantic telephone call from Zeid in the middle of the night, asking him not to send the picture of the third man out on the wire. Originally, the youth was supposed to have died with the others. Clayborne had moved the photograph on the IPS wire and managed to kill the photo just in time. That photograph was filed into the IPS archives and had never made it to the newspapers and magazines. He remembered re-shooting the picture, cropping out the man on the right. It was him, all right. That was when the chemical attack took place. Hundreds were killed. Now why was he here? What was he doing on the steps of the Capitol building a few days before the president's inauguration? Clayborne was tired; he needed to get some rest. He would think more clearly in the morning.

Chris was far too excited to fall asleep. He got out of bed and turned on the television in time to catch the tail end of a report from Yugoslavia, or what used to be Yugoslavia. "Damn, that's one war I'm glad I didn't cover," said Chris to no one. The report was followed by another story on more violence erupting in the Middle East. A poor quality tape showed footage of a car bomb in Damascus that killed fifteen people. The Syrians blamed the Muslim Brotherhood and claimed to have arrested and executed four terrorists. There was more unrest in the West Bank and Gaza. Finally, the anchor announced, *"And this communiqué release by the extremist Popular Struggle Front headed by Doctor Ibrahim Hawali just came in. Frank Delano in Beirut explains."*

Chris recognized the network correspondent standing outside his office in Beirut. *"In a rare press conference, Dr. Ibrahim Hawali, the head of the radical PSF, warned the United States today to stop supporting, I quote, 'the Zionist entity,' unquote. The Doctor, as he is commonly called here, said it was high time the Americans gave some thought to the plight of the Palestinian people. He asked President-elect Wells to discontinue 'his blind support of Israel,' as he put it, and to veto the latest financial and military aid packet totaling more than a billion dollars that Israel is due to receive shortly after President Wells is sworn into office next week. Dr. Hawali warned that unless the United States denounces Israel's aggression and alters its stance on the Palestinian issue before the new president assumes office, the Unites States will bear the consequences. He cautioned the United States that the Palestinian people were rapidly losing their patience and unless the US showed encouraging signs, the PSF would not rule out striking at American interests, even if it meant taking the battle to the very heart of America. 'We will turn the streets of Washington into Beirut,' said Dr. Hawali. This is Frank Delano for News Networks in Beirut."*

"We have Frank Delano on line from Beirut now, where he explains this new turn in policy," said the anchor in New York.

"Frank, this is really the first time the Palestinians have come out with such a blatant warning against the United States, and does that mean we are facing a new wave of terrorism, maybe even here in the US?"

"Well, Bill, actually the PLO, and in particular the PSF, have issued warnings to the United States in the past. What is new here is that Dr. Hawali has set an actual deadline, giving the American government basically until the inauguration of the new president."

"Frank, does it look like it might be a bluff from the PLO or should we, should the State Department, the president, the FBI, the military take this more seriously?"

"Bill, let me clarify something. The PLO, the Palestine Liberation Organization, is not involved here. This is merely a statement made by Dr. Ibrahim Hawali, a radical leftist Palestinian who broke away from the PLO years ago. Hawali is also known to have close ties to the radical Sheik al-Haq, who is known to have financed several operations against the US and Israel. At the moment, his group, the PSF, is at odds with the PLO leadership, whom Hawali labeled a traitor and has even tried to assassinate. The Doctor does not want the Washington peace talks to succeed. His group certainly has the potential to conduct terrorist actions against the United States. They have done so in the past, but never in the US itself. This is a new twist where he threatens to bring the fight to the very heart of America, 'to the streets of Washington,' as he put it."

"Frank Delano in Beirut, thank you."

"These TV guys haven't changed much, have they?" Chris said out loud. "Now they're gonna get all sorts of experts to analyze the statement and the Doctor. They will play it for every cent it's worth."

The sun was already up by the time Chris Clayborne drove out to Annapolis. Charlton MacClarty was an early riser, and when Chris called him at five thirty, MacClarty was already drinking his second cup of coffee and reading the morning newspapers. Chris was greeted by MacClarty, who poured him a cup of coffee and led him into his den. It was a large, comfortable room, decorated with prize-winning photographs, many of which were taken by MacClarty himself in his much younger days. There were copies of several front pages of newspapers, framed and mounted on a wall. Those were the scoops that MacClarty had obtained for IPS over the years. A large television screen was tuned to News Network, but the sound was muted. It was an old habit MacClarty could not get away from. As a retirement present, IPS had offered MacClarty a satellite dish so that he could still receive and view the full IPS photographic service as it went out over the wire. Occasionally, MacClarty would phone Clayborne and critique some of the pictures, or point out spelling mistakes in the captions—another old habit he could not break away from.

"What's on your mind, kiddo?" asked MacClarty. "Kiddo" was a term MacClarty reserved only for people he liked. "It's gotta be very important for you to drive all the way out here, so early in the morning, and this being just eight days before inauguration. I'm sure you must have a number of other fires to put out."

"Well, Mac, that's just it." Clayborne related to MacClarty the events of the last two days and showed him the two photographs: the one from the files and the one he had taken three days earlier.

"What do you suggest I do, Mac?" asked Clayborne. "Journalistically speaking, I feel this is a story. There's no doubt. This man is a terrorist and he was seen scouting the site of the presidential inauguration just days before the event. But on the other hand, if there is a real threat to the president of the United States, is it not our duty to save lives, too? Do I go to the law, or do I try and find an angle to a story? Or do I do both? Right now, all I have is this headshot of a man I know is a terrorist. Not much for a story."

"I understand your dilemma, kiddo," said MacClarty. "But let me ask you this simple question: what were you hoping to accomplish all these years running after bang bang, out there in the jungles of Africa and the deserts of the Mideast, getting your ass shot at? What did you want your news photographs to portray? I believe you were hoping, somewhere inside that mind of yours, that you would show the world the ugliness of war. You remember those words, kiddo? 'The ugliness of war.' Those were your words. You said that to me when I first interviewed you a few centuries ago. That's why I hired you on the spot and sent you to the Middle East. Not because you were some crazy kid out of college looking for bang bang or excitement. Yes, certainly there was that; it's in all our blood. Otherwise we can't get the job done, but there's more to it than that. You as a crusade. Your crusade, your chance to do something. You were hoping that you would maybe save a single life through your images of war. Well, today that life may be the life of the most powerful man in this country."

"So I go to the law." It was more a statement than a question.

"Go straight to the feds, kiddo. Go see my old friend Bill Potter at the FBI. I'll call him and tell him you're on your way. Potter is a good man."

"Thanks, Mac."

"No sweat, kiddo, no sweat. How's that asshole Franklin treating you? Is he still on everyone's case, as always?"

"He sure is; especially these last few days. He's been busting my back about missing his silly meetings."

"That dodo frets every time a big story comes around. He doesn't know shit from Shinola. Keep your legs together, kiddo."

"Mac?"

"Yeah?"

"One more thing. Just what the hell is Shinola?"

"It's shoe shine, kiddo. Go see Potter, and good luck with the inauguration."

Chris Clayborne was heading for the elevators when Julia called him back. The little sleep he had these last few nights had totally exhausted him, as did today's early drive to Annapolis. The meeting with William Potter at the FBI's J. Edgar Hoover Building on Pennsylvania Avenue did not do much to help, either. Clayborne thought he would be in and out in about an hour, hand the prints to the FBI man and return to work. Potter grilled him for over three and a half hours, going over every small detail again and again.

"Chris," shouted Julia. "Urgent phone call. Long distance. Told them to call you on your cell phone, but they insisted you take the call ASAP. She says it's urgent."

"She?"

Julia shrugged her shoulder, throwing her arms in the air. "She, but she wouldn't give me a name."

Chris Clayborne cursed as he returned to his office. He threw his coat on a chair, turned on his desk light and sat down in his large comfortable black leather chair.

"Clayborne here."

"This is Laura, Chris. It's real good to hear your voice."

It took a few seconds for the words to sink in. Laura was the last person on earth Clayborne expected to hear from. "My God. Laura? Laura, how the hell are you? Where the hell are you?"

"I'm calling from Jerusalem. I'm sorry, but I must speak to you. It's important. I wanted to make sure I got you before you left."

"That's all right. No big deal, I was just going home. Laura, I'm delighted to hear your voice. How's Dixie? How are you?"

"Fine and fine. The usual stuff. I've been here for a day and I fly back tomorrow."

But Clayborne could feel there was more to it than that. He could detect the nervous tension in her voice. "What is it, Laura? What's wrong?"

"Nothing's wrong. All is fine, Chris, but there's an urgent matter that I need to talk to you about. I will be arriving in Washington tomorrow afternoon. Can we get together right away?"

"Yes, sure. Yes, we can."

"I'm sorry to impose on you at the last minute, Chris, but this is important."

"What is it? Can you talk?"

"I'll tell you tomorrow. Don't want to talk on the telephone."

"I'm glad you called, Laura. I've been thinking about you. My God, Laura, it's been a while; what have you been up to? I've really missed you."

"I miss you too, darling, I really do, and would love to see you again."

"Laura, it will be so good to see you. God, I've been thinking about you so much," said Clayborne.

"Me too, Chris. So have I—I still miss you very much."

"Need a place to stay?" asked Clayborne.

"Thanks, I might take you up on that."

"Give me your flight details and I'll pick you up at Dulles. Is that where you're coming in?

"That's okay; I have transportation. Why don't we meet at your place tomorrow evening, say around sixish?"

"Sixish. That's great. I'll see you then."

"Chris?"

"Yes?"

"Isn't there something you have to tell me?"

"Tell you? Yes, I miss you. I can hardly wait . . ."

"No Chris, besides that."

"What?"

"How about your address?"

Clayborne sat at his desk for the longest time, unable to put his thoughts in order. He aimed the remote control at the three television sets sitting on a long narrow table that faced his desk, each tuned to a different news channel. As usual, the sounds from the three sets were all muted. Chris noticed a graphic of the Middle East flash behind the anchorwoman. He reached for the remote and raised the volume on the middle set, constantly tuned to the News Network Channel.

"*. . . amid reports of more violence this morning in the Syrian capital, Damascus.*"

Clayborne pulled out a bottle of Jack Daniels that he kept in his desk drawer for medicinal purposes: paper cuts, scrapes and bruises, or moments like these. Julia stuck her head through the door to say she was leaving for the day. With his free hand Chris waved her away as he took a sip from the bottle.

"Everything okay, boss?" she asked.

"All's fine, Julia. Thanks. I'll see you in the morning."

The sounds from the television continued: *". . . a Syrian Ministry of Information official informed News Network this morning that the latest bomb that exploded outside Syria's central bank, killing a dozen people, was the work of the Muslim Brotherhood, an extremist Islamic faction that remains banned in Syria. However, a communiqué delivered to international news agencies in Beirut by the Brotherhood vehemently denies the allegations, claiming Syrian intelligence agents are responsible for the bombs and are using the incidents as an excuse to crack down on their members in Syria. This is Frank Delano in Beirut."*

"Frank, there are reports of troop movements in Damascus tonight. Have you been able to confirm any of this?"

"Well, Arlene, as you know, the Syrians have denied visas to all foreign media, including News Network, saying the mood in the capital is, and I quote, 'not right at this particular time,' unquote. I have, however, been able to talk to several residents in Damascus tonight, including a European diplomat who spoke to me on condition that I not mention his name. All those I spoke to confirm the arrival of large numbers of troops and tanks in the Damascus area. The high-ranking diplomat, whose apartment overlooks the Mezze Highway, a major avenue on the city's outskirts, told me he counted at least 350 tanks this afternoon. He claims he saw a large number of ambulances race past the American embassy towards the central bank. The diplomat mentioned that the tanks were just parked, as he put it, 'they were just parked on the highway.'"

"We'll be back later in the program with more details from Frank Delano in Beirut."

Chris Clayborne left the office earlier than usual the next day. He went straight home, where he spent the good part of an hour tidying the place up—not that his apartment was messy. A Guatemalan maid saw to it three times a week that the place remained impeccably clean. But Chris was nervous and needed to keep himself occupied. He took a long, hot shower, put on some clean clothes, and anxiously awaited Laura's arrival.

Clayborne uncorked a bottle of red Bordeaux he had picked up a few days earlier from the corner liquor store, and allowed the wine to breathe. He placed a Luciano Pavarotti CD on his player and paced nervously around the flat, waving his arms in the air, directing an imaginary orchestra. He was feeling foolish at his boyish anticipation of seeing Laura again.

Laura arrived a few minutes after six thirty. She rang the bell and Chris opened the door almost immediately. She looked lovelier than ever, Chris thought, as she stood sheepishly in the doorway, smiling at him. She was tanned, healthy, and full of vigor. Her hair was a bit longer than before and came down to her shoulders, almost touching them. The black-and-white dress she wore outlined her body perfectly. Chris just stared at her for several long seconds.

"Are you going to ask me in, or are you just going to let me stand in the hallway all night long?" she joked. Chris ushered her in and they embraced for a long time before either of them spoke. They simply held onto one another, feeling each other's warmth.

"It's so good to see you again." It was Laura who finally broke the silence. "I missed you so much," she added. "I really did."

"I can hardly believe you're here. It's so great to see you. Sit yourself down. Let me get your coat and I'll get us something to drink. You look wonderful." Chris Clayborne poured two glasses of the red wine and offered Laura a glass. "Here's to us and old times."

"Here's to better times ahead," replied Laura. "Tell me about yourself. You look great. No, you look fabulous. I guess Washington is treating you right after all."

"Oh, Washington isn't so bad, really. Dull when compared to the Middle East, but then again, what isn't? On the other hand, there is enough going on here to keep me busy, on my toes, and out of trouble. There are plenty of Arabic restaurants to keep me in supply of hummus and other delicacies. But I do miss the old days. The Middle East is never really far though. You want to know something crazy?" said Clayborne, delicately brushing Laura's hair away from her face. "Since I left Beirut, I haven't seen or heard from anyone there in months. As for you, I haven't seen you since your trip to London. I don't even get a postcard all this time, then suddenly, in the space of two days, Beirut seems to be haunting me again. First, Dieter Schiller shows up in a limo, then you call, and finally, I see this Palestinian who was supposed to have died pop up right here in DC."

"Chris," said Laura, looking serious, "this is what I came to talk to you about."

"What?"

"The Palestinian," said Laura, as she opened her black leather briefcase, withdrew a tan folder from inside and handed it to Chris. Inside the folder was a copy of the photograph he had taken on the Hill just a few days earlier. "How did you know he was going to be on the Hill?"

"I didn't. It was pure coincidence. It drove me crazy just trying to figure out who the hell he was. I couldn't concentrate; I couldn't work or sleep until I figured out where I recognized him from. It took me two whole days."

"Chris, I need to know more about him," said Laura, pointing to the folder that Chris was now holding. "What have you kept back from the FBI? What can you tell me that you kept from them?"

"Hold on a minute, how did you know I went to the FBI? How did you know I saw him on the Hill? I never mentioned any of that tonight." Chris opened the folder and almost dropped his wine glass when he saw the Palestinian looking at him. "Where the hell did you get those pictures? That's my picture. Where did you get it?"

"You never mentioned you had a picture of this terrorist either. Yet you had a picture of this bastard all the time. Why the hell didn't you ever tell me about this?"

"What do you mean, 'tell you'? Tell you what?"

"Why did you never mention that you had a picture of this terrorist? That you knew who the third man in the kibbutz attack was?" inquired Laura.

"Look, first of all, you never asked, and secondly, I promised Zeid to kill this picture. It never made it on the wires because this guy, whatever his name is, came back," Clayborne said. "He was not supposed to, but he did. And why the hell are you suddenly so interested in this, anyway?"

"Chris, please listen and calm down. This is what I need to talk to you about. I have to find him."

"Yes, and the Doctor would have found you and terminated your life and mine, Laura. This is no laughing matter. You don't joke around with these people. Zeid had my trust; he gave me the photograph more than twenty-four hours ahead of the competition. He gave it to me before the operation, before the attack on the kibbutz. I couldn't go about handing the picture to other hacks after he asked me to put a stop on it. Hell, that would have been the end of it; the end of me. Don't think I did not lose sleep over this matter. I thought about it a lot, which is why I decided to go to the FBI this time. Laura, if you got to see the Doctor as quickly as you did and visit the training camp in the Bekaa, it was thanks to my good relations with Zeid and his group."

"Yes, I know, Chris, and I am eternally grateful for that."

"You never answered my question. How did you obtain a copy of this picture and how did you know I saw him on the Hill?"

"Chris, did he see you?"

"Did who see me?"

"You know what I mean. Did Omar see you?"

"Omar? So now you know his name too? How the hell do you know his name? Just what is going on here? Laura, you have to tell me. What's going on here? Jesus, this is spooky."

"Chris, darling Chris. I'm sorry, but you must listen to me. I've been on his trail since Beirut, Chris. His real name is Omar al-Kheir, though he never uses it. At least that's the name he is known to us by. He has used a dozen false names and twice as many false passports. More often than not, he used real passports given to him by other intelligence services for whom he's carried out certain favors. The Libyans, the Iraqis, the Iranians, the Syrians, and even the IRA."

"Now wait a goddamn minute. You said 'he is known to us' . . . who the hell is 'us'? Are you a spook? Do you work for the government? And, may I add, which government? You know, maybe we do have a story here. If this Omar guy is as dangerous as you say he is, maybe I should move the photo on the wire? Run a story with it. It could be worth a lot."

"Yes, like your life. This man doesn't kid around, Chris. Please listen to me."

Clayborne sat near the fire, took a poker and moved a log around the fireplace. He took a sip of his wine before speaking. "Laura, how involved are you in this? What are you not telling me? Or rather, what are you trying to tell me—that you're a spook?"

Laura laughed, "Is that what you call it, a spook?"

"Yeah, a spook, a spy, a secret agent, an operative, fucking James Bond." Clayborne poured himself another glass of wine.

"Darling, I can tell you very little and the little I do tell you must remain absolutely confidential. You mustn't move the picture on the wire. There must be no story. Think of the panic it will cause. You must help me find this man in any way you can."

"Laura, do you realize what you are asking me to do? I'm a journalist, not a fucking spook. It's not my job to spy on people. It's my job, though, to deliver the truth. I've already done my duty by giving the information to the FBI. What more do you want now?"

"The truth?" said Laura, raising her voice. "The truth is that this bastard is a dangerous terrorist, probably the most dangerous terrorist in the world today. This man has murdered innocent women and children, not to mention men, simply because they believed in a different god than his, or because they don't agree with his way of thinking. This man used chemical weapons on innocent civilians and is getting ready to do it again, this time in Washington. This man you are trying to protect is responsible for the death of more than a hundred people, brutally killed, slaughtered, like animals."

"Listen, I'm not trying to protect him, remember? I'm the one who went to the FBI. I'm just questioning the ethics of this whole thing."

"Ethics?" Laura's voice changed. She stood up and helped herself to more wine. "Tell me about his ethics. About killing defenseless children in a school, about gunning down diplomats and about bombing street markets in Tel Aviv or nightclubs in Frankfurt while American servicemen dance. Or how about those poor bastards he blew out of the sky? All in the name of what?"

"Laura, Laura, hold on a minute. Let's calm down a bit here. I'm on your side, remember? I'm still with the good guys." Chris walked over to her, placed his arm around her, and pulled her tightly towards him, kissing her on the forehead. "Look, there's a lot more to this than you are telling me. I want to know; I need to know. How involved are you? I have to know. You owe me this much."

"The Mossad has identified him as the third man in the kibbutz attack of a few years ago. That's why I went to Jerusalem last week to liaise with Israeli intelligence. That's why I went to Beirut last August. To track down Omar. They've also identified him as the man responsible for the death of Ambassador Shoman in Brussels. This man is a dangerous terrorist, a killer without a conscience. They believe him responsible for the attack on the TWA plane in Rome. He has assassinated prominent West Bank Palestinians who have voiced their intentions of discussing peace with Israel. This man is far more dangerous than Carlos ever was. He's managed to escape capture numerous times. He brutally massacred a Mossad agent in London and nearly killed another. In Paris, he cut the throat of a lover whom he suspected had ratted on him to the police. He managed to escape only moments before a French anti-terrorist squad arrived. To make his point, he had the nerve to walk into a Paris police station and blow the place up the very next day. There are no known photographs of this man, except of course for the ones you have, the ones you gave the FBI. If he even suspects you to have taken this picture, if he ever remotely thinks you've spotted him, he will kill you without hesitation."

Chris remained silent for a long while, digesting the information. "How do you know all this? No one seems to know much about who was responsible for all those acts you just mentioned. They were claimed by various Pal and pro-Iranian groups."

"We know. Believe me, we know."

Chris noticed the gradual change taking over Laura as she spoke. She was being transformed into a very different person. Her tone was getting more authoritative, more sure of herself. And it frightened Chris. "We?" questioned Clayborne. "Go on."

Laura realized that if she were to convince Clayborne, to obtain his cooperation, she would have to give him something in return. "Yes, we. The intel community. Yes, Chris, I work for the US government; for the CIA. I'm a fucking spook, as you put it. But this Omar is one of the most dangerous men in the world. We believe he now plans to assassinate the president of the United States on Inauguration Day, possibly with the use of chemical or biological weapons."

Laura picked up the color photograph of the Palestinian standing on the front steps of the Capitol and handed it to Chris. "You were right. Your reaction was the right one. It was your Middle East reflex. You guessed right and did the proper thing by going to the FBI."

"It wasn't easy," admitted Chris.

"I'm sure. But now we . . ." she hesitated. "I need your help. Please. What can you tell me?"

"So Beirut was just a big fucking lie? All the time we spent together was just so that you could play your fucking spy games?

186 | INAUGURATION DAY

So that you could use me? You must be out of your mind. You must be mad. Do you realize what would have happened to you, to me, if they ever even suspected? If they ever found out? What right have you got to endanger us like that?"

"No, Chris, I never used you. We, us, what happened between us in Beirut was . . . is, very real. I had real feelings for you. I still do. It's unfortunate that things got in the way. I was doing my job, but I did not use you."

"How can you say that? How can you say that with a straight face? You did not use me? Yet, you disappeared overnight and I don't hear from you until you need me again. You need me because I spotted your terrorist."

"Because it's the truth, damn you! I disappeared because it would have been dangerous to return to Beirut and it would have been dangerous for you had I communicated with you. Yes, I was told to use you. Yes, you did have great contacts that helped me cut through piles of red tape, but my feelings for you are real . . . were real, and still are real," said Laura. Tears started to roll down her face and she dropped her head onto Chris's shoulders. "I never wanted to fool you. I have real feelings for you, Chris. I do."

The lovemaking that followed flowed naturally. They were both hungry for each other's body, for warmth. For several long minutes, it was almost like old times. Chris allowed himself to momentarily forget what he had just heard. He had longed for Laura. He was happy to have her back, even if it would only last a few precious moments.

They kissed, caressed, and touched each other's bodies. It seemed as if they had only been apart for days. Chris looked at Laura. Her face looked even more beautiful than he remembered.

The flames burning in the fireplace reflected off her naked body as she lay on the large Persian rug.

"I missed you, Chris," she whispered in his ear. "I really did. You'll never know how much you really meant to me, with all the madness and all the hatred in the Middle East, you brought a certain comfort and stability into my life. You gave me warmth. I needed that, very much." She placed a gentle kiss on his nose. "But now, I'm hungry. Take me out and feed me or I'll eat you all up," she said, nibbling playfully on his ear.

They were both famished by the time they reached the small, cozy Italian restaurant in Georgetown, one of Chris's favorites. The waiter took their order and Chris remained silent, lost in his thoughts for a long while.

"I'm afraid you wasted your time, Laura. I mean coming here."

"What do you mean?"

"I mean there is nothing more I can tell you, other than what I've already told the FBI. I spent almost four hours with them yesterday. I saw this guy on the Hill, he looked familiar. I instinctively snapped a few frames and nearly went crazy trying to ID him. Voilà, that's all I have. I have no idea where he is, or what he is up to."

"We'll track him down," she said. "We'll track the bastard down. We have to."

They finished their meal. Chris paid and they left the comfort of the restaurant for the cold January air. It had started to snow and Laura held on to Chris's arm as they looked for a taxi. They walked in silence for a while, each lost in their own thoughts, when Chris suddenly stopped, turned to face Laura, and said, "The second option."

"What?"

"The second option, goddamn it. Have you considered the second option?"

"Chris, what the hell are you talking about?"

"There has to be a different goal. A different excuse. The Doctor must be up to something else. He has to have something else up his sleeve. He has to. It just doesn't make sense."

"Chris, just what are you talking about? You're the one not making any sense."

"For Chrissake, Laura," said Chris, looking around him to make sure he would not be overheard, "if the PSF goes to the trouble of taking out the president of the US, which is no small feat in itself, there has to be room for a second option. The Thinker, remember the Thinker? The man I pointed out to you in that restaurant back in Beirut? He would never let an opportunity like that go by without conceiving of some other demonic scheme. A second opportunity."

"Like what?"

"You're the spy. I don't know; you figure it out. But I bet you every last dollar I ever made that the Doctor, with help from his Thinker, have thought up a nice little side dish for you."

"Isn't killing the American president with chemical weapons enough? I mean, what could be bigger?"

"Big enough for me, thank you very much. Far more than I can handle, yes, but not for them, Laura. What would they gain? Directly, I mean. Think about this. What would they gain by killing the president? There has to be a second motive. You see, you have to think like the Doctor. Put yourself in his place. All right, with the American president out of the way, what comes next? What's your next move? How can they take advantage of that situation? What is it that they really want? What have they been after all these years?"

"You can't possibly believe they are going to attack Israel. Don't be daft. The PSF doesn't have the military strength, nor the political clout to take on the Israeli army, especially now with the Soviets out of the way. It would be suicide."

"When was it not suicide—the Middle East, I mean? All that they do there is suicidal. Like the story of the turtle and the scorpion."

"But they couldn't possibly take on the Israeli Army."

"No, not the Pals, they couldn't. But someone else, the Syrians, for example, certainly can."

"But that's insane. Why would the Syrians want to start a Middle East war? Why now, when the peace process is going ahead?"

"Going ahead without them."

"But still, go to war now? Why?"

"Might you have done something that pissed them off during the last forty years, maybe? These people do carry a grudge, you know. And it would give the Assad regime the upper hand in the civil war."

"Be serious, Chris. It's no time to joke."

Clayborne ignored the last remarks. "Besides, with the void left by the absence of US political and military pressure, with the US government safely out of the way, at least for a while, that is, there would be chaos in the Middle East. Utter chaos. It could be the perfect excuse for a short, limited conflict, not a big war, mind you. The Syrians could be in and out before anyone realized what hit them. Especially if Omar creates enough chaos here. If he uses chemical weapons in Washington, it would take weeks, if not months, for the nation to recover."

22

Chester D. Higgins III bore a slight resemblance to the actor Dustin Hoffman. He had the kind of face that made you wonder if you had already met before. He was of average height, not very tall, had the same shape of face as Hoffman, and the same dark hair Hoffman once had. However, Higgins wore wire-rimmed glasses, making him look slightly more intellectual. The other difference was that Higgins was much tougher. Young Higgins had followed in his father's footsteps, joining the Central Intelligence Agency in Vietnam, where he had first served as a major in the US Marine Corps. His father, Chester Delbert Higgins Jr. had joined the Office of Strategic Services during World War II, and then remained with the newly formed Central Intelligence Agency, serving as a field officer in postwar Germany, Hungary, and then the Middle East. Higgins III had spent the first twenty years of his life growing up in Tehran, Cairo, Beirut, and Tel Aviv. He spoke fluent Farsi and Arabic, knew the region and culture better than most locals, and felt more at home in the Arab world than he did on the banks of the Potomac.

Since his return to a desk job at Langley, Chester D. Higgins III had spent every working hour of every day fighting consecutive administrations. He tried desperately to get them to see the imminent danger in the rise of Islamic fundamentalism in the Arab World and of extremist groups like the PSF and fanatics like Sheik al-Haq. The idiots in Washington were far too preoccupied with trivial matters such as sex scandals to take him or the threats seriously. He had seen the dangers coming more than fifteen years ago. He had warned them about Ayatollah Khomeini, but they wouldn't listen. Even the French had passed on their concerns, while Khomeini, still an unknown and unheard-of factor, was preaching in a Paris suburb for the demise of the Shah. Higgins's contacts in Iran, as well as connections in the French Intelligence and Counterintelligence Service, had voiced their apprehension. Higgins relayed the information to Langley, begging the CIA to intervene. The CIA and the Shah had grossly underestimated the powers of the Ayatollah. The rest was history.

Unfortunately for Higgins, most of the Arab world was now off-limits to him. The Iranians had identified him as a CIA operative from files they recovered when they took over the American embassy. Higgins knew that his life would not be worth much if he was caught anywhere in the Arab world. For now, he had to content himself with a house in suburban Virginia and a commute to CIA headquarters every day. And he hated it.

Chester Higgins greeted Laura with a firm handshake outside the Tenth Street and Pennsylvania entrance of the Federal Bureau of Investigation building in Washington, DC. "Good to meet you, Atwood," said Higgins. "I've heard a lot about you from the boss. You have done some remarkable work."

"I'm glad you think so," replied Laura. "I am not so sure the boss thinks along the same lines. Which is probably why he has tasked you to babysit me."

"You may be right about the boss not trusting you and asking me to babysit you, but my admiration of your work in the Middle East is genuine."

"Thanks for the vote of confidence," said Laura. "In any case, most of us at the Farm think that you are one of the few people in this country who understand the Middle Eastern way of doing things."

The two CIA agents entered the FBI building, where they were greeted by an FBI agent who had been waiting for them. The agent signed them in and gave them VIP badges. Higgins smiled, as he knew those VIP badges allowed the bearer into exactly the same places as the regular tourist badges. They just made important visitors feel more important. The FBI man accompanied them up to the top floor and into the sumptuous office occupied by Hamilton Royce, Deputy Director of Operations.

"Welcome to the FBI, Miss Atwood, Mr. Higgins," said Royce in a thick southern drawl. "I just got off the phone with Director Monaghan, who believes there might be even greater trouble brewing back there, that is, unless we stop that S.O.B. first," said Royce, pointing Laura and Higgins to empty chairs.

Laura was introduced to three other people already in the room and made a mental note of their names. "Bruce Whelan, Special Assistant to the Director; Vincent Bonenfanti, head of the FBI Anti-Terrorism Bureau; and William Potter, Assistant Deputy Director of the Federal Bureau of Investigation, in charge of Counterespionage.

"From the US Secret Service, you have Bruce Stravorski, Susan Price, and Muriel Ford. They are respectively Deputy Director of the USSS, Director of the Presidential Detail, and Director of Presidential Travel. We will be joined in a few moments by Alex Vaughn, who is in charge of all advance movements. He is being held up in another meeting."

Royce spoke first, addressing Laura in his southern accent. "Miss Atwood, your director firmly believes that this Omar fellow is here presently in these United States and is preparing to strike at us, possibly with the use of chemical weapons. Mr. Potter, there,"—he gestured with a wave of his arm—"strongly supports the theory. Claims his sources are impeccable, which I don't doubt, as Mr. Potter is an excellent man and an outstanding agent. But quite frankly, little lady, I may be from the great state of Louisiana, but I'm from Missouri on this one." He puffed on his unlit pipe to indicate he was done, for the moment.

Laura realized that she had been living outside the US too long. She had no clue what Royce was talking about. She gave Higgins a quizzical look. "That's Southern talk for skeptical," he whispered.

Laura was about to speak, when Royce raised his hand, to indicate he still had more to say. "Little Lady, all we have to go on is a picture of a man walking by Capitol Hill. Now I ask you, do you believe this is enough to launch a nationwide manhunt? Enough to mobilize the entire Federal Bureau of Investigation and all its resources?"

"Director Royce," said Laura Atwood, "I have been on the trail of this terrorist for years. This is the man who attacked a school full of children in northern Israel and then killed more than a hundred people in the first chemical attack on the country. This is the same man who killed the Israeli ambassador to Belgium, and hijacked several airliners, including American carriers. The list goes on; it's all in the file in front of you. Believe me, he would not be here, in Washington, a few days before the president's inauguration unless he was planning something big. I don't think Omar was playing tourist."

Deputy Director Royce picked up the pictures from the folder given to him by Potter and examined them. "So this is what the son of a bitch looks like." Royce smiled at her, "And just what do y'all think the S.O.B. might be up to?"

"Judging from the tone of the threats delivered so far, it seems that they were all directed against the president's office, urging him to change US policy towards Israel. We believe he plans to strike at the president, sir," said Bonenfanti, the FBI's anti-terrorism man. "The fact that he was seen at the Capitol might indicate he plans to strike around that area, or is still scouting for his ideal target."

"Inauguration Day," said Potter. "That's when the president is most vulnerable. He's out in the open, usually walks down Pennsylvania Avenue after the inauguration ceremony, stops, and shakes hands with people and such. And if the weapon really is chemical or biological, Omar does not need to get up close and personal."

"Mr. Royce, as you know, I went to Tel Aviv yesterday and had a one-hour session with the head of Mossad," said Laura. "He conveyed his concerns. There is more at stake than the US president, if that were not bad enough. Dr. Ibrahim Hawali has been reported by the Jordanians to have been seen traveling to Damascus and Tehran more than a dozen times in the last six months. Far more than the usual meetings he's had in the last few years."

"Surely, Syria isn't going to get involved in the assassination of the president of the United States!" exclaimed Royce.

Bonenfanti nodded in agreement. "But sir, Iran might. Not officially, but Firamarz Kazemi certainly wouldn't pass up the opportunity to strike at American interests." Bonenfanti looked at Higgins for support.

"That's for sure," agreed Higgins, who was thankful that for once someone was taking a threat seriously. "Old Ayatollah Kazemi would certainly jump at such an opportunity. He is the ultra-hardliner and most anti-American of all the mullahs. And again, here too, we have seen large transfers of funds between bank accounts Kazemi manages for the Palestinian jihadists."

***

The president's inauguration was now only five days away. Omar had some final preparations to make before the big day. He left his apartment and rode the Metro to Union Station, only three stops away, from where he boarded an express train to New York's Penn Station. He had studied his maps well over the last few weeks and found getting around was becoming easier. No one would notice another face in the crowd. He would use this to his advantage. A funny place, America, he thought. They would be beaten by their own system. Far too much freedom.

A short cab ride later took him from Penn Station to the United Nations Plaza on New York's East Side. Omar found a working telephone and called a direct number at the Iranian mission at the United Nations.

"This is Nabil," he said in English. "I have not yet received your communiqué."

There was a brief hesitation on the other end before the voice replied, "It is ready for you. Tell us where to send it."

"You have my address on file," said the Palestinian, and hung up.

Omar waited exactly fifteen minutes, then walked to the post office a few blocks from the UN Headquarters at the address given to him by the caller in Athens several weeks earlier. He found the box numbered 3226 and slid a sealed envelope inside it. The Palestinian then positioned himself a few feet away, and pretended to fill out a form, without ever taking his eyes off box number 3226. Less than half a minute later, a man with a Middle Eastern complexion walked into the post office, opened box number 3226, and retrieved the letter Omar had deposited. The letter with Omar's instructions had remained no more than a few seconds in the post office box. The Iranian walked back to the UN and Omar disappeared into the crowd. Omar was back in Washington the same evening.

The next morning, Omar walked to a nearby supermarket. He was always surprised at the abundance of goods available in America. Just look at all the choices there were. Why would anyone need all these different kinds of toilet paper, or orange juice, or cereal? The people in the camps where he grew up never had that much choice. They were lucky to get bread. They would be content just having enough to eat on any given day. Revenge was near. Just let them wait, he thought. Just a few more days now. Things would change.

Omar stocked up on canned food and bottled water to last out the week. He intended to remain in the apartment as much as possible once the equipment he was waiting for was delivered. There was no need to run additional risks. Anything could happen. The landlord might show up unexpectedly, or there could be a leak in the roof. Trouble has a way of creeping up. With the target date nearly at hand, it was silly to risk blowing the operation. Expect the unexpected. His mind floated back to the early days in the training camp with Kifah Kassar. How much had happened since then, how things had changed for him. How he had changed. There he was a simple fighter ready to blow himself up, and now he was about to carry out one of the greatest terrorist feats ever perpetrated. People would talk about this day more than they did about Munich. Killing the American president was by far greater than attacking a group of Israeli athletes. It was far more dangerous, too. He was certain the Americans would step up their security in the capital for the big event on January 20. Already, he noticed there were more men in uniform patrolling his neighborhood; he also noticed more than a few without uniform. Undercover cops, he thought, were the same the world over. They might as well carry a large sign saying "Secret Police."

Ironically, the US Secret Service had done just that with their Uniformed Division. Omar found it hilarious to see police cars with their flashing lights, sirens and all, with large letters on the car identifying it as US Secret Service Uniformed Division.

The day after Omar's trip to the Big Apple, the Iranian diplomat unlocked the special closet in his East Side apartment and removed the two trunks where he had placed the equipment brought into the country over the last few months from Paris. He loaded them onto a small trolley, the kind used by airline travelers, and rode the building's service elevator to his underground garage at exactly two o'clock in the afternoon, where a flower delivery van was already waiting. The driver of the van quickly helped the diplomat load the two trunks into the van. The diplomat returned upstairs and the van drove away. FBI agents positioned outside the front and garage entrances of the thirty-five story building, who kept around-the-clock watch on the Iranian diplomat, paid no particular attention to the van. Dozens of delivery vans pulled into the building every day.

The van drove across Manhattan to the Holland Tunnel to make its way to the New Jersey Turnpike, then headed south on Interstate 95 until it reached Washington's Capital Beltway, some five and a half hours later. The driver had maintained his speed well around the fifty-five mile per hour speed limit. He took the Baltimore-Washington Parkway, which led him into the District of Columbia and onto New York Avenue. Following directions in the letter dropped off in the New York post office box, the driver easily found the Howard Johnson Inn on New York Avenue. It was shortly after nine and traffic was light as the driver pulled into the parking lot behind the motel. As instructed, the driver remained in the van for several minutes. Omar, who was sitting in his rented Ford in clear view of the van, waited ten full minutes before making contact. He wanted to make sure the van was not being followed. It wasn't. No one entered the motel's parking lot, and no car stopped outside either.

Omar approached the driver of the van and identified himself as Nabil. He asked the driver if he had brought the communiqué.

"It's in the back," said the driver.

The two men unloaded the trunks and Omar drove away. No further conversation was exchanged between the two. The driver of the van never even saw Omar's face, as the Palestinian concealed himself behind a large hat and scarf that partially covered his face. The driver took a room for the night in the motel and headed back to New York early the next morning.

***

Laura Atwood was the only woman in a room full of men. Besides Chester Higgins, Hamilton Royce, William Potter, and Vincent Bonenfanti, there was a cluster of Secret Service and FBI agents present. Hamilton Royce spoke first. "Gentlemen, Miss Atwood has been on the tracks of this terrorist for quite a while. It is truly a coincidence, and perhaps a lucky one for us, that this turns out to be the same man she has been tracking in Iraq. The floor is yours, Miss Atwood," said Royce.

"We are faced with a deadly and extremely dangerous terrorist," said Laura, looking at each face around the table. "This man has killed numerous times before and will not hesitate to kill again. Innocent civilians who get in his way die. This man is a ruthless murderer. I myself only narrowly escaped being killed by him and remain one of the few people who has seen him and lived. He is extremely well-trained. Do not think for one nanosecond that any one of our agents can apprehend him. If we have the opportunity to have him in our sights, the order should be 'shoot to kill.' He has killed several well-trained agents and has animal instincts.

"His attacks are always well-planned and executed. He always plans a good escape route, something that he learned the hard way on what was probably his first attack. We believe he will try and assassinate the president on or around Inauguration Day. Statements released by the PSF and Dr. Hawali all seem to indicate that unless the US changes its policy towards Israel, which they know will not happen, they would strike, as they put it, 'at the very heart of America.' His presence in the US points to that. The fact that he was seen by the Capitol is a lucky break for us."

"POTUS's schedule for January 20 is extensive," said the agent in charge of the Secret Service's Presidential Protection Detail. "POTUS's house in northwest Washington is easy enough to secure. In any case, he does not return there after the swearing-in ceremony, but heads directly to 1600 Pennsylvania, the White House. On Inauguration Day, the president-elect starts out at 0800 hours with a church service. The route from the house to the church isn't public knowledge, and isn't announced to the press. It can be changed at a moment's notice. There are three different possibilities. The church is tightly screened and POTUS walks about fifteen yards from the car to the church. Here we can erect visual barriers so that we leave no open angle to a sniper.

"That area can easily be secured. At 0930 hours, he returns home for a short rest. He is expected at the White House at 1030 hours for talks with the outgoing president. Again, the route isn't announced, and we have four possible routes.

"At 1130 hours, POTUS and FLOTUS leave the White House for the Capitol and the inauguration ceremony. Now, here comes the tricky part: the actual inauguration ceremony, where he stands for a good fifteen to twenty minutes on the podium outside the Capitol building. Here, POTUS stands behind bulletproof glass. It's as safe a location as can be. The glass will prevent any known high-velocity bullet. We will have snipers on all adjoining rooftops and scores of agents mingling in the crowd. There are hundreds of uniformed officers on duty, too."

"Excuse me for just a moment, gentlemen," interrupted Laura. "Omar is not an expert marksman, at least as far as we know, and we have documented him pretty well. He has never killed with a single bullet before, not from a long distance. Bombs or straightforward assaults are more his M.O. If he uses a gun, he likes to strike at close range. And as he naturally plans to escape alive, we can assume a frontal assault would be out of the question."

"With the number of security personnel on hand, Secret Service, FBI, Capitol Hill Police, Park Police, DC Police, not to mention the other agencies in DC, a frontal assault seems out of the question. He would never make it past the Capitol lawn," said the FBI agent. "A bomb, therefore, is probably the best guess."

"Then the possibilities are endless," said William Potter, the FBI counterespionage man.

"Not really," replied the Secret Service agent. "Let's not jump to conclusions too fast. This is by far not entirely in the terrorist's advantage. The podium where the president will be sworn in is guarded from the time it is built. It is checked by dogs and bomb-sniffing machines before the president arrives. We will now add chemical and biological sniffers too. The entire perimeter is secured and sterilized. So are all other locations POTUS will attend. What always worries us after the inauguration is when the president heads back towards 1600 and decides to walk, shake hands, and mingle with the crowds. That is the most dangerous time for us."

"Yes, I understand," said Laura, "But you must understand the way Omar thinks. In his mind, he's already sure his plan will work. There are no ifs. He's not counting on the off-chance the president will or will not get out of his presidential bulletproof, bomb-proof limousine to shake a few hands. No one, including you gentlemen, know where or when the president will decide to walk or meet the crowds, right? That's not good enough for Omar. He's already chosen his location. He already knows where and when he will strike. In his mind, he will not fail, and will not leave such a major detail to chance. He has gone over his plan again and again. He is now convinced that he cannot fail and is waiting to strike."

"Well, that really kind of narrows it down a bit for us. It really eliminates a number of options. All we need to do is find out where and when that is," said one of the Secret Service agents.

"What about the rest of the day?" asked Potter.

"There are the usual galas in the evening. Again, no fixed agenda announced, and we don't know until the last minute which inauguration balls POTUS and FLOTUS will attend. What is known is that the First Couple will attend several functions, but with no fixed time. These are issues they decide at the last moment," said the Secret Service agent. "The order in which the First Couple decide which ball they will attend has much to do with how much the Republican Party in that particular state was able to raise and how vital their contribution to the election has been."

"It seems clear to me that he'll need to have visible contact with the president before he can detonate his device, or attack," said the FBI agent.

"It certainly looks that way," agreed Royce.

"All right, that sure makes our job somewhat easier," said Potter, the FBI man. "Let's back up a bit here. I think we hit on something. You say this man already picked out his hit and knows where and how he will strike?"

"Yes, that's right," replied Laura. "I am sure of it. He would not be wasting his time waiting somewhere on the off-chance that the president might or might not pass by."

"Great. In that case, that information is public knowledge, something he picked up from the media. Let's look at the options, see what's been published and go over it. If he has that information, then we can access it too. The agenda is simple. We know there is the church service in the morning. We know there is the inauguration ceremony at noon and we know there is the walk down Pennsylvania Avenue before he reaches 1600. The rest is up for grabs. No other fixed settings or times," said the senior Secret Service agent.

"Cancel the walk," said Royce. "We don't know exactly where it will take place."

"Even better," agreed the Secret Service agent. "That narrows it down to two possibilities: the church and the Hill."

"The Hill. That's where I would strike," said Potter. "That's where the president will be the most vulnerable and that's where we must concentrate all our efforts.

"In the meantime, gentlemen, we have less than four days to track this bastard down. We need to find out when, where, and how he entered the country, where he is staying, and what he has been doing all this time. We must check all Washington hotels for Arab nationals, all car rental agencies and airlines. Mr. Potter will be your point man on this case. Between now and the inauguration, I would like us to meet twice a day, at seven every evening and six in the morning for situation updates. Gentlemen, you have your work cut out for you. Good luck, and may God help us."

"Just one more thing, Mr. Royce," said Laura.

"Yes, ma'am?"

"I'd like to bring in Clayborne to help out. He has also seen Omar. He can help."

"Clayborne? Now who might he be?"

"He's the journalist, sir," interjected Potter. "The one who gave us the pictures."

"No ma'am, I don't want no goddamned newspaper man in on this operation."

"Sir, I think Miss Atwood might have something here," said Potter. "He'll cooperate with us. He's not a threat. I've already spoken to him. He's the one who came to us with the pictures."

"Well, fine, do it, if you must, but by God, keep it quiet. I don't want to read about this in tomorrow's *Post*. Do it, but grab that S.O.B. fast."

It was a gargantuan task to find a man in a city the size of Washington, and in that short a time. Every available FBI and Secret Service agent was put on the case. Additional agents were called in from cities as far away as San Diego and Seattle. Several agents were positioned around the Capitol building just in case Omar returned. They knew it was a long shot, but they had little else to go on. Hundreds of agents visited hotels and car rental agencies. They intended to start with those closest to the Capitol and gradually work their way to the Virginia and Maryland suburbs.

By the afternoon of the first day, they found a bellboy at the J. W. Marriott on Fourteenth Street who seemed to recognize the photograph, but wasn't certain. The face looked familiar, yes, the man had stayed on the ninth, no, the tenth floor. Oh, that must have been about two months ago. He remembered because of the large tip. None of the receptionists could remember, there were so many people checking in and out every day. It was a busy hotel, after all. Names of all Arabs who had stayed in the hotel over the last three months were run through the FBI's and ICE's computers. There were twenty-four names: four Egyptians, seven Saudi Arabians, three from the United Arab Emirates, five Kuwaitis, one Lebanese, and four Moroccans. All were checked and turned out to

206 | INAUGURATION DAY

be legitimate businessmen or diplomats. Next, all the guests' names from the past three months were entered into the FBI database.

The first real break came at Washington's Ronald Reagan National Airport, where the young woman at the car rental agency thought she recognized the photograph. "Yeah, yeah, I remember him. I rented him a car. I remember him because he looked kinda cute, you know, exotic-like. He was, um, tanned and had an accent. A foreign accent. Kinda like Eye-talian, not the Brooklyn Eye-talian, no, not that, kinda like real exotic like, you know what I mean?"

"You keep records, don't you?" asked the agent.

"Yeah, sure we do, hon. We keep meticulous records," said the young woman. "Let me see, now," she busied herself punching keys into her computer. To the FBI agent every second felt like hours. "Here ya go, hon," she announced finally. "Oh, man, I can't pronounce this name. Stav-ros Papa-do-pou-los, ah guess that sounds kinda like Greek, uh, not Eye-talian after all? Rented a Ford Escort, a white one with Virginia plates. Here, y'all wait a minute. I'll print it out for you, hon. It's got the tag number and all."

"What address did he give?"

"Gee, he put down some address in Athens . . , Athens, Greece. Guess he's not from Georgia now, is he?"

"Let me have the printout on that, will you, please?" said the agent grabbing the sheet.

GOLAN HEIGHTS, SYRIA

The snow on the Golan Heights covered the ground in a thick white carpet, giving the usually rocky terrain a clean and serene appearance. Brigadier General Kamal Kader stood behind a wooden barrier, the cold morning wind slapping his face.

He looked proudly at the fluttering Syrian flag flying on a pole above him. A dozen yards away, behind the barrier, were Finnish troops serving with the United Nations Truce Observer Force, UNTSO. Their job was to keep tabs on both sides and report unusual movement to the Security Council in New York. The UN troops had arrived here after the October 1973 Arab–Israeli War and remained ever since.

Less than a hundred yards away from the UN banner, the General could clearly see the Star of David adorning the blue and white Israeli flag. Using a pair of powerful field glasses, the General scanned the horizon, looking at Israeli troops on the other side of their barrier. General Kader spat on the ground.

He conferred briefly with the Finnish UN commander, a young major from Helsinki, returned the commander's salute, and jumped back into his Russian-made jeep.

The maneuvers had been announced nearly two months earlier and his presence on the Heights was not unusual. The General drove to Kuneitra, once the capital of the Syrian Golan Heights. Now it was a deserted, devastated town; a ghost town. The town had been occupied by Israel in 1973 and before their retreat had been completely demolished by Israeli soldiers using bulldozers and explosives. Hardly a single house remained intact. Instead of rebuilding, the Syrians decided to leave the town as it was, a relic and a reminder of the mutual hatred that existed between the two neighbors. Syrian officials made a point of taking every official visitor to view the devastated town.

The jeep stopped outside the building that once housed Kuneitra's public school. Like other buildings in the town, most of it stood in ruins. A Syrian flag hung above the front steps. There were several other vehicles already parked in the courtyard when the General drove in. When General Kader walked into what was once a classroom, six Syrian officers who were chatting among themselves jumped to attention.

"At ease, at ease," said the Syrian general, motioning them to remain seated. "Sit down, sit." To keep warm, the officers had started a fire. They burned scraps of wood in a large tin receptacle that had once contained cooking oil. The General rubbed his hands near the fire. He didn't like the cold, and the snow only made it worse.

"Brothers," said the General, "in three days we will be in a position to savor our revenge against the Zionists, to erase past defeats with the sweet smell of Arab victory. We must stand ready to lay our lives on the path of glory for the good of our motherland and for the benefit of the entire Arab nation." The General looked around the room at the six officers that he had personally hand-picked. He trusted every one of them implicitly. They were all fellow Alawites and came from the port city of Latakia, like himself and like his beloved president. He knew each and every one of these men and their families personally.

"Brothers, for the moment, we must continue to play the game. We are on maneuvers, but I want your soldiers to be ready, for the final hour is now near. In three days, in the afternoon, we will get the green light to tear down these dreaded barriers and retake what is ours. What has been unjustly stolen from us. Brothers, you all know what is expected of you, and I know you will not disappoint your motherland, or your president. May Allah be with you."

"Allah be with us," replied the six in unison, standing and saluting their general.

WASHINGTON, DC

The second break came from the Immigration Service computer, when it matched the photograph taken on Capitol Hill with the one of a passenger who had entered the country through New York's John F. Kennedy International Airport more than two months ago. But after that, the leads simply dried up. When the FBI SWAT team descended on the Brooklyn address the passenger had declared, to no great surprise, they realized the Brooklyn address did not exist. Well, it did exist, but it was a parking lot. It would have been too good to be true if the terrorist had turned up. Too easy. It looked as though the man had simply evaporated into thin air after leaving Kennedy Airport. There was no trace of him. They questioned every taxi driver, every porter, and every airline employee. No one remembered another face in the crowd in an airport the size of Kennedy.

After their initial successes, the special task force set up to track down Omar seemed to have hit a dead end. Their leads from the car rental company, the hotel where Omar had stayed, and the INS photograph led some of the team members to believe these leads would soon materialize into something more concrete, allowing them to close in on their target. But it was not so. Every new lead dried up. One or two restaurants seemed to recognize the photograph, but had no credit card stubs. The man always paid in cash and never returned to the same place twice. Omar had covered his tracks well. The agents combed through every hotel from the center of the District of Columbia to Baltimore and Annapolis on the Maryland side and as far south as Richmond, Virginia. Nothing, nil, zilch. They checked and rechecked every airline computer and still came up blank. There were so many ways for the terrorist to travel. He could have taken the train or simply used a new identity to purchase an airline ticket to any number of destinations. The credit card he used to rent the car turned out to be fake and the agents knew the Palestinian was far too smart to use it a second time. Still, the credit card company was informed to immediately alert the FBI should the card ever be used again.

An all-points bulletin had been put out with the car's tag number and description, not that the agents had much hope the terrorist would use the car again. He probably needed it for a single trip and had discarded it. Most likely the car had been stripped down and sold in the not-so-nice parts of the nation's capital.

"A man cannot simply disappear into the thin air, damn it. He's gotta be hiding out somewhere." The words had come from Chester Higgins. FBI Director Royce had agreed to let him team up with Laura and had assigned one of Potter's men, Special Agent in Charge Tony Billings, to liaise with them. The three had exhausted every possible and logical explanation. Just where could this terrorist be hiding?

"He could be anywhere," said Laura. "It's a big city. He might have rented a room from an individual, to avoid having his name appear on a register. Maybe a boarding house."

"Too many people come and go in a boarding house. He needs somewhere more discreet, quieter."

"So, you just disappear, then," said the man from the FBI.

"Not when you have more than a thousand agents out looking for you. The best agents in the country." Higgins puffed on his cigar and blew a cloud of smoke out of the car's window. "Where would you hide?" he asked Laura. "Put yourself in his place, where would you hole up?"

"I've been doing just that, Mr. Higgins," said Laura. "I've been desperately trying to crawl into that monster's mind for the last week—hell, for years. He is being very, very cautious and is taking absolutely no chances. That's the way he normally operates. He trusts no one and even his people in Beirut don't know where he is. We have been listening to their phones in Lebanon on a continuous basis for the last two months but without much luck. We believe he is passing his messages through a contact in Athens. The calls are always very short, never more than a minute. The only information exchanged were two numbers given to Omar by the Athens contact. At first we thought they might be telephone numbers, but they were not. We cross-checked them for any addresses on our files, or dates, but came out blank. We couldn't make sense of them. He never stays on line more than a few seconds. Not long enough to trace."

Billings swerved to avoid hitting a jogger as they came over Memorial Bridge. "So where would you hide?"

"I'd get out of public places. I'd avoid hotels and rent something and remain low. I'd use a different name from the one I used previously and this is precisely what the bastard is doing," said Laura, slamming her fist into the dashboard in frustration.

"We've checked with real estate offices in the District, Virginia, and Maryland. They have no record of Stavros whatever the fuck his name is, or seen his face. If he's rented directly from a landlord, it'd take months to track him down. And we only have two days left to find him."

"We know the date of his arrival and car rental," said Laura. "One thing we haven't done is go through the classifieds. We need to get the newspapers starting with his date of arrival and go two, three, four weeks from there and track down every possible lead through the classifieds. Contact every number, check every name."

"Marvelous," said Higgins. "Potter will love you for it. You will probably blow his overtime budget for the rest of the year."

"Who ever said spy work was all glory?"

***

Several days had passed since Omar had last been outside his apartment on E Street. He opened the two trunks brought from New York and carefully inspected its contents. Satisfied that everything was in good working order, he replaced the items in the cases and locked them in a closet. He kept the key on a string around his neck at all times. He spent time watching television and cooking simple meals for himself. He played out his plan in his mind over and over. He worked out in the spacious living room to pass the time and keep in shape. He spent hours watching television, switching from one channel to the next; from the home selling networks to MTV, from Court TV to the nostalgic shows of the sixties and seventies. He remembered seeing some of the older shows on a black and white set at a neighbor's in the refugee camp. They were strange people, these Americans. Strange.

The night before Inauguration Day, Omar left the apartment for the first time in nearly a week. He took his rented Ford from the underground garage on Third Street to the commuter's parking lot in New Carrollton, Maryland, locked the car, and rode the Metro back to E Street. No one noticed him or the plates he had stolen off another car a few minutes earlier. His escape was now in place. In fact, he had two different escape routes planned out: the Metro to New Carrollton and car to BWI, or the train that connected the Metro stop to the same airport. Or, if need be, he could always ride the Metro to National Airport. Omar lingered for a while on his balcony, looking over the city whose destiny he was about to change the next day. Nothing would be the same by this time tomorrow. The world would wake up and take notice of the Palestinians and their plight. Yes, they would.

Before going to sleep, Omar turned his television set to CNN and watched a report on the final preparations for the morning's inauguration. He was about to turn off the set when a photograph of the Syrian capital appeared on the screen behind the newsman. Omar turned up the sound.

". . . just in from the Middle East. A series of explosions rocked the Syrian capital over the last few days, killing more than twenty people and wounding scores of others. We've received this footage from the BBC and would like to point out that it carries some strong and rather explicit images."

The screen showed mutilated bodies being pulled out from still-smoking rubble as firemen, police, soldiers, and rescue workers worked frantically to reach the injured. The voice of a British correspondent continued, *"Two bombs exploded in central Damascus this morning, killing and wounding a number of people. As you can see, bodies are still being recovered and the authorities here have not yet been able to compile an exact figure of casualties. This is the fifth explosion in Damascus over the last week that has so far claimed the lives of more than twenty people, and maiming at least twice that number. The authorities are blaming the attacks on the banned Muslim Alliance, an obscure group affiliated with the larger Muslim Brotherhood. Security in the city has been increased and the government has called in reinforcements from other Syrian cities."*

The television now showed footage of tanks with soldiers waving from the turrets. *"In fact, we were able to see this very morning a rather large column of tanks rumble into the city. Damascus is now taking the form of an entrenched armed camp with troops positioned at nearly every street corner, and military encampments are popping up in football fields and sports stadiums."*

The picture returned to the anchorman in the studio. *"That was Nigel Bainbridge of the BBC with an exclusive report. No other media organization, including CNN, has been allowed into Damascus yet, as Syrian authorities continue to refuse us visas.*

"The Middle East remains in the headlines tonight as Dr. Hawali, the radical Palestinian leader, today accused the United States of continuing to ignore the plight of the Palestinians. He warned that the spate of anti-American bombings that has plagued Europe for the last four months would soon cross the Atlantic unless a rapid solution to the Palestinian problem was reached. Frank Delano in Beirut reports."

"Less than twenty-four hours before President-elect Richard Wells is sworn in as the nation's new president, radical Palestinians here have once again issued stern warnings to the new administration to alter what they claim is its blatant pro-Israeli policy. Arab extremists like Dr. Hawali's PSF are generally believed to be responsible for the recent terror campaign in Europe. Although those acts were claimed by unknown groups using names like 'Islamic Victory' and 'Islamic

Obedience,' observers here believe they are really the work of Dr. Hawali's people, possibly backed by the radical Egyptian Sheik al-Haq and some Iranian factions, too. This is Frank Delano in Beirut."

"Frank, would you elaborate on the Iranian connection? Does that mean the Iranians are officially backing such terror campaigns?"

"Not really. As you know, the Iranian government is split right down the middle, with the moderates to one side who very much want to mend relations with the West in general, and with America in particular. They believe diplomacy is the best way to obtain the release of Iran's frozen assets, held in Western banks since the demise of the Shah. On the other hand are radicals like Ayatollah Firamarz Kazemi, who advocates a much firmer policy towards the West. Kazemi blames the West, mainly America, for the country's ills, for supporting Iraq during Iran's eight year conflict with Saddam Hussein, and mostly for supporting Israel. Now clerics like Ayatollah Kazemi are quite powerful and command great support among the people, and especially the Revolutionary Guards. This, of course, makes it very difficult for the government and the moderates to ignore them."

"Frank Delano in Beirut, thank you."

The Palestinian smiled as he aimed the remote control and silenced the set.

***

William Potter thought it would be better if he went to see Clayborne, rather than ask him back to the FBI building. He wasn't quite sure how the journalist would react to his request, and he needed Clayborne's cooperation. Damn it, he needed all the help he could get. Time and options were rapidly running out.

It was still very early in the morning, and except for the two overnight editors wrapping up their shifts, the IPS office was still deserted. Clayborne poured two cups of hot, black coffee and offered one to the FBI man without bothering to ask if he cared for cream or sugar.

"Black okay, I hope?"

"Yeah, sure, that's fine, thanks. Chris, let me get right to the point," said William Potter. "We need your help. We are running out of time and I'm afraid we might not find this guy before Inauguration Day. Let's talk about Inauguration Day. That's where you can help out."

"Just how is that?" asked Clayborne, taking a sip of his coffee.

"I need you out on the stands, scanning the crowds, looking through your long lens. You've seen him before, and I'm sure can recognize him again much easier than many of my agents can. I'll have an agent with you, relaying the information and protecting you."

"You're nuts," said Clayborne. "On a day like this, this big a story, I have to be inside, to stay here and run the show. You think I can just get up and leave?"

"This is a matter of national importance, Chris. The life of the president of the United States may be at stake. Possibly even more that just his life."

"And so is my career, if I walk out on Inauguration Day, especially if there is an attempt on the president."

"We'll handle that. My director will talk to your director, if need be. We can take care of that."

"Can I sleep on it?"

"Sorry, but we don't have time."

Clayborne was silent for a few seconds before replying. "Tell you what," said Chris finally. "Let's make a deal. I give you my time. I will go and stand on the podium, scan faces for you. No agent with me though. Just wire me up, give me a radio. I'll be in constant contact with you, or with your people."

"Fine," said Potter.

"In return, you give one of my people access."

"Access to what?"

"Total access to whatever happens," said Chris. "Unlimited access to any situation. If you nab the terrorist, I want my person there, in front of him, in his face, unhindered, able to work. If you shoot him, I want my person there. If there's a gunfight, a hostage situation, a bomb, an arrest, or whatever, I want my person to have exclusive access."

"Not sure I can make that happen."

"Make it happen, you're in charge. It's not negotiable. That's the only way it'll work, the only way I can justify doing this," said Chris. "I cooperate in return for exclusive coverage. And it remains inside this room. No one but the two of us will ever know about this deal. Understand?"

"Where did you ever learn to bargain like that?"

"The souks of the Middle East. I take it we have a deal, then," said Clayborne, extending his hand.

William Potter shook Clayborne's hand, hoping he would not live to regret this arrangement.

Delphine Muller-Hoeft was the best person Chris Clayborne could think of to handle such a delicate and potentially dangerous assignment. She was the daughter of a French Foreign Legionnaire, Sergeant Frédéric Muller, a Frenchman from the

Alsace region, and a beautiful Vietnamese woman whom her father met while serving with the Legion in Indo-China. The last part of her name came from Wilhelm Hoeft, a Swiss tax lawyer she had married and divorced several years ago. It was a brief and unsuccessful marriage that lasted barely six months. There could not have been two more diverse personalities under the sun.

Delphine had remarkable features, a mélange of Asian and French-German. On some days she looked Vietnamese, while on others, she seemed totally European. Her looks were much like her languages, totally mixed: she was fluent in English, French, Vietnamese, German, and Russian, yet spoke all with an accent. When she spoke English she had a French accent, and a Vietnamese accent when she spoke French. It came from the multicultural upbringing and constant moving between her mother's house in Saigon, her father's family in Strasbourg, and Corsica, where part of the Legion was based.

Delphine Muller-Hoeft's career as a photojournalist began in Vietnam, where she freelanced for IPS and some of the major American magazines. She won two Pulitzer prizes for her coverage of the war, one of which was for the photographs she took on Hill 54. The battle for Hill 54 lasted twelve days, during which time the US Marine Corps and the North Vietnamese People's Liberation Army each captured and then lost the hill numerous times. When the battle finally ended with the Marines raising the Stars and Stripes on its summit, hundreds of fighters had died on both sides. Delphine Muller-Hoeft had been there the entire time, documenting the conflict with her camera. She was grazed in the right thigh by mortar shrapnel, but continued to work after a medic patched her up. She even encouraged young and wounded marines to keep on going. Her work won her the respect and admiration of the Saigon press corps, as well as that of the marines who fought on Hill 54. It was reported, jokingly, that some of the language she had used on Hill 54 even made the marines blush.

While Clayborne was covering wars in the Middle East, Delphine was doing the same in Southeast Asia. After Vietnam came Cambodia and Laos. When those wars ended, Delphine found smaller, more obscure conflicts in Malaysia, the Philippines, and Indonesia, until she was assigned to the Moscow bureau, where she could cover various conflicts erupting all over the former Soviet republics.

She and Clayborne had only worked together once, in Tehran, during the Iranian Revolution, during which time they had a brief affair. Clayborne knew she could do the job and keep her mouth shut. She was not one to brag.

Delphine Muller-Hoeft seemed amazingly refreshed after an all-night flight from Moscow as she walked into Clayborne's office.

"Morning, Chief. So how does it feel to have the weight of the world resting on your shoulders?" She threw her camera bag in a corner, placed her coat on a chair, and walked around the desk to hug Clayborne and place a friendly kiss on his cheek. "So what's the fire that makes you have me fly all the way here from Moscow? Don't tell me it's the inauguration, because I know you have more than enough capable people in this country to handle that."

"Thanks for coming so quickly, Del. I have a very hot potato on my hands and know you can handle it. The boys in this town talk too much and would never be able to keep this kind of thing quiet. As you know, there are no secrets in Washington, especially not among the press corps." Chris opened his top desk drawer and pulled out a note, which he handed to Delphine. The note was typed on official FBI stationery and simply stated:

"TOTAL ACCESS To All Federal and District of Columbia Law Enforcement Agencies: The holder of this letter, Miss Delphine Muller-Hoeft (see photograph), is entitled to pass, unhindered and without restrictions, all police and other law enforcement lines. No restrictions shall be placed on the bearer of this note, who shall be allowed to photograph and report on any situation under the jurisdiction of the aforementioned law enforcement agencies. The directors and Chiefs of the FBI, the USSS, the US Capitol Police, and the US Park Police order all law enforcement agencies to respect this order.

This note expires at 2359, January 21, at which time this note will be surrendered to the FBI."

A passport-sized photograph of Delphine Muller-Hoeft was attached to the upper right-hand corner and the letter was signed by the Director of the Federal Bureau of Investigation.

Delphine let out a long whistle and dropped the letter on Chris's desk. "Wow!" she said. "How on earth did you ever manage to get this? And the next question I have is what did you have to do to get it? Sell your soul to the devil? If Hoover was still in charge I might have suspected you sold your body."

"Almost," said Chris. "Grab your coat and I'll brief you over lunch."

23

It was a bitterly cold day in Washington as a chilly wind blowing south from Canada brought the temperature well below ten degrees Fahrenheit. Chester Higgins III cursed as he scraped the snow and ice off his car's windshield. It had snowed a little in suburban Virginia and it was at times like these that Higgins cherished the warm climes of the Levant. If only these fools weren't so busy killing each other, he thought, the Arabs and Jews could outsell the French Riviera any day. But who wants to bask on a beach and risk being blown up, kidnapped, knifed, or hijacked?

His wife came out of the house wrapped in a robe and handed him a cup of hot, black coffee. At fifty, Phyllis Higgins was still a very beautiful woman. She and Chester had been married for twenty-three years now. She had followed him to all sorts of weird, crazy, and exotic places; places where she couldn't speak or understand the language. Places where she couldn't even pronounce names correctly, where she ignored the local customs. Somehow Chester felt more at home in those strange places than in America. She, on the other hand, never did like it there. She was happy now, living back in America. She wanted her two children to grow up in the United States, not in some godforsaken land where women still had to cover their faces. She loved her husband dearly and had agreed to follow him wherever he went, but she was glad to be back. At least Virginia was almost home. The daughter of a marine colonel, she was born and raised in North Carolina, outside the Marine Air Station at Cherry Point. Phyllis Higgins knew that her husband was unhappy working at Langley. "Far too many kings and not enough king's men," he always complained.

"What time do you think you'll be back?" asked Phyllis.

"Don't know, sweetheart." He took a sip of the hot coffee and kissed his wife. "Get back inside before you catch your death out here."

"Think you'll be home for dinner?" She knew her husband had been under tremendous pressure this last week. Something to do with the president and Inauguration Day. Chester never liked to discuss his work; he tried hard to keep it out of the home, but this time he seemed different, he seemed preoccupied. He had even started talking in his sleep. First time he had done that since they returned to the States, since that time in Iran when things went real bad for him.

Phyllis noticed the .45 automatic holstered under her husband's jacket. Chester had never carried a gun before, at least not since they came back to the States. "You're not working on anything dangerous, darling, are you?" she asked, pointing to the bulge under his suit.

"Huh? Oh that. Nah, nothing to worry about. It's just with this case I'm working on and the inauguration, I just feel it would be better, safer. Hey, you know I always said the commute around the Beltway would be the death of me. Hell, I face greater danger driving to and from work here than I ever did in the Middle East. Gotta go. Bye, sweetheart."

"Be careful," shouted Phyllis as he pulled out of the driveway.

"Always am, dear, I always am," replied Higgins.

Laura did not sleep much that night. The nightmares would not go away. She kept seeing the terrorist's face appear around a corner. He was chasing her down the darkened, narrow back streets of south London, only it was not London, it was Tel Aviv, no, it was Beirut, but the Capitol building was there. She tried firing her pistol at him, but the weapon jammed. Her legs were heavy and she ran in slow motion and the more she ran, the more she remained in place. She was attending a funeral for the victims of a terrorist bomb, and Omar was there, standing beside the grave laughing at her, pointing his finger at her and holding a large box with chemical agents. She was in a refugee camp in south Lebanon while Israeli war planes screamed overhead, dropping their deadly cargo; only when the bombs fell, they would not explode. Omar appeared, smiled, pointed at the planes and fired a machine gun at her. She awoke with a scream.

"What's the matter?" asked Chris Clayborne, turning on the bedside light.

"Had a bad dream. I'm sorry I woke you."

"That's okay. What time is it, anyway?" He looked at the alarm clock on the bedside table. "Almost five. I've got to get going in an hour anyway. Today's the day," Chris said, putting his arm around Laura. "God, you're drenched in sweat. Must have been a real bad dream. You know, I used to have the same nightmare over and over after I left Beirut. Sometimes it still comes back. Here, let me massage your neck; that'll make it go away."

Clayborne sat up and started caressing Laura's back. He removed the goose down comforter and sheet, revealing a perfectly curved and svelte body. His hand started moving down her back until he reached her hips.

"I guess my neck must have slipped down to my hips, huh?" said Laura, closing her eyes. Chris stopped and looked at her. "Don't stop; it feels good. Mmmm, real good." Chris ran his hand over her slender legs. "That's good, that's real good. Mmm, that's heaven," she mumbled, her head buried in the sheets. Chris laid on top of her and kissed her neck, moving her silky hair over her head. He was fully aroused and she could feel him. She arched her back, turning her head towards him until their lips met. Chris turned her around, falling on his back and allowing Laura to get on top of him. He looked up at her perfectly shaped breasts as she ran her hands across his chest. Laura started moving in a slow, gentle motion, bending further and further backwards, supporting herself on her arms pressing down hard on Chris's legs. Chris knew she was about to explode. He arched his body upwards and the two collapsed in a sensuous moment. They remained still for several long minutes, holding onto each other in silence.

Laura was savoring this instant, holding on to these precious moments. She knew the day ahead was going to be a long and painful one, a day where she would be hurled into a world of hatred and violence. A world where she might have to kill, or even be killed. She had never taken a life before. Except of course that one time when five Iraqis tried to rape her, but that was different. Yes, she had trained for it, was instructed in the use of weapons, but never actually killed someone herself. That was different. She had never given it much thought in the past; it was something she had always accepted. These terrorists were cold-blooded assassins who killed innocent people; they had to be eliminated. But her job consisted of gathering intelligence that allowed other people to do the dirty work. There were dozens of people who could do that and not give it a second thought. She herself had never actually pulled the trigger and thus felt somewhat absolved, at least partially. That's what she kept telling herself. She was fighting for something she believed in. Her country was threatened by ruthless enemies and she had taken an oath to help protect that country.

She was brought back to reality by Chris. "Hey Laura, are you still here?"

She smiled at him and hugged him closer to her. "Yes, I'm here my darling, I'm here."

"Laura, what are you up to?"

"What do you mean?"

"I mean just that. What are going to do today? And what comes next?"

Laura Atwood looked momentarily lost. "I don't think we should discuss this matter further, my darling. Not right now."

"Please level with me, Laura. I lost you once before and I don't want to lose you again."

Laura stared at the ground. "Just trust me, Chris, trust me."

"I love you, damn it. That's a lot more than simple trust. It's you who's not trusting me. What are you holding back?"

"Chris, I also love you. I have since Beirut, only I couldn't let myself admit it. I had a job to do, a career to pursue. I was torn and couldn't back out. A lot of people depend on me, Chris; it's very complicated. But let today slide. There is just too much to do. We have to stop this madman. You are part of it now; you are on the team."

"Just be careful out there," said Clayborne as he got up and went to the kitchen to make coffee.

"Chris, my love," said Laura, following Chris into the kitchen. She hugged him from the back, pressing her body against his. "When this is over, let's get away. Let's go to the islands, to the sunshine. Let's go lie on a warm beach and bask in the sun. Let's swim naked in the sea. Forget this madness, get away from all this hatred. A vacation, just you and me."

"Sounds wonderful. Let's."

"Promise?"

"Yes, of course. I promise," replied Chris.

"Can you get away?"

"I'll resign if they don't let me go. They owe me time anyway. It's been a while since I took any time off."

"I'll hold you to that," said Laura.

"Will you promise to spend the rest of your life with me?"

"Is this a proposal?"

"You could call it that," said Chris, planting a kiss on her forehead. "You might live to regret this."

At about the same time that Chris and Laura were savoring their first cup of coffee, Omar woke up and made himself a cup of tea. This would be his last day in the apartment. The day ahead would be a long and busy one. Today he would change the course of history. This would also be the last chance for a decent meal, at least for a while. He needed to be ready and rested, both mentally as well as physically. Tired men make mistakes. There would be no room for mistakes today.

He showered, shaved, and packed his one carry-on suitcase. Not that he cared much for the contents of the case, but a trans-Atlantic traveler without luggage would arouse suspicion. He placed the suitcase by the front door and checked the entire apartment for any telltale signs he might have inadvertently left behind. He made a quick telephone call to United Airlines to confirm his flight out of Baltimore Washington International. It would be silly to be caught simply because he forgot to reconfirm a seat. He confirmed another seat from National Airport to Boston, on an American Airlines flight. His backup plan was now in place.

Satisfied that all was in order, he unlocked the cupboard where he had placed the equipment brought to him by the man from New York. He opened the first case and took out a 60 mm mortar, complete with a specially designed folding baseplate, sight, and bipod. All together, the mortar weighed exactly 45.2 pounds. It took Omar three minutes to assemble the mortar, which he placed in the living room, not far from the sliding glass door leading out to the large veranda. The advantage of a mortar was that he could fire over the other buildings that stood between him and the Capitol steps, and in doing so, did not need to see his target. The enormous advantage was that if he could not see them, they of course could not see him either. He could easily calculate his distance from his target from the map he had purchased. He also had the best spotter in the world working for him, helping him correct his aim: live television. Thanks to the TV cameras, he would see exactly where his shells landed, and, should the need arise, correct his aim.

Next, he placed the ten rounds neatly on the ground next to the mortar tube. There were eight shells with yellow markings. Those were high-explosive shells that had a range of eighteen hundred meters. High explosive rounds break up into small fragments upon impact, sending lethal shards of burning hot metal flying in every direction. A single mortar round can neutralize an area twenty meters across by ten meters deep. Three rounds fired from the same mortar will neutralize an area about thirty-five meters wide by thirty-five meters deep.

Omar then removed the two rounds with the red labels. Those were white phosphorous: WP, or "Willie Peters." White phosphorous rounds have a range of only fifteen hundred meters, but Omar was well within his killing range. What Omar did not know was that the two WP shells had been fitted with the anthrax VX toxins mixture. The rounds contained enough to kill everyone within a three-mile area. With the January winds blowing through the streets of Washington, thousands more would be killed within minutes. The deadly solutions had been placed in the mortar rounds by Sheik al-Haq's people.

Omar turned the television set to CNN and waited. Soon the president of the United States, the vice president, the president-elect and the vice president-elect would be standing on that now empty podium. So would the secretaries of state, defense, treasury, justice, interior, and others. So would the president of the Senate, the speaker of the House and other members of the American government. And Omar planned to kill them all. It would take him less than thirty seconds to wipe out the entire cabinet. There would be such confusion in the American government that it would take them months, if not years, to sort it out.

Omar would launch the two white phosphorous rounds first. Those would have the effect of setting fire to everything in the area and would badly burn everyone standing in the immediate blast area. It would also cover the podium in a cloud of thick white smoke, rendering it impossible for Secret Service agents to react and save the president. It would also allow him time to rectify his aim, should he need to. Omar felt sure he would hit his target with his first shot. Then hundreds of others would be killed within minutes by the deadly chemical mixture.

He would immediately follow those with the eight HE (high explosive) shells. In all, ten rounds of deadly hot, burning metal would rain down within milliseconds of each other on the entire American government before anyone even realized what had hit them. A good mortar man could fire off twenty to twenty-five rounds before the first shell even hit the ground. The maximum rate of fire for a 60 mm mortar is thirty rounds per minute. In other words, Omar would have finished firing his ten rounds and be well on his way out of the apartment before the last shell landed. And there was nothing the American Secret Service or the FBI or the CIA or the police or the army could do about it.

The seats around the podium were gradually beginning to fill up. Omar looked at his watch. It was a little past ten in the morning.

Chester Higgins collected Laura outside Chris's apartment near Dupont Circle. The streets were practically deserted as they drove to the J. Edgar Hoover Building, where Special Agent in Charge Tony Billings was waiting outside the Tenth Street entrance, stomping his feet to keep warm.

"Brought you guys some doughnuts," he said with a smile as he entered the car.

"Thanks," said Higgins, "but we're spies, not cops."

"So, where do you guys want to start?"

"Let's go to church," said Laura.

"Think we'll get lucky today?" asked Billings.

"Your guess is as good as mine," replied Laura.

Delphine Muller-Hoeft kick-started the Yamaha 750cc motorcycle that IPS had rented for her a couple of days earlier. A motorbike would be easier to maneuver and get around on. The cold did not bother her. She clipped a police scanner onto her belt and inserted its earphone in her right ear. The two-way radio that would keep her in contact with IPS and Chris Clayborne went into her left jacket pocket. She donned her crash helmet, lowered the plastic visor, and headed for the Washington Cathedral. She checked the radio to make sure it worked properly and called in to Clayborne. "Just leaving now, Chief."

"Read you clear," replied Clayborne. "And don't call me Chief. It makes me feel like Perry White."

"Who?"

"Didn't you ever read Superman comics when you were a kid?"

"I was never a kid," said Delphine.

Security around the cathedral was extremely tight. The cathedral had been checked and rechecked and triple-checked, as were the grounds surrounding it and its roof. The Secret Service and the District police had combed through it with trained sniffer dogs and electronic devices. Extra security had been assigned to secure the perimeter all night long. Every manhole along the possible routes the president-elect would take had been checked and then welded shut. All mailboxes along the route were removed. There were four possible routes in all. As an added precaution, several streets abutting the cathedral were closed to traffic. Everyone, including the minister performing the morning service, was searched and checked and had to pass through metal, explosives, and chemical detectors set up by the Secret Service. All guests were asked to show their invitations and some form of identification. Secret Service marksmen were positioned on all rooftops overlooking the cathedral, as well as on top of several other buildings along the route.

Laura and Higgins entered the church while Billings remained in the car, concentrating on the traffic coming over his walkie-talkie. There was a lot of traffic over his radio set. None that really mattered much.

Quite a few people were already inside the cathedral. Laura scanned every face, studying every feature. No, it made little sense. Omar would not be stupid enough to show himself in person in such closed quarters. Still, she and the CIA man positioned themselves outside the front door, along with several Secret Service agents and members of the uniformed division of the Secret Service and the Washington Metropolitan Police force. They scanned every arrival as the guests were made to walk through multiple detectors. Secret Service agents held smaller copies of Omar's photograph, which they looked at from time to time, comparing the pictures with guests that might fit the description. Some of the agents carried a gadget similar to an iPhone that could take a picture of the guests arriving at the church and then morph it to see if it could be someone wearing a disguise.

If only she could get inside Omar's head. Where was the weak link? There had to be one. Somewhere in the president's schedule, Omar must have found a gap, a small breach in their security. That's where he would strike. That's what she had to find. Laura pulled out a schedule of the day's events given to her a day earlier by the Secret Service. The events that were public knowledge were printed in bold letters. It was here, she thought, somewhere in this list, somewhere in here was the weak link that the terrorist would strike. The question was where? How?

The presidential advance team was already positioned outside the church. One of the agents who had attended several of the joint task force meetings recognized Higgins and Laura. He nodded to them, and they nodded back.

"Seven minutes," said the agent. "Thunder will be here in exactly seven minutes. No one else goes in between now and the end of the service."

The sound of wailing sirens from the approaching motorcade could be heard nearing the cathedral as the first of the motorcycle police escort came into view. The Secret Service agent in charge of the security detail spoke into his small microphone.

"Thunder approaching. Rooftops, check in."

"Roof one, north side clear," replied the Secret Service marksman positioned atop the closest building to the church.

"Roof two, south side clear," came another voice over the radio.

"Roof three, west clear."

The Secret Service agent spoke again: "Street points, check in."

"East side, clear."

"West, clear."

"Front clear."

"Back. All clear."

"Bring Thunder forward, all clear here," said the agent into his concealed microphone.

Higgins motioned to Laura, who joined him at the bottom of the steps. "We've done all that we can here. It's up to the Secret Service now." Overhead, a Park Police helicopter flew by and disappeared over the church in a large circle, darting between the low clouds. Laura looked up at the sound above her. "Can you get us in that machine?" she asked, pointing to the chopper.

"Sure," replied the CIA man. "Let's get Billings to earn his money. Remember, you and I are just observers here." It took Special Agent Billings about seven minutes to contact the appropriate authorities from his car phone.

"Let's go," shouted Billings to Laura, who was watching the president-elect walk briskly up the stairs into the sanctuary of the church, surrounded by a gaggle of press photographers and television cameras. "We've got a ride. They'll pick us up at the Pentagon, just across the river."

***

Omar pulled back the living room drapes and stepped out onto the large veranda. It was a glorious day. Cold, but glorious. Today would be a great day in history. It would mark the beginning of a new dawn for the Middle East. The world would no longer continue to ignore them. This was only the beginning. In time, the West would learn that unless the Palestinians were given back their land, there would be no safe haven, anywhere. Even this great America, the country that claimed to be the last bastion of democracy, until now far removed and unhindered by terrorism, would learn what it was like to live in perpetual fear. Just like he and his people did all those years.

***

The service ended and the president-elect and his wife returned to their residence in northwest Washington. Tonight, and for the next four years—maybe even the next eight, if they got the votes—they would sleep in the White House.

Laura, Chester Higgins, and Tony Billings flew ahead of the convoy, scanning rooftops and every person they could set their sights on. All looked normal as a white blanket of snow gently enveloped the nation's capital. With the president-elect safely home, the helicopter pulled away to refuel. They had another thirty minutes before the president-elect left for 1600 Pennsylvania Avenue. Thirty minutes of respite before taking back to the air. It was going to be a long day.

Delphine Muller-Hoeft rode her motorcycle back to the IPS bureau. She had another hour or so to kill.

Thousands of miles away, on the peaks of the Golan Heights, Syrian troops were preparing for a large-scale nighttime military exercise. The weather was even colder here than in Washington, and the soldiers were not particularly pleased at having to prepare for a make-believe assault, just to please their officers. The snow was almost a foot deep and the cold bit right through their winter gear.

A few hundred yards away, most Israeli soldiers felt exactly the same way. This was probably as close as the two sides would ever come to agreeing over anything. In response to the Syrians' maneuvers, the Israeli Defense Force had stepped up its readiness on the Golan Plateau. This was normal procedure that happened at least twice a year. It was fine in summer, but these winter exercises were hard on the body. However, since the previous night there were more soldiers than usual. The newly arrived troops could not help but notice scores of tanks and armored vehicles inching their way up the slopes of the Golan.

Captain Yosi Castell brought his binoculars up to his eyes and took a look across the dividing line. He was only a few hundred yards from the front-line Syrian soldiers. He had never seen so much armament piled up on the other side before and it frightened him. Yosi Castell had never trusted the Syrians much. Having fought them as a young recruit during the Yom Kippur War, he knew they could be formidable foes. He remembered the harsh battle his elite unit fought to capture these heights. Castell shivered, but not from cold. He picked up his portable field telephone and reported the latest developments to brigade headquarters. This was unusual, he thought. He had seen maneuvers before, but this was not right. He could almost feel the tension. He took a last look across the dividing line. Anyway, these silly war games would be over in a day or so and then he could go back to his comfortable seaside apartment in Nahariya with his wife and two kids.

In six different small Mexican towns in close proximity to the US border, six groups of heavily armed men were guarding six trucks packed with their best grade of cocaine. Each of the six Latin American drug lords had chosen a town to use as a forward base for what would no doubt be the largest cross-border drug run ever undertaken. The street value of the cocaine inside each one of the six trucks was easily fifty million US dollars. That would quickly make up for the ten million they each had to pay to have the gringo president killed. There were additional expenses, such as purchasing the trucks, security for the convoys, and buying off local police. In the rare instances they would refuse, they had to be "taken care of."

With that much investment, the drug lords had to make sure that no one would be tempted to double or triple his investment by double-crossing one of their fellow drug lords.

Paco, who had thought of the idea at the outset, was the most nervous of all. If the plan failed, his "friends" would be coming after him to reclaim their initial investment, and in addition they would demand to be reimbursed for whatever they would lose in this transaction. With a street value of fifty million, there was no way in hell Paco could ever repay any of it. As a backup, Paco had dispatched twelve of his men, six sniper teams, each comprised of two men, the shooter and the spotter, to each of the other six cities. Their orders were to kill the drug lords who were his partners if something went wrong. As an added precaution, Paco had his private Learjet fueled and waiting at a local airstrip with an air crew standing by to take off with less than five minutes' notice. Just in case, thought Paco. Just in case. What the drug king of Mexico did not know was that the six other drug lords had anticipated a possible double-cross from Paco, and just in case something happened to their shipment and Paco conveniently tried to get away, a hefty bribe to the airport officials where the plane was being serviced allowed one of their men to sneak aboard for just thirty seconds and place a barometric bomb in the cargo compartment. It would be triggered by a cell phone call and would explode once the plane commenced its descent and passed three thousand feet. Just in case. Just in case.

The president-elect was on the move once more. Secret Service agents escorted him into the waiting bulletproof limousine and it sped toward the White House at 1600 Pennsylvania Avenue NW. The presidential limousine was escorted by units of the District Police and several large, black four-wheel-drive Secret Service vehicles, often referred to as the "war wagons." Each one of these vans carried enough firepower to repel a small army. The convoy remained in constant radio contact with the Secret Service Presidential Protection Unit, whose job was to oversee all movement of the president, vice president, and their families. The accredited White House Press Pool followed in one of the Secret Service vans, never far from the president.

Chester Higgins, Laura, and Billings were back aboard the helicopter, flying ahead of the motorcade. Laura knew the terrorist would strike today. He had to. The question was where and when would he choose to hit?

It took the motorcade fifteen minutes to reach the White House. It was only ten thirty in the morning. The president-elect waved to waiting journalists as he and Mrs. Wells were greeted on the steps of the White House by the outgoing president and his wife. The four then disappeared inside for a tour of the presidential residence.

Omar al-Kheir looked at the television monitor. Most of the guests had arrived and had already occupied their seats. He recognized the secretaries of state, defense, and treasury from photographs he had seen in newspapers and magazines, or on television. The Palestinian opened the large glass door leading to the veranda and laid out a square rug he had purchased a few weeks earlier. The thick, deep wool of the brown shaggy carpet would hold the mortar tube steadily in place, as if he had planted it on grass, or dirt. Omar turned the television set around so he could see it from outside. The cameras were his spotters. He placed the map of Washington and his compass on the floor and calculated his angle once again. He was ready now.

The outgoing president and his wife arrived on the podium minutes before president-elect Richard Wells and Mrs. Wells. The two vice presidents were already there. It was eleven fifty five and Governor Paul Ricardo of New Jersey was sworn in as vice president of the United States. There was applause, cheers, and a short prayer by a Methodist minister.

David Peterson, Special Agent In Charge of the president-elect's Secret Service detail, was well aware of the possible threat against his new boss. He lifted a finger to his ear to hear traffic coming in on his walkie-talkie. Agents were reporting in.

"Front clear."

"Back clear."

"East approach clear."

"West approach clear."

All was clear. "Bring Thunder forward," Peterson said quietly into the small microphone concealed in his sleeve jacket. This was going to be one hell of a long day for him and his team. And the day was only starting. He prayed silently for it to be over. Get this day over with. Get POTUS safely back to 1600.

Delphine Muller-Hoeft was back on the streets, back in her element once again, cruising on her motorcycle around the empty lanes of Pennsylvania Avenue and Capitol Hill. The special pass issued to her by the FBI worked wonders. Every police barricade she came across opened up and allowed her through, no questions asked.

Clayborne meanwhile was standing on the press platform, braving the icy wind. He was looking at the crowds through his powerful camera lens, searching for a face he knew he would not find. He was beginning to regret giving in to the FBI's demands. He was stuck here until the end of the ceremony, unable to leave, even if he wanted to.

It was time now. Omar moved the mortar out from the living room and placed it in position on the veranda. It took him barely two minutes to correct his aim and secure the deadly weapon. Next he brought out the ten rounds, placing them on the ground next to each other and within arm's reach of the mortar. He was ready. Only a minute to go. He had to wait until the new president was sworn in. He could see Senator Wells place one hand on a bible, the other raised as he started taking his oath. Omar turned up the volume. *"I, Richard Randolf Wells . . ."*

It was Laura who first noticed it. There was something different about that top veranda. Yet they had just flown over it a moment earlier. The color of the veranda had changed, there was a big dark blotch in the snow. This had not been there moments earlier, and there was something, or rather someone, moving about. She looked towards the Capitol and noticed that the man on the veranda didn't have a direct view of it, or of the presidential podium. For a moment, she turned her head away, but somewhere inside her, an alarm bell went off. What was someone doing on a veranda in this weather? She looked again and noticed the man run inside.

"Get lower, get us lower," she shouted into her headphone to the pilot. "Over there by the beige building to your left, there's a brown spot on the snow. On the upper floor. I need to take a closer look. Move, now!"

The pilot banked the chopper to the left, slowing it down and cautiously edging his machine closer to the roof. There was not much room to maneuver and he had to be careful to avoid hitting the chopper's blades on the opposite building. The man on the veranda had reappeared and seemed to be pointing at them.

"Gun! Oh my God, he's got a gun," shouted Higgins. "Take me down on that roof immediately, now! Move it, man, move, go, go, go, go!" His adrenaline was pumping hard. Higgins pulled his .45 automatic out of his belt holster, glad that he had thought to bring it. He pulled back the chopper's door and leaned out, letting the cold air swoop inside the cabin. Billings was stepping over Laura, trying to reach the door. "Let me through," he shouted. "Let me through; move, damn it, move!"

Laura had already armed the pistol given to her earlier that morning as the helicopter descended, closing in on its prey. The man on the veranda fired an entire magazine into the air, ejected the empty magazine, and reloaded.

"We're hit, we're hit," shouted the pilot, a Gulf War veteran who kept his cool and control of the bird. "Can't keep it up here much longer, sir. Mayday, mayday, mayday. We're hit. Going down. I need a clear place to land, ASAP. Advise, advise."

"Just get me on that roof. Get me down there," Higgins was leaning out of the door, already standing on the chopper's narrow skids. Billings was close behind him, urging him to move, to jump. They were still too high and too far from the terrace. If he jumped too soon, he risked falling to the street below.

"Wait 'til I hover the bird, sir," shouted back the pilot. "I'm having trouble keeping her steady. There's too much wind. Just a few secs more. Hold on."

Billings was frantically shouting instructions into his radio. "Just where the hell are we?" he shouted to the pilot. "What's the fucking address?" He looked around trying to identify some landmark, to see if he could read a street sign, but they were too high and the helicopter was swerving from side to side.

"Third southwest and echo," shouted back the pilot.

"Third Street and E. Third and echo, southwest," Billings said into his radio, then removed his gun from his shoulder holster and prepared to follow Higgins down. "We've got the S.O.B.," shouted Billings. "We've got the bastard now. Go, go, go."

"... and to protect the Constitution of the United States . . ."

Omar was cursing. Damn them. Damn those Americans. Another thirty seconds was all he needed. Thirty seconds more and he could fire his mortars. Just another half minute and he would have delivered his ten mortars and no one would have been able to stop him. Mad with rage, he placed a new magazine in his gun and fired at the approaching helicopter. Omar was determined to complete his mission. No matter what it took, he would fire those mortars. The Americans were too late. He was not scared of them. He had died a hundred deaths already and would die once more, if that's what it took.

Delphine Muller-Hoeft first noticed the hovering helicopter. Years of living in war zones had taught her to notice the unusual. She kept her eyes on the helicopter and her ears tuned to the police scanner. Moments later she heard the address come across on the police scanner. "Third and echo, Third and echo, southwest." She revved the bike and jumped over a curb to get past a metal barrier blocking the street, shouting into her radio as she went. "Chris, I think we have something."

Clayborne was still in the press stands with dozens of other press photographers and cameramen, unable to leave.

Higgins felt the first bullet tear into his thigh. He looked down and saw a large hole in his trousers, then blood starting to ooze out. The pain was intense, but bearable. He had to get that bastard. He was no more than ten feet above the veranda now. That was as low as the chopper could descend. The mortar was clearly visible and Higgins knew he had to stop the man. Laura was on the other side of the helicopter and unable to get a clear shot at the terrorist; her view of the Palestinian was further blocked by Billings' large shoulders. The helicopter was beginning to swerve violently, its blades narrowly missing the building across the street.

"Gotta put her down now," screamed the pilot. Higgins jumped off the skids and landed on the terrace, just feet away from the terrorist. His ankle shattered on impact and he thought he was going to die from the excruciating pain that shot right up to his brain. The terrorist, who had picked up the first mortar round, turned and fired repeatedly at the CIA man. Higgins caught two bullets in his left arm and another in his chest.

"*. . . So help me God.*"

President Wells smiled and waved to the cameras. Now, thought Omar, now! He released his grip on the yellow-labeled round. It fell to the bottom of the short tube and instantly shot skywards with a dull thud.

Higgins knew there was more than the life of the president at stake. He had to stop this man. Crumpled on the veranda floor, with a superhuman effort he mustered all the energy left in him and yanked as hard as he could on the edge of the rug just as the mortar was exiting the tube. The movement was enough to deflect the mortar's angle. The Palestinian fired one more shot at the American. It caught him right above the heart and Chester Higgins III collapsed. Omar rearranged his mortar and was preparing to lob his second round when Special Agent Billings lunged out of the chopper, crashing right on top of him and the mortar. The pilot continued to hold his smoking helicopter in place as Laura prepared to jump onto the roof.

"Ma'am, I've got to get outta here or we'll crash," screamed the pilot, suddenly veering away to avoid hitting the building across the road.

"Get me down there first," screamed Laura back. "Then crash if you have to!"

Thanks to Chester Higgins' last effort, the first shell fired from Omar's mortar landed twenty-two seconds later in the large pool on the west side of the Capitol, between the Capitol's lawn and Third

Street. The mortar round landed almost at the same time as the US Marine gunners fired their first round of a twenty-one-gun salute in honor of President Richard Wells. The mortar shell fired by Omar exploded in the shallow water, sending a geyser of water into the air. The impact also sent deadly shards of shrapnel flying around, killing two bystanders and maiming eight others. Upon contact with water, the lethal combination of anthrax and VX toxins was instantly transformed into a nearly harmless gas. Some within a few feet of the impact would die, and more would suffer nausea and various side effects, while others would recover within hours.

Bystanders thought it was a shell fired by the Marine Honor Guard that went astray. Some believed they might have mistakenly fired a real shell instead of a blank. People screamed in horror and started running away. A District policeman standing nearby radioed for help.

Omar recovered faster than the FBI man and fired three bullets repeatedly into Special Agent Billings' back and head.

The Palestinian quickly rearranged the tube and was preparing to fire his second round as Laura jumped from the crippled helicopter just as the metal bird struggled to fly away. Laura landed two feet in front of Omar, her sudden appearance momentarily stunning him.

The Palestinian, still holding his mortar round, rushed at Laura as she fired at him, hitting him in the left shoulder. The shot slowed him down but did not stop him. Omar lifted the mortar with his right arm, and using it as a hammer, lunged at Laura, aiming for her head. Laura turned to avoid the full impact of the heavy object, shrinking her head down between her shoulders, while at the same time closing the distance between her and her opponent. She could feel the Palestinian almost on her.

She thrust her right elbow into the Palestinian's stomach with full force, pushing it further in by pressing with her left hand on her clenched right fist. Twisting her right hand so that her knuckles were now facing upwards, she brought her hand up to a forty-five degree angle, hitting the Palestinian in the face. The Palestinian missed Laura's head but was able to bring the heavy object crashing down on her ear. Laura stumbled forward, caught her leg on the mortar's bipod and fell backwards, momentarily stunned.

Omar looked at Laura as she lay on the floor in front of him. He recognized her eyes. They were the eyes of that dreaded woman! He had seen her before, but where? In London! Yes, that's right. He thought he had killed her; she was supposed to have died. But did it matter now?

Omar realized he had only minutes left to complete his mission. Already he could hear the sounds of several police cars converging rapidly towards the building. For the first time, he realized that his plan might fail. He only hoped his first shot had found its mark. He aimed his gun at Laura, now lying dazed on the ground, and shot. The bullet was a fraction of a millimeter too high. It grazed Laura's skull, causing her to bleed profusely, but caused no real damage. Omar aimed lower and fired again. The gun produced a dull click. He had already fired his last round. He shot a quick glance at the television set to see if his first mortar round had hit the presidential stand, but in the general confusion he could not tell.

The pain in Omar's shoulder was getting worse. He looked at his arm. Blood had seeped out of the wound, covering part of his upper arm, and it was still bleeding. He couldn't tell, but believed the bullet had gone right through his upper shoulder. Damn, it hurt. Damn, damn, damn. Think clearly. Must think clearly, he told himself.

Laura quickly recovered. She touched her hands to her head. Blood from her wound had covered her clothes and made her hair stick to her head. Her head throbbed with pain, but she was still alive. Then she noticed Chester Higgins' inert body lying a few feet away. He looked dead. Billings was sprawled next to him. She knew he was dead.

Laura looked straight into Omar's eyes. She could see the hate they reflected. The same eyes she had seen in London, full of hate. Her head was hurting, as was her arm.

"It's too late," she said. "It's too late. You have failed. The president is alive and we know about the Golan."

"Shut up, you stupid woman. Shut up, I will kill you, too."

What happened next took Laura completely by surprise. Omar looked at her and screamed, "Shut up, you stupid, stupid woman. Shut the fuck up. You have absolutely no fucking idea of what you are getting yourself into. This is far bigger than you and your fucked-up CIA. You have no idea. But I will kill you, too."

What surprised Laura was that Omar's English was . . . well it was ENGLISH. He spoke with a British accent. How could he have suddenly developed a British accent unless he already had it. But this was not the time to ponder such questions.

Omar lunged at the remaining mortars lying evenly on the shag carpet. He picked up a round and inserted in into the tube. He would kill the president and then he would kill that woman.

Laura watched in horror as the mortar round descended into the tube. Although the round took less than a second to reach the bottom of the tube and bounce back out, to Laura it seemed like an eternity. She had the impression the scene was being carried out in slow motion. Laura wiped the blood from her face and leapt up at the terrorist. She had to stop him. It was now up to her. Both agents had died and it was up to her. Laura threw herself on the Palestinian, but it was too late. The round flew out of the tube after hitting the base with a sharp bang and exited with a soft swoosh. The deadly round flew into the sky, arched over the buildings and fell with a loud explosion.

In his haste to fire the round, the Palestinian had failed to rectify his aim. The mortar fell a few feet from where the first one had landed, sending another geyser of water into the air. It killed three District policemen responding to the first attack.

Laura was sprawled on the ground. The mortar tube had hit Omar on the head, giving her a few precious seconds to react. Both she and Omar knew they were fighting for their lives. Laura spotted Agent Billings' automatic lying a foot from his hand as he lay dead. She kicked at Omar with all her strength, pushing the Palestinian away from her as she lunged for the weapon. Omar followed her look and realized what she was attempting. He tried to get up, but the last kick from Laura had caught him straight in the face. His nose was bleeding and was probably broken. The throbbing shoulder did not help. Laura picked up the gun, spun around, aimed for Omar's heart and fired twice. But Omar rose as she pulled the trigger and the bullet caught him in the abdomen.

Omar fell back. He looked at the television set and saw President Wells waving to the crowd as agents pushed him quickly into his heavily armored limousine. The president's smile surprised Omar. He should have been dead. He looked closer at the television screen and saw his father. His father was the president. Omar smiled back. His father waved to him before getting into the car. Omar blinked. But when he opened his eyes, it was not his father any longer, but the ambassador. The ambassador from Brussels! The ambassador was laughing and waving at Omar, as if inviting him to join him. Omar shook his head. His nightmares were back. They would not go away! He looked again at the screen, but now the ambassador was that horrible woman. And she was holding a gun.

Omar tried to get up. He had to stop her. She would ruin his plan, his perfect plan. He stumbled to his feet and picked up the mortar tube. With all his remaining strength, he lifted the forty-five pound object and screamed at the dreaded woman, "It's your turn to die!"

Laura was still lying on the ground as Omar approached her, screaming at her. She fired the remaining three shots at Omar. The first shot missed, going high over his head, but the next two caught him straight in the heart. Omar dropped the large tube and fell forward on top of Laura, hitting her on the head with the heavy metal tube. But he was dead before his head even hit the ground.

The last thing Laura remembered was the sound of the apartment door being flung open and several men in black uniforms converging on her, their weapons drawn. They were wearing face masks and goggles. It amplified their eyes. She remembered thinking how they looked like men from another planet, like giant insects, and she thought she had died. She heard one of them say into his radio, "Christ, there's a bunch of dead bodies here, there's blood everywhere." The men in black approached with caution, their guns drawn and ready. They were speaking into their headphones as they approached. She could hear other men whom she could not see call out "Clear" as they went from one room to the next. Then she remembered hearing one of them say into his radio, "We've got him, we've got the bastard; he's been neutralized. Thunder is safe."

She also vaguely remembered a photographer bursting into the apartment, taking pictures, a woman, and the masked men trying to stop her. There were voices, arguments, shouts. Then the sounds faded away and then everything went dark.

Clayborne was still standing on the press platform, cursing the very idea and regretting that he had agreed to waste his time in such a manner, when he heard Delphine's frantic call come over the radio. "Shootout at Third and echo, southwest. On my way."

Long, tense minutes ticked by and Clayborne was tempted to call her back, but he knew that Delphine was a professional. She would communicate again when she had something concrete to report. He would only slow her down if he tried calling her back. Several agonizing minutes passed until he heard her voice crackle over the radio.

"Jesus, Clayborne, it's a massacre up here. Bodies, blood all over the place."

"Is there a woman there?" asked Clayborne. "Is Laura there?"

There was a muffled sound as Delphine managed to snap a few frames before the FBI SWAT team reacted, grabbed her, and pinned her to the ground. It was, after all, what she was good at. She got the job done. IPS would have exclusive photographs and the inside story. Delphine Muller-Hoeft remained pinned on the floor, with several agents pointing their automatic weapons at her head, before one of them found the typewritten note from the FBI director.

EPILOGUE

Later that night, Chris Clayborne and Delphine Muller-Hoeft drove to George Washington Hospital, where Chester Higgins was fighting for his life. Delphine's *total access* pass allowed her entry to the intensive care unit where Higgins was being treated. A quick telephone call from Potter saw to it that Chris got in too.

The bullet had barely missed Higgins' heart, causing some damage to his left lung. But Higgins was a fighter; he had always been one. Although he was still listed in critical condition, he had taken a turn for the better and was now out of danger. He would live, the doctors told Chris.

Laura fared far better. She required only a few stitches to her head, and after a complete checkup, was released. Clayborne took Laura back to his apartment where they snuggled comfortably on large pillows placed on a thick Persian carpet in front of the fireplace. They sat there in silence, watching the flames flicker and slowly consume the large wooden logs. Chris uncorked a bottle of Dom Perignon that had been chilling in the refrigerator since the morning. He gently stroked Laura's cheek with the back of his hand and placed a tender kiss on her lips.

"It's all over now, Laura. It's over," he said.

She nodded and replied softly, "Yes. It's over. I can rest now. I'm tired. No more violence; I'm through."

The only sounds came from the wood crackling in the fireplace.

"Is it really over?" asked Chris. "Can you pull out? Will they let you pull out?"

"Yes," said Laura, "they have no choice. I can't go on."

"Where do we go from here?"

"Where do you want to go from here?" she asked Chris.

"Are you sure you want to leave the Agency? Will you be happy doing something else?"

"As long as I'm with you? Yes."

"Are you proposing? Isn't that the role of the guy, usually?"

"Yes, perhaps, but there is nothing 'usual' about us."

"Will you live with me?" asked Chris.

"Yes, I will if you want me to."

"No more guns, no more spooks?"

"Yes," said Laura, as she buried her head in Chris Clayborne's shoulder and cried. She cried for a long time.

They were interrupted by the ring of Chris's cell phone. It was Delphine. "Hey Chief, are you ready for this?"

"Where are you?" Chris asked.

"At the hospital. Those SWAT guys are a tough bunch of fuckers. But they are good and they don't mess around. I thought they broke my wrist, but I'm okay. And to make up for jumping me as they did, they showed me the body of your terrorist. However, here's a story for you. I saw the autopsy report. His DNA shows absolutely no ties to the Middle East whatsoever. And another thing, judging from his anatomy he was neither Muslim nor Jewish if you know what I mean. This is formal and I have a copy of the report. I will email it to you in two seconds.

Have fun, thanks for the assignment. I'm going back to Moscow in the morning."

Turning to Laura, Chris said, "What the fuck. If he wasn't Palestinian or Iraqi, nor Syrian or Arab or even Muslim, then what the fuck was he? More to the point, who the hell was he?

"I'm afraid that we will never know . . ."

"I wouldn't bet on that," said Laura. "I have a feeling that we have stumbled onto something huge."

***

Colonel Aref Attiyef stood on the snowy slopes of the Golan, scanning the Israeli lines with his powerful field glasses. Something was wrong. Word had not yet arrived to attack, and even worse, the Israelis had been moving men and matériel all night long. He looked across the UN buffer zone and spotted an Israeli officer looking straight at him. For a brief instant he lowered his glasses, believing the enemy would go away. But when he raised the powerful scopes again, the officer was still there, looking straight at him, as if taunting him. He could now see the Israeli lower his binoculars and saw his face. The man was clearly smiling, as if to say, "We know what you were planning. We've had you figured out all the time."

Colonel Attiyef picked up his field telephone and spoke to his general, in a bunker some hundred yards away. Both men had been present a few days earlier when Brigadier General Kamal Kader briefed them.

"They have been moving troops up all night, sir. Thousands of them. And armor too. I haven't seen anything like this since 1973."

On the other side of the Golan, Brigadier General Eliahu Ben Yahar looked back at the Syrian officer. "We've had you all along, my friend, all along," he said in a low voice.

Brigadier General Kamal Kader stood silently at the large window of his office on the second floor of the Ministry of Defense in Damascus. From here, the Syrian general commanded a clear view of the snow-peaked Golan Heights. In the streets below, traffic was gradually subsiding after the evening's rush hour, although heavy fumes from old battered buses and cars still lingered in the cold January night. The general stared out the window. Behind him a television set was still broadcasting live images of the American president, proudly parading down Pennsylvania Avenue. The general realized that somehow the Palestinian had failed. Tears slowly filled his eyes and the hatred inside him grew even more. The general would not take his revenge today. Not today.

He looked away from the television images being broadcast "live" on Syrian state television showing that life was normal in Damascus. The "live" shot showed the large square outside his office at the Ministry of Defense. The general looked away from the television and out the window. What he saw was another reality. There were three tanks guarding the entrance to the building and about half a dozen carcasses of blown-up cars, debris, and soldiers in full combat gear protected by a wall of sandbags guarding the approaches to the ministry. He looked back at the television set now broadcasting images of a gardener planting flowers along the narrow strip of road between the north and southbound traffic lanes. He looked out the window and saw another picture altogether.

He barely heard the news coming from his television set. *"Just a few hours after Richard Wells was sworn in, the American president said he would convene the Washington peace talks next week in the US capital, and promised he would push both sides to seek a quick and lasting solution."*

***

In Tijuana, just a tram ride away from San Diego, Paco was watching the news on CNN in Spanish as it was projected on the huge plasma screen that took up almost half the wall in his study. He was in a jovial mood, though somewhat nervous about the next few hours. If everything went well, he would become the most powerful drug lord in the world. No, not if—there could be no ifs today. He had gambled much. Today had to work. He was sure it would. Although he was assured as late as the previous evening that all was on track, there was always the chance of something going wrong.

He held a large tumbler of cognac in one hand and a cigar, Cuban of course, in the other. As a precaution, he had his plane readied with orders for the pilot to be ready for a quick takeoff from the private airfield about one mile from his residence. He also had his driver waiting in the car, with the engine running. One could never be too careful in this business. If something went wrong he would have the Americans, the Mexicans, and—worst of all—his fellow drug barons after him.

What Paco didn't know was that the US Drug Enforcement Agency had been onto him, and given the gravity of the situation had shared the information with the CIA.

A special task force was put together in utmost secrecy, with special forces from the US working with a special unit of the Mexican Federal Police, whose members were all hand-picked and then sent to a secret CIA facility in Panama, where no communication with the outside was possible. There, the joint task force trained on the mission ahead. No one was told who the target was or when the operation would take place. The evening before the inauguration, the task force was divided into seven groups, each composed of twelve men, six Americans and six Mexicans. They were flown in unmarked planes to holding operation centers close to their target areas where they went through a final briefing. They studied the layout, watched surveillance videos, and examined photos.

The next morning, on Inauguration Day, each team boarded two helicopters—six men per craft—and headed for their target areas. At precisely noon, as the American president-elect was sworn in and the attempt on his life unfolded on international television, and the seven drug lords were busy watching what they had paid for, and therefore captivated by the events unfolding on their screens, the special joint task force units repelled from the helicopters onto the roofs of their targets' villas.

Before any of the guards had time to react, the first men out of the choppers had already silenced them using guns equipped with silencers. In under four minutes, all seven drug lords were apprehended, handcuffed, had a black hood placed over their heads, and placed aboard a helicopter. The choppers were flown to a heavily guarded remote airfield, where the prisoners were transferred onto a Hercules C130 military aircraft. The plane took off instantly for the secret CIA facility in Panama.

In Langley, Virginia, the Agency, through a meticulous process of surveillance and telephone taping and Internet monitoring and intercepts that required a task force of more than one hundred people and that took months of hard work, had finally paid off. The list of suspects was narrowed to two possible candidates. And a couple of months later all the analysts were leaning heavily in favor of one candidate and just as they were about to make an arrest new evidence surfaced that made their existing evidence circumstantial. They were not much more advanced than when they had first started.

The head of the task force at Langley opened his combination safe and took out a bottle of twelve-year-old Scotch. He poured himself a glass and raised his glass in a mock toast.

"Here is to HUMINT over ELINT any day of the week and any week of the year." He downed the Scotch, called his secretary, and told her to arrange a meeting of the section chiefs.